Dark Road
Punished

Krys Fenner

"Thou shalt also consider in thine heart, that,

as a man chasteneth his son,

so the Lord thy God chasteneth thee."

Deuteronomy 8:5

Dark Road Punished

To Niki
Congrats!
Krys Ferner

Chapter One

Bella believed God hated her.

Her best friend Vick called a couple of hours ago and said he needed a ride from his parents' summer home before the storm hit because his car died and he couldn't reach his parents. Her mother worried about Bella's quick departure, but Bella hadn't hesitated to leave, and believed she could beat the onslaught of wind and rain. Except Vick didn't stand on the other side of the door. Jeremiah, stood in front of her. They hadn't really spoken since he walked out of her hospital room. She didn't count the arguments or texts. Her stomach churned all the emotional ramifications she'd worked to bury over the past few months. Yep, God really hated her. She crossed her arms over her chest, and spun around on the porch and moved toward the steps.

"Bella, where do you think you're going?" Jeremiah followed after her.

"Home!"

He pulled her arm and she almost toppled into him. "Absolutely not! No way you'll make it back before this thing hits."

"Not if you stop me from leaving!" She yanked free of his grip with a sudden sense of de ja vu.

"Are you insane? Look at the sky! I know you're not stupid. You're smart enough to know you'll get stuck and being in a car in a storm is suicide. Come on, there's a storm cellar over there. We should head that way."

She snickered. "You must think I'm crazy if you believe for one second I am going to get holed up in a shelter with you to wait out this damn storm!" *No way in hell is he getting me in there!* Her plan for the day did not include her ex-boyfriend. She'd spent two and a half months away from Jeremiah, which included a month with someone else, and it had been good for her soul or so she'd tried to convince herself. Realistically she couldn't avoid him. She and Jeremiah went to the same school and church. She no longer attended the Tuesday night Bible study group her parents hosted since... Unfortunately in a small town, every godforsaken person knew what happened to her. She couldn't stand the look of pity a lot of people wore on their faces around her. Few people forgot that night ever happened and treated her normal, the two things she wanted. She'd kill to beat the vivid memory into submission and bury it six feet underground.

"No! But I will think you're crazy if you keep pushing to drive in this storm," Jeremiah quipped.

She crossed her arms over her chest again and looked at the sky beyond him. As much as she refused to admit it, she knew she wouldn't make it back before the storm.

"You have two choices. One, you walk nicely with me to the storm cellar or two, I toss you over my shoulder and carry you."

She maintained her stance and narrowed her eyes. "You wouldn't dare."

He grabbed her by the waist and threw her over his shoulder.

"Jeremiah! Put me down!" She hit him on the back and kicked her feet doing whatever she could to get out of his grip. Angrier than before she yelled again, "Put me down!"

Jeremiah remained silent as he carried her into the storm cellar. Once inside he placed her on her feet and put some space between them. He walked over and locked the door, then found a spot at the end of the stairwell, leaned against the wall, crossed his arms and ankles and dropped his gaze.

Too angry for words, she started to pace the shelter. She couldn't walk out the front entrance because Jeremiah strategically perched himself between her and the door. *What the hell is he thinking? What is wrong with him?*

While she huffed and puffed around the room, he just watched her beneath hooded eyes. "Bella, talk to me."

One month earlier...

Chapter Two

Bella looked at the door marked "New Mexico Rescate County Chief of Police." She hated being there. She sighed and walked over to the door. It was halfway open. She knocked. "Chief Detrone?"

"Hey Bella. Come on in. You know you can call me 'Jamar'." The man rose to his feet and stepped around the desk.

"I know, but it doesn't feel right." She headed over to one of the chairs and took a seat, while he closed the door. Bella liked the man. He'd always been nice to her. Chief Detrone's features reminded her of her boyfriend who ignored and avoided her. She practically saw Jeremiah in his face whenever she came to see his father.

"Why's that?"

"If I call you 'Jamar' then I have to think of you as Jeremiah's dad and not just the man handling my case." She desperately wanted to separate the two.

Chief Detrone approached and sat in the chair opposite her. "You're his girlfriend. You should think of me as both."

"Am I?"

"What?"

"His girlfriend."

Chief Detrone leaned back in the chair. He frowned. "If things have changed, he hasn't said anything to me."

"That makes two of us." Bella shook her head. "Look, I don't want to talk about Miah. My mom said you needed to see me."

"Yes. I needed to clarify some things regarding your case." Chief Detrone stood, reached over his desk and grabbed a couple of files. Then he returned to the chair across from her.

"Okay. Fine." Bella sighed. She couldn't count the number of times she'd been in the police station over the past six weeks. Just when she thought all the questions that could possibly be asked had been, another one would pop up. It probably wouldn't be so bad if she didn't have to deal with Jeremiah's dad every single time she came in. At this point, she would rather speak directly to the prosecutor.

"On October 2nd, when you and Jeremiah arrived at your house, where did you find your mom?"

"She was in the living room with a couple of paramedics."

"What did she tell you happened?"

"She didn't remember much. Just that she had gotten inside the door when she felt something hit her on the head. The neighbors were the ones who called the cops. Mrs. Sanford had come over to see if my mom had seen Pugsie. The trunk of my mom's car was open and the front door was too. Mrs. Sanford called for her husband. Mr. Sanford found my mom crumpled on the floor of the main hall."

Chief Detrone notated a couple of things. "How did you find out what Mr. and Mrs. Sanford saw?"

"When Jeremiah and I stepped out of the house for some air, they were still there. They told us what happened and asked if my mom was okay."

"You and Jeremiah were the ones who walked the house?"

"Yes. Detective Russell wanted me to see if anything was missing and I didn't want to go alone."

Chief Detrone nodded and closed the file before he moved onto the next. "Now let's go to October 9th."

"Do we have to?" Bella never liked talking about the night of her attack.

"I'm sorry Bella. I know this is difficult, but we do. I'll try to make it as short as possible."

She sighed. "Fine, let's just get this over with."

"The men that attacked you, had you ever seen them before?"

Bella shook her head. "No. And I only saw the one man's face. The other kept his face covered."

"And there were no distinguishing marks on the second man? Anything that stood out?"

"Not that I remember." If there had been, Bella still wouldn't remember. She'd used all her power to block that night out.

"The first man we identified as Quincy Harlem. Did he say anything to you?"

"A lot. Can you be more specific?"

"I need you to tell me everything he said Bella."

God, why? Bella sighed. "He called me his honey bear. Told me that he wanted to make sure I could see his face to know who he was. He said I was my father's payment."

"Payment? Did he say for what?"

"Not until the shooting at the Fall Harvest Production." Another day Bella wanted to forget. Eleven days between the two events, but they were linked by a never ending nightmare. Her bruises had healed by that point, but her arm had been in a cast and her ribs cracked. She had been determined that Quincy Harlem would not take her life away. She'd refused to relinquish her position as producer to the Halloween event her church put on every year. All the people in town came and enjoyed the festivities. She hadn't expected Harlem to show up and shoot both her and Jeremiah.

"What did he tell you then?"

"I was payment for his brother."

"Did he explain what that meant?"

Bella nodded. "My dad is the Youth Pastor at the juvenile detention center his brother was sentenced to. I guess my dad counseled his brother and led him to God. From what my dad told me, Quincy's brother Jeffrey decided he wanted out of the gang. He said Jeffrey told him Quincy considered him as good as dead. Since my dad took something from him, Quincy said he was returning the favor."

"Do you think that's why he marked you?"

Of all the questions to ask, you ask that one. Bella glared at Chief Detrone. Among the pictures of her bruises and broken bones had been one of a brand she had on the back of her neck. A pair of crisscrossed scythes had been the only thing to link the crimes to Quincy Harlem's gang, The Twin Reapers. She got to her feet. "And we're done."

"Bella — "

"'Bella' nothing. I can't answer that question and you know it. Now, I'm done." Before the Chief had another opportunity to ask anything else, Bella walked past him. She had half a mind to slam his door shut behind her, but somehow found the composure to leave the office as if nothing happened.

****

"I don't care what you have to do, just take care of the problem." A man in an orange jump suit stated into the phone. Even though a piece of flexi-glass stood between Quincy Harlem and the kid on the other side, the kid still winced.

"I understand sir. We just wanted to clarify any limitations."

"Whatever it takes. I can't be any more clear than that." He snarled.

"Yes sir. I'll report back in a week."

"No! Come back in two. I don't want to see you before then. Do you understand?"

The kid nodded.

"Good. And Swifty?"

"Yes sir?"

Quincy reached into his pocket and pulled nothing out. His gaze honed in on Swifty as a sinister smile spread across his lips and pronounced the jagged edges of the scar on the right side of his face. "There's a piece of paper under your seat. Pull it out."

Swifty reached under the seat. An envelope had been taped to the bottom. As he pulled it out he looked across the way. "What's this?"

"Something you need to deliver. That is your first assignment."

"Yes sir. Is there anything else?"

"No. That is all."

Swifty waited.

"You may go." Quincy watched Swifty return the phone to its placeholder. Quincy hung up his phone as well. "Guard."

Chapter Three

A black Volkswagen Beetle Coupe pulled into the driveway next to a mailbox marked "The Naughton Family." Bella stared at the modern day Victorian style house. From outside, a portion of the dining room could be seen through the den's large bay window. At the angle she sat she caught a glimpse of an older woman moving around the kitchen as it connected to the dining area. She sighed. Her mother was home. The wagon to her right should have been a dead giveaway.

Since the incident, Bella spent as little time as possible at home. When she got her car, she found a way to be more independent. She'd been independent before, except her parents always knew where to find her. She did as they asked. Now she didn't care what they wanted unless they threatened to take away her car. The car made it easier to come and go as she pleased. It was her lifeline and she couldn't be without it. Life would be different if she could have forced herself to walk anywhere. Her first car had always been one of the big "firsts" she looked forward to. Then a horrific tragedy turned what should've been a reward into a reminder of an ugly and unwarranted experience.

She sighed. It was pointless to hide in the car. At some point her mother would traipse outside and yap at Bella until she forced her daughter to hide in her bedroom. If she vanished into her room until she could escape again, sooner would be better than later. Bella turned off the ignition and climbed out of the car. Never before had she such disdain for life. Her friends and family stepped carefully around her as if shattered glass constantly surrounded her. Nightmares and lack of sleep contributed to her feelings. On some nights when the pills didn't cut the pain she'd entertain the idea of just ending it all.

She couldn't recall if the Bible actually condemned people who committed suicide, she'd still think twice about getting into heaven. Then she'd wonder if God would let her in anyway. As a young child she'd served and loved Him. As a teenager, she no longer felt as if He loved her. Now she believed He had turned His back on her. The one thing that didn't make sense, if He intended to punish her, why didn't the bullet pierce her heart? Why did she survive? With no answers and a constant feeling of loneliness, ending it all often seemed the only way out. Nothing would make that go away, not even pills. She struggled through every day hoping it to be her last.

She headed up the walkway and barely noticed the fresh lilies planted beneath the window. They were her favorite. Bella paused long enough at the double doors to stare at the flowers for a moment, then quietly disappeared inside the house. Two months ago she would've announced her return home, but now she didn't bother.

Her mother's voice called out to her. "Bella? Is that you?"

"Yeah mom, it's me." Her stomach rumbled and reminded her she hadn't eaten in several hours. Bella walked into the kitchen, but didn't say hi or give her mother a hug. She stopped and opened the refrigerator.

Behira glanced over as she dried her hands on the apron around her waist. "How did it go at the police station?"

"Fine." There weren't many options in the fridge. Either leftovers that had to be heated up or she could throw a peanut butter sandwich together and snag a glass of milk. While the first would be quick and easy, the last sounded better. Reaching in, she grabbed the jug of milk, then pulled the loaf of bread from the bread box and put it on the kitchen island. Then she went back for the peanut butter, knife, and glass. Throughout the process of making the sandwich and putting everything away her mother just watched, while neither said a word.

"Dinner will be ready shortly." Her mother commented perhaps under the illusion she planned to eat with them.

"I won't be here. Sarresh is picking me up in an hour and a half and we're going shopping. I have plans to stay the weekend with her," Bella replied without looking up.

"Isn't she still living with that man?"

"Yes."

"I don't think you should stay there. You have a car. Call and tell her you'll meet her at the mall. Then you can come home."

For the first time in the five minutes she'd been in the kitchen she looked at her mother. "Porque?" Bella paused as she had no desire to argue with her mother. Typically they argued in Portuguese and spoke normally in English. After a calming breath, Bella continued, "He's not skivvy. Just because he's older shouldn't make a difference. Besides, she told me she was already out. And I don't want to waste gas."

"Your father and I pay for the gas so it doesn't matter."

"I pay for it with my allowance."

"Which we provide."

"Are you telling me that if I ran out of money, you would give me more?"

"Of course," her mother replied.

"Would it be any amount I asked for or enough to get me by?"

Crossing her arms across her chest, Behira sighed. "I would feel more comfortable if you came home."

"That's what I thought. I'll be back on Sunday." Turning back to get her sandwich and glass of milk she completely dismissed how her mother felt. Discussing nothing further Bella left the kitchen and went to her room. Closing the door behind her she walked over and settled into the chair at her desk, where she typically sat. Her bed hadn't been touched since she returned to their house. She could only see the pool of red that had covered the bed every time she looked at it. Not to mention the animal all that blood came from.

****

Bella and Jeremiah walked through the house advising the officer of any missing items. Nothing appeared to have been taken, simply destroyed. So far only the living room and the bathroom remained untouched. The remainder of the house had been violently ripped apart. Bella and Jeremiah saved her room for last. All the destruction had been aimed at her parents from what she gathered. She truly expected her room to appear as tidy and organized as she had left it. With the door open, her eyes widened in horror and she desperately wanted to turn around and run back into the hall, instead she gripped Jeremiah's hand tighter and buried her face into his shoulder.

As soon as Jeremiah saw it he pulled her in closely and wrapped his arms tight around her. Instinctively he tried to protect and shield her from the assault of her bedroom. This room had received the worst blow. It looked as if someone had taken a hammer to the walls, an axe to the dresser, and a knife or screwdriver to her bed. It looked as if straight scissors shredded her clothes, strewn all over the place. Holes were spread across all four walls. The dresser and drawers had been chopped into pieces and flung across the room. Apparently one of those pieces had been hurled against the mirror that used to hang on a wall. It had been shattered into pieces scattered all across the floor.

She could have handled the nominal destruction. The pug faced shar pei she knew well forced her to look away. Rippling shocks throughout her body split her heart in two.

Officer Russell slipped in past the couple who had not moved from the door way. Kneeling down at the end of the bed he shifted his gaze to Bella. "Do you know this animal?"

Closing her eyes and burrowing deeper into Jeremiah's body she swallowed, nodded and muttered, "That's our next door neighbor's dog, Pugsie. She belongs to Mr. & Mrs. Sanford." While she understood the destroyed furniture, broken fixtures and paintings, and even the torn clothing, she couldn't fathom why anyone would hurt an innocent dog. No matter how close she got to her boyfriend, the image of the thick red glossy pools all over her bed wouldn't escape her mind. She couldn't rid the memory of death in the dog's face either. It was simply cruel.

****

Bella shuddered as the memory danced all over her brain like it planned on hanging around a while. One of the many things she refused to talk about because it only led down one path and she hated going there. Forcibly she turned away not wanting to be reminded of what she considered the first step down a long road of tragedy. Stopping mid-bite she glanced down at the reflection of her face in her small hand held mirror. The full length mirror had been replaced and hung back on the wall, but she had it covered.

The majority of her physical injuries had disappeared. Only one remained because the cast had come off two days ago. She still had physical therapy to go through. One devastation became a never ending nuisance like a CD stuck on the same song. She really hated God for allowing Quincy Harlem to do those things to her. Yet she still hoped he rotted in hell. Such hate had never existed in her heart before that terrible night.

Finishing the sandwich and the last of the milk she tossed her trash into the can beside her desk. Stealing a look, the clock told her she'd killed all of about thirty minutes. She had at least another hour before Sarresh picked her up. Bella laid her head down on her arm across the desk, and reached into her back pocket and pulled out her cell phone. It had been a present from Jeremiah a couple months ago. Stroking the phone with her thumb she stared at the object serving as the invisible tether tying them together.

When the phone itself stopped being enough she set it down on the desk and pulled up his contact information displaying his picture. He cared about her a lot and convinced his parents to get a cell phone and pay for it for her so she could be reached at all times. Smiling she remembered the first few nights spent with endless texting which amused him. He used to tell her she didn't have to type long hand, but she never could get the hang of the shortcuts. All the LOLs and smiley faces confused her. She glared at the phone as if it would make him call or unexpectedly show up. Looking at the clock again she moaned, only ten more minutes gone. Waiting would kill her if she had to sit there one more moment. Snatching the phone she shoved it into the back pocket of her jeans.

Her determination didn't prevent her from pausing in front of the closet. She swept her fingers across the blouses and jeans that occupied the hangers. Tonight she'd shop for some of the same things with her friend. These type of clothes hadn't filled her closet three months ago. Three months ago she had been the feminine advertisement for Christian women: full length skirts, button up blouses and modest shirts. Short sleeves were okay as long as they weren't any shorter than three inches from the elbow. The shoes that lined the floor used to be flats, now it consisted of ballet slippers, flip flops, wedged sandals, and a few pairs of heels. *That night* really did change her whole life. Shaking her head free of memories, she disappeared into the bathroom, quickly brushed her hair, touched up her make-up, popped two Oxycodone with a small sip of water from the faucet and brushed her teeth. She'd driven by Jeremiah's house a lot of times before this. In fact, tonight would be more like the fortieth. She didn't care if he was ashamed of her. She planned to drive by again.

Am I thinking straight? No. Am I crazy? Absolutely! Do I care? Nope, not at all. Okay, not the smartest move in the book, but Jeremiah would never find out. Sometimes stealing peeks at him at school didn't cut it. Neither were the pictures she had stored in her phone and often the memories seemed so far away they were surreal as if they never happened. She missed him down to her core, no matter how much he angered her. Nothing kept her from doing these drive-bys. Sometimes they were the only thing that made the pills work and got her through the day and she needed to cling to that right now. Grabbing her keys she stepped out of her bedroom and shut the door behind her. "I'm heading off, Mom. I'll be back." Bella didn't say anything else as she walked out the front door. She climbed into the car and drove away from the house.

Jeremiah lived on the outskirts of Nautica Valley about twenty minutes from her home. With it being a family neighborhood she easily found a spot along the curb opposite his house. A single stone pathway led up to a wooden porch with matching doorframe. She knew intricate details of the house, but those weren't nearly important as one of the two bedrooms she had been in. Even though she had been in his sister's room, only Jeremiah's room mattered.

Bella's mother ended up spending a night in the hospital for observation after the raid on their house. Her father stayed at the hospital. Needless to say the visit Bella expected to last a few hours had magically turned into an overnight stay. Jeremiah woke up during the night and found her curled up on the couch in the living room. Like in his sister's room, Bella had been attempting and failing to fall asleep. She woke up the next morning in Jeremiah's room, in his bed. The first and only night she could recall actually sleeping peacefully without any nightmares in months. Now she'd give anything to have that type of peace back in her life. Inhaling quickly and deeply, her eyes widened when she spotted the man running a marathon in her brain step outside with a bag of trash in hand. She hoped he wouldn't spot her, but nearly wanted him to see her too. She didn't know what she'd do if he did. *That's not true. If he doesn't want to talk to me, then why should I talk to him? Shit!*

Chapter Four

Whistling, Jeremiah walked barefoot around the side of the house and dumped the bag of trash in the bin. He turned around and started back when he paused. He walked to the edge of the driveway past his mother's van and his father's car. Suddenly vehicle lights flooded the street and he stood there watching someone speed off in a VW Bug.

The car hadn't really caught his attention, but the girl did. She had the same dark hair and round face as his angel. Unfortunately the driver took off before he could get close enough to confirm his theory. He had heard through the grapevine she'd been driving, but he didn't know the type or color of the car. If it was her, what did he plan to do? Chase after her? Not to mention he'd have no clue why she'd be there. God, he wished he'd gotten closer before the car took off. He believed the driver to be his girlfriend. Even if he had gotten close enough to talk to her, he had no clue what he would say. Brushing a hand atop his brown hair, he turned around and headed back inside.

He missed Bella like crazy, but had no clue how to begin to explain what happened. God knew how bad he wanted to talk to her. Leaving her alone hadn't done either of them any good. Even with all the wealth of information Amanda and Vick shared, Jeremiah had been unconvinced. He saw it whenever he passed her in the hall at school. Bella may have fooled them, but not him and he didn't have half the facts they did. The two of them had information he didn't, which was exactly why he knocked on his sister's door then cracked it open.

"Hey sis, you decent?"

"Come on in." Amanda sounded annoyed.

He suspected she knew what he came for. Yes he'd stopped talking to Bella, but he hadn't stopped thinking or asking about her and nothing could make him do otherwise. Mentally he expected he'd walk into Mandy giving him the finger, but he didn't. Instead she sat at her desk focused on a book. Obviously he interrupted her working on homework and he didn't care. "I need some information."

"And?"

He sat down on her bed. Leaning his elbows on his knees he rubbed his face. "Look, I know you and Vick are tired of me asking questions."

"Yet you always have more." Amanda sneered.

"Hear me out? Please?" He wanted to know Bella was okay. Even unconvinced, his sister's and Vick's confirmation made staying away worthwhile. Doubts constantly crept in, but he believed it to be the Devil trying to get at him. If for one second he thought he hurt Bella more, he'd never forgive himself.

Sighing, Amanda spun around in her chair and faced him. "I'll listen, but you need to stop coming to us. You need to talk to her. Even if she brushes you off, you should try."

"And you think I haven't thought about that?"

"Then why haven't you?"

An extremely logical question. Except nobody ever liked his answer. "If I have to stay away for her to be happy, then that's what I'll do."

"Even at the expense of your own happiness?"

Burying his face in his hands he sighed. He hated she had a point. Misery set up a nice little hammock in his heart and got comfortable like it always did when he thought or even talked about Bella. If the car belonged to her, what would he do with that news? Could she be seeking him out? Did she miss him too? Slowly he lifted his head from his hands as more and more thoughts pummeled his brain. For the first time in a long time they were good, not hopes or desires or wants, but likelihoods and he loved that. "What kind of car does she drive?"

"A black Volkswagen Beetle. Why?"

Jeremiah mumbled, "I saw her."

"What?"

"Just a minute ago, when I was taking out the trash. I wasn't sure it was her because I didn't know what car she drove, but it was. She was just parked there, but sped away when I started toward her."

The corners of Amanda's lips pulled into a warm smile. "Then maybe it's time you return the favor."

"And then what?"

She shrugged. "I don't know, but you and Bella need to figure that out. Now, are you going to stay here and annoy me or are you going to go tell your girlfriend you love her?"

Blinking at the blatant question she asked, he wondered what led her to the conclusion he loved Bella. At the same time, he knew his sister spoke the truth. He absolutely loved his Bell.

"Thanks sis!" Without another thought he bolted to his feet and jogged out the door around the corner to his room. Grabbing a pair of sneakers and socks, he shoved them on his feet then headed to the living room. His parents watched television.

"Can I borrow the car?"

His dad looked up at him for a split second then nodded. "Sure."

He assumed his father saw the determination in his face. Snapping to attention Jeremiah snatched the keys and headed out the front door. Unfortunately Bella was a good ten to fifteen minutes ahead of him. He hoped she only planned to go home and had no intention of leaving. He had no clue what he would say, but he could start with "Hi." From there, he'd wing it.

Either he was extremely lucky or God was on his side. The car he saw parked across the street from his home sat in her parents' driveway. He still had no clue what he would say once he got her to the door or if she'd even let him in, but he knew how to start. Pulling his dad's Navy Blue Dodge Avenger behind Bella's bug he came to a stop and parked with a broad smile on his face. After weeks of silence he planned to talk to her. He paced his steps although the urge to run felt better. No way to hide the wide grin on his face as he knocked on the door. Waiting sucked. *One... two... three... four... hmm,* how long should he stand there before knocking again? What was suitable? Five seconds, ten... maybe twenty? Too short made him seem eager and too long made him appear nonchalant. He needed to knock again. *One... two... three... four... five... six...* six seconds after the second knock the door opened.

Except Bella hadn't answered, but that could be a good thing. Gave him a chance to breathe before he talked to her. Speaking would be good about now.

"Sorry Mrs. Naughton. Is Bella here?"

She blinked. "I'm afraid not. You just missed her, Jeremiah."

Brushing his fingers over his short hair he half nodded. "Oh. You know when she should be home?"

Softly she sighed. "Sunday? Even then I'm not positive. Would you like to come in for a little while?"

"Sure, Mrs. Naughton." Uncomforted by her answer, he considered denying her offer, but he was eager to know more. Walking in past her he took in the changes made since the last time he'd been there. There had been so much destruction and the threat that told Mr. Naughton to *Stay Away or Else Someone Gets Hurt.* That hadn't been the greatest experience. Jeremiah remembered when he had escorted Bella through the house. Mr. Naughton presented to the Chief of Police threatening letters. From what Jeremiah heard from his father, Bella's father hadn't taken them seriously until that night.

Walls were together now, portraits and paintings returned to their appropriate locations. The entire house appeared untouched by the harsh issues of life. He followed Bella's mother into the kitchen and took up a seat at the dining room table.

She smiled. "I've told you before you can call me Behira. Would you like something to drink?"

"Water would be nice, thanks." Yes, she had told him several times to call her by her first name and so had Bella's father. Neither of which would happen. His parents raised him to treat his elders with respect.

She nodded, grabbed a glass from the cabinet, filled it with water from the refrigerator and set it down in front of him. "How are you doing? It's been a while since we've seen you around."

"I'm making it through. Healed up pretty nice. Doctor says I should be good as new with a few more therapy sessions." He'd learned to deal with seeing Bella and her family in church, just like he handled crossing paths with her at school. He befriended Vick and William at Bible Study Group, but going and seeing his girlfriend there and not talk to her, it hurt less to rip out his heart. Heck, he would rather take the bullet that could've killed her five times over than to have to see her in a church function, only to ignore her. Yes, ignoring her was torture. Now he would do something about it.

"That's good. I prayed you would be okay. I know you were just trying to protect Bella. You probably saved her life. But I wouldn't have been able to accept you getting hurt in the process." She released a heavy breath.

"Thank you, I'm grateful for any prayers and to you and Mr. Naughton for letting me date your daughter." *Not that it seems like it.* He hated the truth that banged around in his head. And he knew why, it reminded him of how much he hadn't done. For all the work he did avoiding her, in theory trying to talk to her would have been easier. He couldn't argue the accuracy of his departure in the middle of her giving her statement to his father. Bad enough she had to talk about the rape in all the detail she remembered. Seeing her laying in that hospital bed close to death's door scared the hell out of him and pissed him off to no end. To this day, he still had no clue if she knew he punched a hospital wall on his way out.

He still remembered the look on her father's face when he got to the church and they both discovered Bella missing. Jeremiah blamed himself for her rape. He'd made frequent trips back to the alleyway where she'd been found. He re-walked the path through the alleyway she took to get to church, the one he himself would have taken if he hadn't been running two hours late. One of his friends in the dance group he belonged to gave him a ride. The walk would have taken him twenty extra minutes, which meant he would've found her sooner rather than later. Blinking he realized Bella's mom said something.

"I'm sorry, what?"

"Have you talked to her recently?"

He shook his head. "I tried to talk to her a few days after I left her hospital room, but she wouldn't hear me out. I don't blame her. She has every right to be upset with me." He thought about that more, he also tried to talk to her upon her initial return to school, but she blew me off. God, and that freak David took full advantage of it, didn't he? The guy walked right up, draped an arm around Bella and told him "The lady said, 'Leave her alone.'" Groaning, Jeremiah really wanted to kick his own butt because he didn't interfere more and hadn't made any more attempts. Why the heck had he waited so long? Why didn't he come here sooner? He sighed. God he was such an idiot.

"I wish you were the only one she was angry at."

"What do you mean?"

Mrs. Naughton briefly steepled her fingers together. "She doesn't spend much time at home anymore. When she does she shuts herself in her bedroom. If we see her for meals she doesn't talk to us. She stopped going to the Bible study sessions, I think she only goes to church out of habit. But I'm afraid it won't be long before she stops that too."

He blinked because he couldn't do anything else. All this time and he'd seen what his sister and Vick weren't telling him and yet he still insisted on staying away. Could Jeremiah actually say he did it for Bella? No, not anymore. If he were brutally honest, which he absolutely needed to be, he did it because he was a coward. Too scared he would do the wrong thing, say the wrong thing, or be able to do nothing at all. He freaked out and pushed his girlfriend away. Fumbling for words he started. "I, um..." Fairly certain no matter what came out of his mouth, his foot would surely be in it, he paused. The trains in his head were prepared for a head on collision, so he said the first thing that came to mind. "I heard she's been seeing a psychiatrist. Is that true?"

"Yes, starting a few weeks ago, but I don't think she's really talked to the doctor. We've had a few group sessions, but she doesn't talk during those. I feel like we're losing her and we can't stop it. We don't know what else to do."

Where the hell did his voice go? It would be nice if it made an appearance, any time now. Rubbing the top of his head he wondered if he could find a way to help. All he wanted was for Bella to be okay and here he sat doing nothing to ensure it. He wasn't even positive he could convince her mother of it. Again, he failed Bella again. Reaching for the glass, he picked it up and took a sip of water. Thinking out loud, "God I wish there was something I could do."

"There is. Talk to her. I think if you do, she can move forward from this rape."

Talk to her. Seemed like an easy solution. He'd been prepared to do just that, but things were much worse than he'd been led to believe. Even if he did talk to her, would she talk to him? Would she listen? He didn't know how receptive Bella would be. While he had no clue what he got himself into, he loved this woman's daughter and would do anything to save her. He just prayed he wouldn't be too late. Looking up to the brown eyes that pleaded with him, he nodded. "I'll try."

****

Still in a stupor from the conversation he had with Bella's mother, Jeremiah walked into his house and locked the door behind him. He paused just outside the living room. His parents were no longer curled up on the couch. His sister had taken their place. Without a word he stepped around the couch and chair, gripped a poker by the fireplace and stoked the fire.

"That bad?" Amanda looked up from her phone.

He returned the poker to its rightful place, leaned a hand on the wall and just stared at the bright flames that popped and cracked.

"Jeremy?"

He couldn't bring himself to tell her what happened at Bella's house. The men in his family didn't fail. And he had done that more times than he cared to count. Not once could he recall his father failing at something. The man worked, helped raise six kids with another on the way, and always remained there for all of them. Jeremiah strived for the relationship he witnessed between his mother and father. When he and Bella first got together Jeremiah had faith he had found that. Was it something rare at sixteen? Yeah, but he didn't care. His heart wholly belonged to one person and yet he constantly failed her. He had no right to ask Bella to love him back.

"Jeremy?" Amanda stood beside him. "Hey, would you talk to me? You're starting to freak me out."

He glanced over to his sister. "Sorry Mandy. I didn't mean to."

"Then I need you to talk to me."

He sighed. "She wasn't home. I missed her by a few minutes."

"Then what has got you so distracted?"

"I talked to Mrs. Naughton."

"And?"

"It's not good."

Amanda's phone beeped. She ignored it and never looked away from her brother. "Meaning what?"

"You going to answer that?"

"It can wait. Stop stalling. What does 'It's not good' mean?"

He sat in the chair. The couch carried too many memories of him and Bella with one in particular always singing in his brain. He hadn't sat there since that blissful night when she fell asleep in his arms.

His sister plopped back down on the couch and forced him to look away.

"You know how you told me Bella's been seeing a psychiatrist?"

"Yeah."

"Her mother doesn't think it's doing any good. She doesn't believe Bella is talking to the doctor."

"Why would she think that?"

"Apparently she's hardly around and when she is, she locks herself in her bedroom and hardly talks to either Mr. or Mrs. Naughton. Not even when the three of them are in session together."

"You mean she's not talking period?"

He nodded. He had no clue what to do. If she hadn't been talking to a professional, what would make anyone think she'd talk to him? Provided she accepted his explanation and forgave him for being such a fool.

"Makes sense," Amanda muttered.

Whether she meant it to or not, she caught his attention. "What are you talking about?"

The look his sister gave him said that she didn't want to talk about it, but he wouldn't stand for that.

"Don't even. You pushed, now spill."

She sighed. "Up until the rape, the only time I'd ever seen Bella get frustrated or annoyed with something someone said was our first day of school when she snapped at Heather. Even after the rape when she came back to school and that bitch called her a slut, Bella didn't react. I did. But a few weeks ago Bella and I were at her locker and I overheard Missy saying she asked for it. I went to say something, but Bella beat me to it."

"What did she say?"

"That at least she wasn't claimed as being a bad lay by the entire football team."

"What?"

Amanda's phone beeped again. She got on her phone and texted whoever back, then returned her attention to Jeremiah. "Missy then called her a skank. And Bella said that she'd rather be a skank than a lousy whore who would do anything for a buck."

He couldn't believe these kind of things were coming out of his girlfriend's mouth. The fact he hadn't heard about any of it before now surprised him more. Given, all schools gossiped. But at Jackson Heights, you weren't important if you didn't gossip. He rubbed his face and shamefully dropped his gaze to the floor. "Please tell me there isn't more."

"I wish I could. Bella and I were walking down the hall one day heading to class when some guy bumped her from behind. Next thing I know she spun around and smacked the boy then she huddled up against the wall like she was hiding. I wasn't able to get her attention until after the bell rung."

"Maybe it was a panic attack."

She shrugged. "I don't know. I mean it's not just the outbursts. Sarresh tells me Bella doesn't participate in class as much. She won't even do things with me and Sarresh. I see Bella in school, but she doesn't say a lot in the hall or at lunch. Some days she just stares into space and other days she can't stop looking around like someone is out to get her. I've seen her stand at her locker like she's in a trance. A couple of times I've said something to her about class then come by an hour later and she'll still be in the same position. I don't really see her eat. I've caught her a few times throwing up in the bathroom, then spending the rest of the day in the nurse's office. She's got to be holding it all in."

"You don't think it could be anything else?"

"No. I know she's still on her pain medication, but Sarresh says that's to be expected. Bella stays the weekends with her, so Z would see if she were abusing at all."

"I wouldn't put my faith in what Sarresh says."

"Why won't you give Z a chance?" Amanda asked.

"I don't trust her. Why do you hang out with her?"

"Aside from Sarresh being family, we get along."

Jeremiah shook his head. "I don't care if she's our cousin. There could be more going on with Bella and Sarresh would either ignore it or refuse to believe it."

"Except this makes sense for Bella. Kind of like a slow-building volcano. And we're the ones waiting for her to erupt."

Jeremiah sighed. Logically his sister's answer made sense. He didn't care if their cousin agreed with her. Unfortunately other things made sense too and he didn't want to think about either of them because they worried him more than an exploding volcano. No matter what the reason for all of her unexplained outbursts, he couldn't be sure she needed him. He looked at his sister. "Can you answer me something honestly?"

"Yeah."

"How much of her reactions do you think are my fault?"

Amanda opened her mouth and snapped it shut.

"It's okay, you don't have to answer."

She shook her head. "I told you I would, so I will. The truth is, I can't give you an estimation. Rape isn't easy for anyone to deal with and Bella seems to be trying to bury it so she never has to deal with it. But I would be lying if I said your actions or lack of haven't contributed to her emotions in some way. If I had just been raped and my boyfriend turned his back on me, I would be devastated. I would blame myself thinking I did something or that he was ashamed of me. Not to mention she was a virgin. She may feel you won't talk to her because she's unclean and isn't the same pure girl you fell in love with. I can't say one impacts more than the other. Personally, I would weigh them equally."

"I feel like crap, but thank you for the honesty."

"Jeremy, you know I love you. And not just because I'm your sister and I have to. You had a tough choice to make. I've seen Dad struggle the same way when he thinks no one's looking, especially since Mom got pregnant again. Half of us are teenagers, the other half are ten and under and he's about to have another one. Like him, you carry a lot of pressure on your shoulders to be everything for the people you love. You can't do it all and you can't beat yourself up when you don't. There's no telling what would've happened if you had been there. Maybe you both would've been killed, maybe nothing would've happened. Or maybe it would've happened another night or not at all. You don't know. And you handled it the best you knew how at the time. Now you know better."

He snickered. "I hope that wasn't meant to make me feel better."

She smiled and patted him on the shoulder as she stood. "Nope. If you'll excuse me, I'm going to bed."

Jeremiah remained in his seat as she headed for the hall. "Hey sis."

She stopped at the doorway and turned to face him. "Yeah?"

"Thanks."

She shrugged and disappeared around the corner.

Jeremiah looked at the fire. Soon it would burn out. What his sister said didn't comfort him, but he felt he got some perspective. Maybe he didn't have all the answers, but somehow he would find a way to save Bella... even from herself.

Chapter Five

Bella filled a small paper cup with water from the bathroom sink, then set it to the side. She picked up the unlabeled bottle and stared it for a moment before she shook out a couple of pills and popped them in her mouth. Recapping the bottle she lifted the cup of water to her mouth and swallowed. A few weeks ago the bottle had a label on it from a prescription she'd gotten from her doctor. When it stopped being enough she found other means of obtaining what she needed. That was how she met Tommy. He was only significant when she called for a refill.

Bella set the bottle on the counter and glanced at her watch as she slipped it on. With a small sigh she grabbed her brush and quickly pulled her hair into a ponytail. She looked in the mirror and studied her reflection for a moment. For the day she had selected a pair of ultra-low rise destroyed skinny leg jeans and a black and white studded graphic short sleeve cropped tee that had *Miss Your* above and *Kiss* below a pair of lips. She sucked in her bottom lip, grabbed the pill bottle and turned off the light on her way out of the bathroom. She slid on a pair of black round toe ballet flats. She grabbed her purse off the night stand, dumped the pill bottle in it and nearly slammed into Sarresh as she exited the room.

Sarresh gripped Bella's arms. "Whoa! Slow your roll Bella."

"But David should be here soon."

"Yeesh, I never thought you'd be so excited over getting a tattoo."

"I'm more excited to see what he designed." Bella bounced on the balls of her feet.

"So he got you to rethink the tombstone?"

"For God sakes, I told you yes already."

Sarresh held up her hands and laughed. "All right, I'm just making sure."

"Good. Now can we go downstairs?"

"Yeah. Cook has breakfast waiting."

"It's not more grapefruit and soy milk, is it?" Bella whined.

Sarresh laughed. "No. Pancakes."

"Now that's what I'm talking about!" Bella grinned, slapped her hands together and ran past Sarresh down the stairs, hooked the corner and plowed through the doors that led into the smaller dining hall. Bella's parents may not have liked her being there, but she loved it. The house was huge, large enough for the acres upon acres it rested on. There were two dining halls (formal and informal), kitchen, den, living room, office, greenhouse, servant quarters, and guest rooms. On the grounds were a tennis court, indoor pool, basketball court, and a track, a recent addition. Yet none of these things delighted her. No, what she loved about this house was the fortress that protected it. No one knew how to find her and even if they did, it wouldn't be easy to get in.

"Good Morning."

Mike already occupied the table in the informal dining room. Bella smiled when she found a seat to his left. Aside from being the father of Sarresh's baby, Bella had no clue about the type of relationship he and Sarresh had. They never kissed or hugged in front of Bella, and only ever talked shop. They were so easy to be around because they had no relationship to throw in her face.

"Good morning," he replied.

Like a lady she slid a napkin across her lap while she waited to be served. A minute later Sarresh walked in with the baby and settled into a seat to Mike's right. Between the two of them sat a bassinet. Sarresh had their little girl, Takina, about a month ago so she still breastfed. This had become the normal morning routine whenever Bella stayed the night. During the week with Sarresh in school and Mike working they had a nanny who took care of the baby. On the weekend Mike tended to her. He loved his daddy/daughter time. Most of the time Bella was okay, but sometimes she focused on eating rather than anything going on in her surroundings. She liked Mike, he was nice and a good father, but occasionally he reminded her of the relationship she used to have with her own father. Often it hurt to realize she didn't think she'd ever trust her dad again.

Right now what she thought about was David Warren. During last night's shopping trip, she and Sarresh had run into him and his friend Tyler. David insisted that Bella go to his tattoo artist because his guy was cleaner than the place Sarresh had intended to take her. With the importance of safety he didn't have to work too hard to convince her. David and his friend ended up spending the rest of the night with them. He officially surprised the heck out of her.

Three years ago David's family moved to Rescate County Estates. They met when she tutored him in Geometry half way through her freshman year and his sophomore year. Being in advanced math she'd been perfectly capable of helping him pass. As taken by her as he had been, she knew he hung out with the popular crowd and she didn't fit in. So she hadn't cared to learn about him at the time and nothing had changed until last night.

David made sure she saw a whole new side of him. She discovered he was thoughtful, kind, funny and genuine. He answered all of her questions honestly, even when he seemed uncomfortable by her inquiry or when it regarded her. Bella hadn't been prepared for the last two qualities. Over the past two months whenever she worked with David at the Fall Harvest Production she had unintentionally flirted. That ended last night. Jeremiah ignored her for weeks. Yes, he ran toward the car last night, but what did that mean to her? *What does it mean? Why did he run to me? Does he miss me? If he does, why did he leave me? It doesn't matter. He hurt me. I don't think I can forgive or trust him again.*

Bella had been lost in her mind and barely caught the end of Sarresh handing an envelope to Mike. She didn't catch what Sarresh said. "What's that?"

Sarresh shrugged. "I don't know. Uncle Jamar asked me to give it to Mike when I was at the house the other day."

"Oh. What were you doing?"

"Mandy and I were watching a movie."

"Did you see..." No. She didn't need to ask about Miah. *I have to stop this!*

"No, I didn't." Sarresh sighed.

Bella stared at her pancakes and pushed them around a little. "Is your brother visiting soon?"

"He's coming up after Fall Semester is over."

"Is he going to see your mom while he's here?"

"No one's going to see that bitch."

"Language!" Mike said.

Sarresh frowned. "She's almost two months old. She doesn't know what I'm saying."

Bella smiled in amusement. Jeremiah's mother and Sarresh's mother were sisters, but his mother never really talked much about her family. Bella understood why. Sarresh's parents were tolerable up to a certain point. She hadn't spent a lot of time around them, but their personalities weren't hard to pinpoint. Sarresh's father was arrogant and selfish. Sarresh's mother was bossy and selfish. They made quite a pair.

"When was the last time you saw Ron?"

"At your fifteenth birthday party." Bella didn't like to think too much on that day. She had gotten into a huge fight with Sarresh. They made up a week later, but their two year friendship had been damaged. After a few months they stopped talking and hanging out altogether. Just over a year had passed by since then. They only reconnected when Sarresh showed up in her hospital room a couple days after her attack.

"I'm sure he'll want to see you again. He used to tell me you were like a second sister, annoying."

Letting the memories go, Bella frowned and tore off a piece of her pancake, then threw it at her friend.

"Hey! What was that for?"

"I think I'm offended."

Sarresh grinned and threw a piece of food back at Bella.

Mike interjected. "Ladies, ladies. Food is meant for eating, not playing."

Bella and Sarresh exchanged a look and simultaneously threw a piece of pancake at him.

"Oh come on!"

Bella laughed and looked at Sarresh. "You ready?"

"Yeah."

The two of them left the dining room just as a buzz sounded from the front gate. David had been given the address because he insisted on picking them up. With everything they talked about the night before not once did she find out what kind of car he drove. He rounded the driveway as she and Sarresh stepped outside. Bella whistled low. She had no clue what type of vehicle it was, but she knew it - was - beautiful! Common sense told her that it was an exquisitely sleek, black convertible and she recognized the BMW logo. When he answered on exactly what type of car he drove she could easily play stupid. If she hadn't seen it, she'd have no idea what a BMW E64 M6 Convertible looked like. With it being a two door, Sarresh climbed into the backseat with Tyler and Bella took up the passenger seat. Although it was winter, the weather was perfect for riding with the top down. They chatted a little, but mostly listened to music and sang during the forty-five minute trip. David pulled into a parking spot and she turned to him. "What tattoo design did you come up with?"

He reached into his pocket and handed her a piece of paper before he shut the ignition off and got out of the car.

She unfolded the paper and stared at the drawing. She looked up when he opened her door. "Did you do this?"

Offering her a hand he shook his head. "No. I don't draw. That's Tyler's handiwork. I just gave him the specs to work with."

"I like this." She accepted his assistance.

Sarresh got out behind her. "Let me see."

Bella handed the paper over her shoulder. "How did you come up with it?"

"Not sure really. It just popped into my head after thinking about the verse a bit."

Feeling the drawing being returned to her hand she couldn't help but smile. "I'm curious though, I don't see the eight or five anywhere."

Moving around behind her he pointed them out. "There and there."

Her eyes snapped wide open as she followed his hand. Nothing like this would have crossed her mind. A skull and bones with a tattered pirate flag seemed too perfect for words at the rebellious nature it symbolized. But having *Deuteronomy* in Old English between the tips of the dagger-shaped bones as if it was the name of a ship fell right into place with the rest of the image. Yes, this was perfect for Deuteronomy 8:5. Feeling David take her hand into his he tugged her to the door. She watched as he took command and told the lady at the front who they were there for. When he presented his ID she stole a glance at it and instantly refocused her attention back to him. "Why didn't you say it was your birthday?"

"Because it isn't a big deal."

"But eighteen is supposed to be a monumental birthday!"

"My parents travel a lot. Heather and I celebrated together until we moved here. Besides I can't imagine a better way to spend my birthday than with you." He grinned. "Now, do you know where you're going to get this?"

She stared blankly at David then nodded unable to do anything else. "Yeah, my lower back."

The design may have changed, but the location hadn't. Once again a flush crept through Bella's body as she watched his lips broaden into a devious grin. If she didn't know better, sometimes she would swear the Devil incarnate possessed him. His gaze slipped from her after a minute, realizing the guy she presumed to be their artist stepped into the room. The two exchanged a hand grip, clap on the back and split-second chest bump. Amused she brought a hand to her mouth and hoped to cover the snicker.

David slid a hand around her waist. "Bella this is Bobby. Bobby, Bella."

"Nice to meet you," Bella said.

"Likewise." Bobby turned to David. "Is it just you or the two of you?"

"Both of us. We'll go back together, but you'll do her first then me." He glanced over his shoulder. "Sarresh, are you wanting something too?"

"Yeah, but you guys go first."

Bobby nodded. "Cool. Come on back and we'll start."

David kept his arm around Bella as they walked to the back room. Inside were a few different tables, one of which had a small chest of drawers and butt loads of bottles of color. Taking up half the back wall was a huge mirror she could see herself in and everything behind her. A chair had been placed against the right side wall, a stool by a lap top on a table against the left wall and in the middle of it all - a long chair without arms.

"Do you have something in mind?" Bobby asked.

Bella handed him the design. "This. On my lower back."

"You sure? You don't want something a little more feminine? Like a sugar skull?"

"I don't know what that is, but no. I want that exact design."

"Okay."

Easy enough. People usually argued with her. Her family and friends always seemed to think they knew what she wanted more than she did. Like they knew what was best. She watched as Bobby headed into a back room of some sort. While he did whatever she rested her head against David's chest. "So, do you have one already?"

"Two actually."

Shocked by his response Bella lifted her head and looked up to him. "Are you serious?"

"Yes. Why do you look surprised?"

"I guess I just didn't peg you for someone who would defile himself."

David laughed. "I don't consider it being defiled. It's a form of art. Besides if it's defiling, then why are you doing it?"

With soft eyes she tilted her head. "What? I don't look like the type of person who would get a tattoo?"

"No."

"I think I'm deeply offended."

"Then tell me what I can do to make it up to you."

What could he do? Good question. His statement hadn't really offended her. Simply a misconception people often had about her. Until a month and a half ago she would've never gotten a tattoo. Her parents raised her to treat her body like a temple as the Good Book said. David was right. Except she wasn't the same girl any of her friends knew a month and a half ago. Maybe he did need to do something to make up for his assumption. Bella grinned as an idea popped into her head. "If you want to make it up to me, then we need to go out for your birthday tonight."

"But I—"

"No buts, you asked and I answered. Take it or leave it." She pulled out from under his arm. Bobby returned from the back and patted the chair in the middle of the room. Purposely she swayed her hips as she walked. Redirecting her attention to Bobby. "How do I sit in this thing?"

"Low back, right?"

Bella nodded.

"Straddle it."

Good thing she knew what he meant. She glanced over her shoulder to David before she climbed up and swung a leg over. Yes, very unlikely that she would straddle him, but that didn't mean she couldn't give him a show. As she leaned forward on the back of the chair she felt paper get tucked into her pants and then something cold swiped along her back.

"I'm just wiping your back. I'll get the design transferred, get the colors together and then we'll get started. Let me know if you need a break at all."

"Do you think I'll need one?"

"It depends on your pain tolerance. This is a fleshy area so it's a good place for a first tattoo."

First? Bella had no idea if she planned to get more than one. Right now it seemed like the perfect thing to do. It made the most sense. If God could turn His back on her, then she would turn hers on Him. Although she chose a Bible verse to include in the tattoo, she knew it would serve as a permanent reminder. Not even a child of God could be protected from His wrath. She never wanted to forget she could be punished just like anyone else. Whether or not another tattoo would be in her future, well she didn't want to think too much about that. After all, who knew if she would even have a future. The whirring noise she heard pulled her back into reality and she instantly flipped her gaze to Bobby. She stared at the device in his gloved hand with wide huge eyes. *I wanted a tattoo. Then why does that thing freak me out?*

"You ready?"

Bella inhaled and exhaled a couple of calming breaths. A pair of fingers snapped in front of her. Quickly she looked over to the person they belonged to.

"You don't have to do this," David said. "But if you're positive you do, you can hold my hand if you need to."

She took another set of deep breaths. Right, she didn't have to, but she would. Finally relaxed Bella looked back over to Bobby. "I'm ready."

"Okay."

Returning her attention to David she couldn't help but smile a little. Not only had he been nice about everything, he'd been patient. Tilting her head she studied him and wondered if he had always been like that. If so, why had she never noticed? Easy. She never gave him the time of day. She tutored him because she had to, but he hadn't been the type of person she would spend time with outside of school. Had she always been so judgmental? Ashamed of her prior actions she said, "I'm sorry."

"For what?" David asked, confused.

"Of the way I've treated you. I always figured you were like your sister and I hated her. I'm sorry. I shouldn't have just written you off without getting to know you."

"Hey, no need to apologize. We're human and naturally protective of ourselves. Maybe that's why the Bible teaches things happen on God's time, not ours."

Bella's lips tightened as she bit her tongue. She wanted to tell him to keep that crap to himself, but she didn't. Instead she curtly nodded. Funny, with all this talk she'd hardly noticed the sting as the needle danced across her skin. But David's last statement pushed her to change the topic. "You said you have two tattoos. Tell me about them."

"I got the Arc de Triomphe in ruins as a reminder that I can only depend on myself. I was sixteen and my parents went to Paris without me or my sister. I decided I'd do something to piss them off. I figured a tattoo was the way to go. I befriended Bobby not too long after we moved here and knew he did tattoos. I came up to the shop and he said he'd hook me up. That's how I got my first one."

"What about the second?"

David stared at her in silence. She could see he hesitated on telling her about the second, but she couldn't figure out why. Her brows lowered as she studiously waited. Impatience getting the best of her. "How come you don't want to tell me?"

"It's a little embarrassing."

"You said you would only ever be honest with me."

He sighed and nodded. "Okay. The second one I got about three months ago. It was just after the first Bible Teen Group I attended." David paused there and shifted around in the seat he'd taken across from her.

He lifted his sleeve. On his left arm he had an intricate band of thorns. Just when she thought she'd seen all of it he turned his arm around and showed her the cross that had been incorporated into the thorns on his bicep. She shook her head and grinned. At least now she understood his embarrassment. He hadn't been raised a Believer like she had. And somehow she couldn't help but feel like teasing him a little. "Either my dad is good and you accepted the Lord Jesus as your Sovereign Savior or you really wanted to fit in."

David shrugged. "To be honest, I'm not sure. I was just compelled to get it."

She nodded. "I get that. Sometimes things we want just can't be explained." For a moment she wondered why he only showed her the second and not the first. "Can I see the first one?" Again she watched him hesitate. She lowered her gaze at him. "It isn't in someplace, private, is it?"

He blinked at her then busted out laughing. "No. Nothing like that."

"Then I do believe you should show me." She grinned.

"Okay, okay. You don't get told 'no' do you?"

"No."

David sighed and stood up. He turned so his back faced her and he pulled his t-shirt over his head.

"Come closer."

He didn't move and he needed to be closer so she could reach. Curiously she glanced to the mirror and noticed the frown on his face. "I see that."

"And."

"Come on. Come closer or I'll pout. I swear I'll do it." As he stared at her reflection in the mirror Bella slowly puffed out her bottom lip, rolled her eyes up, lowered her brows and pouted.

He shook his head, but complied with her request. Finally close enough, she studied the image and traced the lines over his back. The tattoo took up nearly his whole back, but it worked well with his natural musculature. The Arc de Triomphe had been done in three dimensions, which made sense. If any one of the sides had only been done then it wouldn't have been as detailed, nor would it have looked right. Half of the arc stood facing away from the body. About three quarters of one side had been drawn over most of his left side between the base of his neck and the middle of his shoulder. The soldiers that should have appeared along that portion of the arc were nearly missing as if chunks of stone had been ripped out. Partial lines had been drawn as if to demonstrate the destruction of the arc with the entire top of it gone. To complete the tattoo, the design had been done in various hues of black and gray. Slowly she continued to trace the lines. Bella had never seen the Arc de Triomphe, but she didn't believe it to naturally be this dark. Unsure if David noticed or not, she felt him shiver every time she touched his back. Biting the bottom of her lip she couldn't help herself as she traced more lines. Grinning widely she pulled her hand back. "Very beautiful."

David nodded and tugged his t-shirt back on.

"Now I see why you wanted me to come here. You knew I'd be getting worked on by the best."

"Something like that."

"Well, I appreciate it." She smiled and canted her head as a thought crossed her mind. "So, what new tattoo are you planning to get?"

Chapter Six

Bobby wiped down David's right arm, "All right, man. You're done. Want to check it out?"

"Yeah." David got up from the chair and walked over to the mirror and looked over the work. He glanced at Bobby. "Exactly what I wanted."

"Cool. Let me get it covered and you guys are set."

"Can I see before he does?" Bella asked since he had refused to answer her question earlier.

David turned to face her and bobbed his head back and forth for a second as he contemplated her question. With a sigh he nodded and headed in her direction.

Oh. My. God! What was he thinking? Scrawled in the same Old English font her last name glistened back at her. *Insane! Holy crap!* She pulled herself together and forced a smile to her face. She got out of Bobby's way when he stepped in to put some lotion on David's tattoo and taped plastic gauze over it. Just the opportunity she needed to collect herself. Right now he needed to believe her flattery. His attraction to her she had to have. Once David got set up, he walked to her. She looked up at him and slid her hand in his as they headed back down the hall.

When they came into view, she saw disappointment crawl on Sarresh's face at the hand holding. Bella dropped her gaze to the ground and felt grateful when Bobby took Sarresh back and Tyler followed. She and David took their place on the couch.

Yes, the fact he got her last name permanently embedded in his skin unnerved her and she questioned it considering they weren't dating. Though they could, couldn't they? Sure she occasionally went by her boyfriend's. *Does that mean I stalk him? No. That's too strong a word.* She only drove by, but they never talked. Although Jeremiah ignoring her didn't actually end their relationship. She would at least break up with someone first. And he hadn't done that. And she certainly *did* enjoy spending time with David. She may not be able to manage any kind of intimate contact with him, but that could be dealt with if they crossed that bridge. Bella shuddered.

David pulled her hand into his again. "Are you cold?"

She nodded and figured it easier to lie than tell the truth. Amazing how easy lying had become. Until a few weeks ago she'd never lied once in her life and now it had become second nature. Needing to get out of her own brain, she looked to David. "So about your birthday."

"Right. We have to do something so I can make up for my earlier actions."

"Yep. What should we do?"

"Let me think a second."

She shook her head. "Come on, you already know don't you? Stop messing with me."

"How well you read me." He grinned wide. "A friend of mine is a DJ at that new club downtown, T2, and he's been trying to get me to go for a few weeks now. We could check it out."

"Can I get in?"

"Yeah, it's specifically for teens and I'd absolutely love to take you."

"You've been thinking about that for a minute haven't you?"

"Yeah. At least since the club opened." He rubbed his chin. The devious grin returned.

"Will it just be you and me, or will there be others?" Bella shivered.

"I'm sure Tyler would like to go and you can invite Sarresh."

"As long as Mike doesn't mind staying home with the baby. Then again, he hasn't complained any time she says she's spending time with me."

"Baby?" David quirked a brow.

Of course, he didn't know. Last night had been the first time she'd spent with David outside of tutoring. *Duh, Bella.* "Sorry, I forgot. You remember all the rumors floating around school about a pregnant girl?"

"Vaguely, I don't really pay much attention to them. More my sister's territory."

Snickering, she mumbled, "That's an understatement." His sister - *Bitch* with a capital B. Of all the times Heather's attitude came out, the one that will forever be imprinted in Bella's mind with absolute joy occurred just after her first return to school. Bella laughed and shook her head. As much as the memory shouldn't make her smile, she loathed David's sister enough that it always did.

"What's so funny?"

"Nothing." Intending to talk about anything beside the memory that amused her, she continued. "You think we can stop for some lunch after this? And maybe you can run me by my parents' house so I can pick up enough clothes for the week."

Silently he studied her face in contemplation. "On one condition."

She hesitated. "All right."

"Tell me what made you laugh."

A wide grin spread to her cheeks. "Only if you can promise me you won't be offended."

"If it has something to do with me, I can't promise that."

As bothered by his response she suspected she should be, her smile still wouldn't go away. She needed to smile. Sometimes it gave her the opportunity to bury the anger and hurt. "Indirectly it does."

"Then I might indirectly be offended, but I want you to tell me anyway."

"Just remember you asked for it."

"I think I can handle the punishment."

"Okay then, I was thinking about the time Mandy punched the shit out of your sister and knocked her on her ass. Every time I replay that moment of Heather landing on the floor, I can't help but laugh. And not just because it's funny, even though it is, but because I know how much she deserved it."

He raised an eyebrow just before he burst out in laughter. David almost sounded like a thundering, cackling hyena. A little creepy. When he finally caught his breath. "You think I would be offended by *that*?" He shook his head. "Not at all. Fact, I like to recall that myself. Reminds me my sister isn't as untouchable as she likes to think she is."

"My, my, my. I'm not quite sure how I should react to this. I mean aren't brothers supposed to love and protect their siblings?" Since she had none of her own, she could only assume. Her best friend Vick was the closest she had to a brother. The only other interactions she'd been exposed to had been with Jeremiah's family. Quickly she squashed that thought. She had to be fair and not think about him while spending time with David.

"Oh, don't get me wrong. I love my sister, but sometimes I detest her just as much. If I didn't know any better, I would swear she's adopted. I mean, we're so different."

"You mean because she's a Class-A bitch and you're not an asshole? Or is it because you have class and she doesn't."

"Little bit of both." David chuckled.

"You know if I didn't like you before, I think I really like you now."

Inquisitively he stared at her. "Part of me feels like I should be thrilled and the other part questions that."

"You shouldn't. Instead you should just look pretty, smile and nod." Bella giggled.

Busting out into another bout of laughter he shook his head. "Where would you like to go for lunch?"

"Hmm, I think there's a burger joint a couple blocks from here."

"I know the place." He paused. "And I suppose this means afterward I'm running you by your parents'."

"That was the deal."

"Will your parents mind that you're with me?"

"Doesn't matter. I mean how would they react if they knew I got a tattoo? Or that you took me? You running me by my house for clothes should be the least of your concerns."

"Point taken."

Yeah, her parents wouldn't like him being in her life, let alone driving her around. And that seemed all the more reason to do it. She wondered if they would be home when they arrived. For a moment, she wished they would be.

Chapter Seven

At lunch, Bella started a french-fry fight between the four of them. David promptly tickled Bella to get her to stop throwing fries. Sarresh and Tyler laughed at her and David. She had fun for the first time in what felt like forever. Having gone without fun for weeks, she'd forgotten what it was like. She couldn't wait to see how the rest of the night went. Both Sarresh and Tyler agreed to go to T2 with them. The drive to her parents' house went just like the drive to the tattoo parlor, music and singing. Finally David pulled into her driveway. Bella glanced to her friends. "Do you guys want to come in or wait out here? I shouldn't be long."

"I'll come in with you," David answered.
Sarresh said, "I'll hang out here."
"Me too," Tyler followed up.
Quickly nodding, Bella and David climbed out of the car and headed to her front door. The house was empty. She reached into her jeans and pulled out the key. After they walked in she paused for a moment and shuffled through the mail. Only one thing had her name on it with no return address. Unimportant she folded it up and shoved it in her back pocket. With a vivacious grin she nudged David and walked on down the hallway. "You know I've never had a boy in my room before."
"Guess I'm just lucky then." He followed after her.
"Guess so." They stepped through her bedroom door. Once inside she moved over to her closet, grabbed her suitcase, placed it on the chair and popped it open. She started at the dresser, then moved to the closet where David took up space. Without grabbing any clothes she studied him for a second. "Anything you like?"
Running his fingers over her clothes he paused on one of her tops. "This one. I like this one."

The blouse he picked was a white sleeveless mock neck zip back. "Really?"

"Yes."

She snagged the blouse off the hanger and started back for her bag. "Guess I know what I'm wearing tonight." She returned making sure she got the three inch tan heels purchased to go with the top and then stopped at the dresser to fish out the shorts and belt that went with it. "Got to have all the right stuff."

"Of course."

Ten minutes later they headed back down the hallway with him carrying her bag as they stepped out the door. He opened the passenger door for her before putting her suitcase in the trunk. Back on the road she remembered the unmarked envelope she'd tucked away. Reaching into her pocket she pulled it out and opened it only to wish she hadn't. One time, she read over it one time. Slowly her hands dropped into her lap loosening their grip on that awful sheet of paper. They said there shouldn't be any contact. Even though no signature or return address appeared on the letter, she knew who sent it. Who else could it be? Where had all the air gone? Glancing around she needed assurance the top remained down and the tightness in her lungs was all in her head. When a hand found hers, she jumped as far as the seat belt would let her go, forcing her to pull it together.

"Hey," David spoke low. "You okay?"

No! Hell no! "Yeah," she mumbled averting her eyes from him. If she looked at him she wouldn't be able to keep the tears at bay clawing at the corner of her eyes.

"You sure? We don't have go to out tonight." He squeezed her hand.

Forming the best fake smile she could. "I'm okay. And we're going, no objections."

"Okay." He stroked her hand.

****

On the way back to Sarresh's house Bella managed to fold the letter up and return it to the envelope and re-tucked it in her back pocket. She'd barely spent two minutes in the house before she asked to borrow Sarresh's car and bolted. Being a Saturday she prayed Chief Detrone would be at the station, but knew better. Of all the time she'd spent at Jeremiah's house, how often had his dad been at the police station over the weekend? Once. As much as she wanted to go there first, logically it didn't make sense. That pissed her off more as she headed to the one place she didn't want to be. Bella sped across town like her life depended on it. Typically this drive took thirty minutes. Making it in twenty she screeched the tires to a halt when she parked the car in the driveway, shut off the ignition, got out of the car and slammed the door. Unfortunately the front door suffered her approach too. She banged as hard as her fist allowed.

Amanda answered the door. "Hi," she barely said when Bella shoved past her.

Unusually aggressive Bella hollered, "Where's your dad?"

"In the kitchen."

Bella stomped to the kitchen. "I thought you said he couldn't get to me!"

Jeremiah's dad turned around. "Well hello to you too."

"You said he couldn't get to me!" She yanked the letter out and threw it on the kitchen island. Finally unable to contain her emotions any longer, she sobbed.

Holding up his hands. "Calm down, deep breath for me. Now what are you talking about?"

"That!" Bella cried out pointing to the letter. "You said..." She hadn't been able to complete the sentence as he walked over and picked up what she'd placed in front of him. Unable to look away as he read the letter, she wrapped her arms tightly around her body. She knew what every line said.

> *My slick and sweet honey bear*
> *How I wish, I was there.*
> *Your innocence, so hot and pure*
> *Is my only hope of a cure.*
> *To feel your lips on mine*
> *And taste your strong, lovely wine.*
> *When we're chest to chest*
> *Bare breast to breast.*
> *There is a song beating in my heart*
> *That reminds me we'll never part.*

No longer able to fight the shakes, tears came hard again and forced her to recall all the things Quincy Harlem did to her. Every bruise he left, every bone he broke, every piece of her soul he took - all of it. The rancid smell of rotting meat, the reek of sweat pouring off his body, the horrid stench of stale cigarette smoke on his breath, the rough voice whispering "Honey bear" in her ear - the memories hurt so much.

Shaking more, a pair of warm soothing arms came around her with a gentle voice. "It's okay."

Unaware of how much time she allowed the pain to break free, she found a way to put a cap on it and tuck it away. Pulling away from Jamar's arms she wiped her eyes. "Why did he send this?"

"It's a psych out to keep you from testifying."

"What are you talking about? You said I wouldn't have to testify. There was enough evidence to get him without my testimony."

"Haven't your parents talked to you?"

Shaking her head Bella curled her arms around her body again suddenly fearing what would come out of his mouth. Again. God punished her again! *What the hell did I do to deserve this?*

"The DNA evidence we had from your rape kit was contaminated by the lab so it was thrown out. Your testimony and ID are the only thing keeping the rape case alive. Trial is scheduled to start December 20th and you'll be the first one to take the stand. That's why I asked to see you yesterday."

"No! No! No!" She implored. *This can't be happening! Please God, don't let this happen!* Firmly shaking her head. "No... I won't testify." Unwilling to hear anymore she ran out the front door.

****

Jeremiah stood off to the side of the entranceway and heard the entire conversation. As she ran past him he grabbed her arm. "Bell!"

She yanked her arm free. "Let go of me!"

"Bell, please. We can get through your testimony." He beseeched, desperately wanting to be there for her.

"Stop calling me that!" Turning around she stared at him hard. Tears pouring down. "And what 'we,' Jeremiah? You walked away from us. There is no 'we'!"

"Bella, I'm sorry." He attempted to respect her request and used her nickname and not his nickname for her. Though she would always be his beautiful angel.

"You're sorry? That's all you can say?" Turning away she screamed. "Go to hell!"

Yeah, he deserved that. He grabbed her arm again and noticed part of a bandage peeking out of her jeans. "What is that?"

"None of your damn business!" She snapped, freeing herself from his grip.

He hated when she got like this. Still, he hadn't planned to let her go. Especially with all her mother told him the day before pointing him in one direction for the bandage. "Did you get a tattoo?"

"Like I said before, 'none of your damn business.'" She walked away again.

"No, Bella." Anguish firmly snaked a hold of his heart at the truth of what she didn't say. Leaving and never telling her parents where she planned to go, what she did or who she was with was one thing. This took rebellion to a whole new level. Instead of grabbing her arm, he ran around her until he blocked her way to the car. "Bella, please. I just want to be there for you."

"Like hell you do! You left me! Or don't you remember, because I do! Can you even tell me why?"

I want to, but I can't tell you. Jeremiah shook his head. "I'm here now."

"Yeah, just so you can leave again like before."

Low and brutal, but honest. With his words having no effect, he knew he had to do something drastic otherwise he would lose her. No one could've prepared him for what made the most sense. Feeling for sure he'd get her attention and scream his seriousness to her, he stepped forward and pressed his lips to hers.

For a second she may have returned his kiss, but then she hauled back and slapped him and yelled. "Leave me alone!" She stared hard at him and said coldly, "You should be used to it by now." Stepping away from him she shook her head. "I can't go through this with you anymore. You pleading and kissing me isn't going to change that you haven't been there! I can't trust you will be. And right now there is someone who is." Walking past him to the car she paused and murmured, "I'm done."

The sting in his face matched the ache in his heart, especially when what she said hit him. Jeremiah spun around. "You're right, I haven't been there. And I get you need that. If you've found someone, I can accept it. As long as it's not David Warren." From the moment Jeremiah met the guy he knew something was off. David's attraction to Bella had been obvious and strong bordering close to creepy stalker. David was still suspected for slashing the tires on Jeremiah's dad's car a few months back while Jeremiah and Bella were on a date. Although nothing had been proved Jeremiah knew for sure he didn't trust the guy. Not to mention, according to rumor, David had a temper.

Now at the driver side door she stopped with her hand on the handle. "You lost all rights to give me any opinions about who I do or don't spend my time with when you walked out of my hospital room and stopped talking to me."

Lifting his gaze to hers, he got a glimpse of everything happening behind those hazel eyes for the first time in weeks. Remembering how full of life they used to be, staring at them now he would swear the joy had been ripped out, leaving them lifeless. Anger, hate, and despair filled what once sparkled. Her rapist could claim partial blame, but the rest of it belonged to him. The tears that began in the kitchen were from reliving the rape again and again, but the tears that streamed full force now, those were from him. Not once had he helped and he couldn't change the truth. He may not like David, but if he could bring the light back then Jeremiah needed to step aside and let him. Quenching his own tears at what he planned to do, he rubbed his face with a brief nod and decided he would once again respect her request. "I'm sorry Bella. You're right. I'll leave you alone."

He watched as she stood there blinking at him. Reading those eyes for a moment he believed the hurt that overwhelmed them when he said he'd let her go and for a split second he wanted to run to her, pull her against him and hold her forever. Then she tore her gaze away, climbed in the car and left. Once out of eyesight, he did the most unmanly thing he could, he crouched down, buried his face in his hands and cried.

Jeremiah couldn't be sure how long he stayed outside once Bella drove off. After a while the crouching position had become uncomfortable, which made him sit on the concrete with his face still buried in his hands. At some point he stopped crying and stared down the driveway. Maybe if he did that long enough he could will the car back. He wanted her to come back. He needed her to come back. He needed his beautiful angel, his Bell.

Chapter Eight

Bella drove a couple of blocks down the road. Out of sight from Jeremiah's house she pulled over to the side, put the car in park and shut off the ignition. Tears flooded her eyes as she dropped her forehead against the wheel. She cried and shook letting all her anguish free.

Unsure her heart could break any more than it just did, she tried to force the truth out of her head. No matter what happened, she loved Jeremiah. In the month they dated her heart became his. Someone might as well have just cracked her ribs and removed the organ that beat beneath her chest because she felt horridly empty, worse than how she felt after her attack. She didn't want to break up with him, but she couldn't ignore how easily he left or his failure to explain anything. She couldn't trust he would stay. Even if it didn't fix anything, she would hold one thing dear in the worse argument she's ever had. A one second kiss where their lips touched and reignited their spark. The one she had missed for months. All for nothing.

Needing a way to calm down she reached over to her purse and dug around until she found the bottle she never left home without. Mental, emotional, and physical pain overran her body; which exhausted her to the point that she needed it to go away. It took four times to get out the right number of pills because two wouldn't cut it right now. Reaching over for the bottle of water she popped three in her mouth and followed it with two swigs to make sure they went down. Fifteen minutes later she finally stopped crying enough to pick up her phone and press a couple buttons.

Before she met Jeremiah, she had one person she always depended on - Vick. They grew up together. If she knew anything about siblings, he was it. He was a year older and the closest she had to a brother. Like a brother, he didn't approve of her choice in friends or guys, except Jeremiah. The two became friends a couple of months ago. As for Amanda, she couldn't figure that out. Bella thought Vick and Amanda were dating, but that remained unconfirmed. Bella could call Sarresh, but she couldn't handle bad situations. Like many times before, Bella turned to Vick.

Two rings later a voice answered, "Hello?"

"Hey Vick." She cleared her throat twice before speaking. It didn't help, she still sounded hoarse, stuffed up, and broken.

"Bella? You okay?"

"No," she whispered. "I need time away. Is anybody — Is your summer home open?"

"Yeah. Key's in the birdhouse. You want to talk about it?"

Whimpering she muttered, "It's over."

"What?"

Unable to stop the tears now any more than she could thirty minutes ago. "I can't...." she rocked back and forth. "I just can't... No more..."

As if what she said made complete sense Vick said, "I'm sorry, Bella."

The next four words weren't anything she'd planned to say openly. Until that moment. She whispered, "I don't want this."

Based on what she said, his next question shouldn't have surprised her. "Do you love him?"

"Yes," she cried between staggering breaths.

"Okay," Vick said. "You go on to the house. But first I need you to calm down so you can drive. Take a deep breath with me." Following his example she inhaled broken spurts of air and exhaled once. "Good. One more." Again, she took another one and managed to get a better grip this time.

For good measure she took another one and wiped away her tears. "Thanks."

"Anytime. Now, go on. Relax a little. Okay?"

"Yeah," she answered before disconnecting the line. While she couldn't be sure if the calm that finally claimed her came from the numb sensation of the pain killers or from the three deep breaths at least now she could drive. Starting the car she pulled back onto the road and got on her way.

****

No matter how hard he stared or prayed, his beautiful angel, his Bell never did come back. Jeremiah couldn't believe he let her leave. He'd give anything for a second chance, a way to re-do that entire argument and replace it with a conversation. There were many things he needed to tell her and this time instead of fearing what she would say, he'd tell her all of it. From how much he screwed up when he left her hospital room while she gave her statement to his dad to how cowardly he'd been in not going back. Breaking up with him made so much sense he wanted to kick his own butt. He barely heard his name called, but paid more attention the second time.

"Jeremy, you've got a phone call," his sister told him.

"Who is it?" he asked without taking his gaze away from the driveway.

"Vick."

Unsure he had the energy to talk to him, Jeremiah thought of his feelings for Bella and reconsidered taking the phone call. Whether they were together or not, he wanted to make sure Bella would be watched out for, especially if she would be dating that creep David. Placing his hand on the ground he pushed up to his feet and walked toward his sister.

"Everything copacetic?"

"No, but don't ask right now. I'll come talk to you after I get done with Vick."

"Whatever."

The two headed back inside the house. He picked up the phone. "Hello?"

"Hey man."

"Hey," he replied closing his bedroom door behind him. Wanting to be as close to his angel as possible he settled on his bed choosing the side Bella had slept on the one night she spent there.

"I'd ask how you are, but I know."

"Did she tell you?"

"Yeah, I just got off the phone with her."

"How is she?" Jeremiah asked with a little prayer.

"Bad," Vick told him. "Listen, you guys are meant to be. I grew up with her and I've never seen her the way she is when she's with you. Obviously you guys need some time though."

"Tell me, how bad is she?"

"Worse than I expected." He paused. "She told me one thing, but I don't think she meant to."

"What's that?"

"She loves you."

Jeremiah's heart stopped the second those three beautiful words came out of Vick's mouth. *Can it possibly be true? Did he really just say that? Did she? Did she mean it?* Jeremiah swallowed. "Do you believe her?"

"With as broken as Bella is, I do. Let her calm down. Staying away like you have, you can't fix it with one conversation. Remind her why she fell in love with you and that you can be there for her, even if right now it's just as a friend. And she'll come around."

Jeremiah rubbed his face willing his heart to mend a little in order to survive. If he could just hold on, he sighed. "I need you to look out for her. I picked a bad time. I should've waited."

"What are you talking about?"

"She showed up here with a letter that apparently came from her rapist. I haven't had a chance to talk to my dad, so I don't know what it said, but it was enough. And to make matters worse, the DNA evidence was thrown out."

"What?"

"Yeah. I didn't know until my dad told her. That isn't the bad part. In order for the case to stick, the prosecutor needs her to testify when the trial starts on the 20th."

"Please tell me you're joking."

"I wish I were."

"That explains a lot," Vick mumbled. "She's had such a hard time with the rape as it is. I can't imagine she could handle having to relive it in front of people, especially with that guy in the room."

"Yeah." Jeremiah rested a hand on the midnight blue comforter covering his bed. He remembered what it felt like to curl up to her and wake up beside her. Her body conformed perfectly to his and they both slept on their side. He loved her natural scent of lavender. Lying next to her had been like sleeping under the sun in the spring. What he wouldn't give to be able to do that again. He suspected Vick was right. So he would try being her friend, if she would let him, and show her his true strength. "Will you look out for her?"

"Don't I always?"

"You do. I'm glad she has you." Knowing he needed to forewarn Vick about David, he took in a deep breath. Didn't help, he still growled lowly at the next bit of information he shared. "Just a heads up. She might be seeing, David Warren."

Silence filled the other line. Jeremiah was great at bomb dropping, wasn't he? Just when he started to ask if he was there, Vick spoke up. "You're serious aren't you?"

"Unfortunately. I don't have confirmation, but she didn't deny it either."

"I'll be nice, but if he hurts her, I have the rights of a brother. Feel me?"

"Yeah. Thanks man. I'll holler at you later."

"Sure thing." The line went dead.

No desire to stare at the phone or remain in his room any longer Jeremiah rose to his feet and stepped through the door back into the hallway. Pausing at his sister's door he remembered he still needed to talk to her, but he should put the phone up first. Heading into the kitchen he returned it to the cradle and overheard the tail end of his dad's conversation.

"Good, I'll see you then," his dad said then pulled the cell phone from his ear and disconnected the call.

"Dad?"

Glancing over his shoulder Jamar slowly turned around. "You okay, son?"

He shook his head. "No, but I'll survive."

"I'm here if you need to talk."

"Thanks, but I'm more worried about Bella right now."

"You care about her. I'm not shocked by your concern, especially with this coming in." He tapped a plastic bag on the counter. Upon closer inspection Jeremiah realized it must be the note Bella came by with, envelope too.

"You think you can get something off of it?"

"Don't know, but we'll try."

"There anything you can do about her testifying?"

"No. He won't take a plea bargain and he has a right to face his accuser."

"And there's really only less than five weeks to convince and prepare her?"

Jamar nodded. "I'm afraid so."

"Okay." Jeremiah said before turning back down the hall. This time instead of pausing at his sister's door, he knocked and waited for it to open. Once it did he stepped inside shutting it behind him.

"You want to tell me what's going on?" Amanda dropped down into the chair at her desk, crossing her arms.

"She broke up with me." He didn't know why, but he spoke so low he might as well have whispered a secret. Maybe because he didn't want it to be true and saying it out loud made it such. Meaning he had to acknowledge just how bad the fight got. Or maybe because his lack of emotional support for his girlfriend... *ex-girlfriend* mentally correcting himself, embarrassed the hell out of him. Brushing the top of his head he looked at the ground away from the hard stare his sister gave him. "Vick's going to keep an eye on her. And I need you to do the same, but if you see her with David Warren, you need to be cool, even if they start dating or are dating."

"David? David who? I don't know a David."

Her frustration hadn't been directed at him, but he sure felt the sting behind her words almost as if he'd been slapped again. "Mandy, you know who I'm talking about."

"No, I'm afraid I don't. And if I don't know who you're talking about that means any dickwad who tries to steal my brother's girlfriend is likely to get his ass kicked."

Glancing back up at her he dropped both hands to his hips. "Please, don't make this harder than it already is. If she needs him right now, then you have to let her."

Grinding her teeth she huffed. "Whatever! But if I so much as see him kissing her in the hall at school, I can't promise I won't hit him."

Acknowledging the best promise he would get, he nodded. "Just remember you're being supportive of her."

"You really are a buzz kill. I punched his sister, why can't I do the same to him?"

Her sarcasm made him smile. "Because I have first dibs."

"Buzz kill!"

Laughing he headed out of her room back down to his own.

****

What is that noise? The smell didn't match the sound. The air had a wonderful light and fresh perfume. *Damn ringing!* The noise kept irritating the hell out of her. Two seconds later beautiful silence returned. The ringing started up again forcing Bella to open her eyes. Looking around she tried to remember where she was. Judging by the proximity of the lake she figured she had to be in the backyard of Vick's summer house laying in the hammock. As the sun set exquisitely, she wondered again about the noise? Ringing didn't make any sense. Then the quiet came back, only to be interrupted by that god awful high pitched shrill sound. When the neurons in her brain started firing back up it occurred to her the noise belonged to her cell phone. She reached into her back pocket, which caused the hammock to swing a little as she shifted around and brought the thing to her ear. "Hello?"

"Where the hell are you?" The voice on the other end snapped out.

"Sorry Z, I didn't mean to take off with your car."

"I don't care about the damn car," Sarresh replied. "What I care about is that we're getting picked up in an hour and half and you're still not home."

"What?" She moved too fast off the hammock and landed face first on the ground. With a groan she rolled over onto her back. "What time is it?"

"It's eight o'clock. You've been gone six hours."

"Oh shit!" She jumped to her feet. "I'm on my way back now. I'll be there in an hour."

"Where the hell did you end up?"

Quickly she brushed off her clothes and headed toward the front of the house. "Not important. I just needed to get away. Now I'm hanging up. I'll be there in an hour."

"Fine. You just better be able to get dressed in a short time. You know I hate running late."

"Z, it's a club. There is no running late unless we get there after they close. Which won't happen."

"Whatever. And call your mom. I'm tired of her calling me."

"All — " Bella wanted to get upset at Sarresh for hanging up on her, but thought about the consequences of getting mad since she took off. Sighing she dialed her house number and headed for the car. Feeling refreshed she stretched before climbing in and took off hoping like hell to get there soon.

"Hello?"

"Hey Mom. Sarresh said you called."

"Yes. I wanted to remind you about our therapy appointment on Monday. And don't forget your father and I are going on our annual couples retreat with Vick's parents next weekend."

Therapy? Like she could forget. She only attended the sessions so her parents wouldn't take away her car as had been threatened on more than one occasion. She hadn't forgotten about the retreat either. For the first time in years she looked forward to having the house to herself. "I'll be at the session Mom."

"Okay. Be safe. Call if you need us."

"Sure Mom. Bye." Bella disconnected the call and tossed the phone into the passenger seat. Time for some fun.

Chapter Nine

The back of T2 had a wooden porch high enough that most of the city could be seen from the view. Thrilled by the reaction to their performance Bella took a breath as she stepped outside with David. She had worn exactly what had been picked out earlier causing her steps to be heard against the wood. As if he was trying to match her, David had on a pair of tan slacks and loafers with a white un-tucked button up. The sleeves had been rolled up to his elbows.

Bella smiled. "That was so much fun! And you were good. I've heard you sing, but not like that."

"Thanks, but you were better. I'll never get tired of hearing your voice."

"Well I thoroughly enjoyed it and we definitely have to do that again." But she might have to reconsider letting him pick. Of all the songs in all the world, he had to pick *Meet Me Halfway* by the Black Eyed Peas. Bella liked the song, but David seemed more passionate about it than she did. Of course, her mood could be attributed to one of three things and they all sucked.

Draping an arm over her shoulders he said, "I'm sure I can arrange that."

They stopped as they approached the edge of the balcony. She'd worn her hair down for the first time in a while. She hadn't had much time to do a whole lot with it. Her only option had been to blow dry and let it fall. She half looked to David when he trailed his fingers through her dark tresses.

"Did you cut your hair?" he asked.

Growing up, her hair had only been cut when the dead ends needed to be trimmed. Other than that it had never been cut until after her attack. Once her mind wrapped around what happened with that man, she knew she had to cut off the hair he had touched. If she'd had her way she would've cut all of it off, but her parents wouldn't let her. Bad enough her mother cried watching the inches fall to the ground when her midnight black hair went from her butt to her mid-back. She sighed without looking at David. She didn't want to answer his question, let alone think about it.

"I'm sorry," he whispered. "You don't have to say anything."

"It's okay." She offered a small smile.

"If you want to go I'll understand," he said in an apologetic tone.

Snapping her eyes up to his. "Go? Why would I want to do that? I'm having fun and after the day I've had, I need that."

Quirking a brow he reached a hand up and tucked a loose hair behind her ear. "I want you to have fun. I didn't mean to..."

"Hey, you can't stop that from happening. I'm always reminded of it except when I'm with you. I don't think about it as much and I can't ask for anything more."

Grinning a little, he brushed his fingers against her cheek. "If you're trying to make me feel better, you're really bad at it."

Bella laughed. She couldn't help it.

"As much as I don't want that smile on your face to go away, you want to talk about today?"

Her gaze lowered. She frowned.

"It's okay, you don't have to." David wrapped his arms around her and hugged her against his chest.

Bella wrapped her own arms around his waist and snuggled deeper into the safety of his arms. She didn't have to, but wondered if she should. The case seemed somewhat safe. Even then she wasn't sure. "They want me to testify."

"You weren't going to?"

"No. They had enough evidence for a plea bargain, but the DNA got thrown out. Now I have to testify."

He rubbed her back. "I'm sorry. I wish there was something I could do."

"You are. Just by being here." She looked up at him and smiled. Watching his face she realized something tumbled around in his head.

"What about Jeremiah? Isn't he there for you?"

She slipped out of his arms and stepped back. Dropping her gaze to the ground she crossed her arms and said, "No. We broke up."

David uncurled her arms and grabbed one of her hands. "Come on, let's go impress some more people with our vocals."

"I can handle that." She smiled brightly.

****

Four o'clock Monday afternoon and she sat on that stinking couch. Keeping her parents happy sucked. But she liked access to her own car too much to do otherwise. As usual she sat in a chair by the window and watched the outside world, while her parents droned on and on about how disobedient she had become. *If only they knew the half of it.*

"Bella, do you have anything to add?" Dr. Filmore asked.

"No."

"This is what we get," her mother said. "She gives half answers or none at all. She never tells us where she's going anymore. I've gotten reports from her school her grades are falling. We just don't know what do."

"Sometimes therapy can only do so much. If you'd like I could prescribe mood stabilizers for her."

Bella's attention snapped to the three people discussing her. "Excuse me?"

Dr. Filmore looked to Bella. "You've undergone a tragic situation. That can make you anxious or depressed."

"You think I'm depressed?"

"It would explain things," her father replied.

Bella stood. "I'm not depressed! I'm pissed off because nobody can do what I ask."

Her mother turned her gaze from the doctor to Bella. "You're right. I can't do what you ask because I'm worried about you. I'm afraid if you don't come to these sessions, if we don't come here, then I'll lose you."

"Lose me? I haven't gone anywhere. I've just changed. Why can't you accept that?"

"Because we raised you better than this."

She hated when her mother made sense. *I can't fight logic.* Bella mumbled damn it, "Porra!"

Her mother gasped. "Observa sua lingua!"

Watch my language? Really? She must be out of her mind.
Bella crossed her arms and told her mother that she couldn't make
her. "Nao pode me obrigar a fazer isso."

"Eu sou sua mãe e eu posso obrigar fazer o que eu quero." Her
mother rose to her feet as well. Behira stared at Bella.

She's my mother so she can make me? Ha! "Porque? Para que
eu possa ser como vocē? Eu nunca vou ser como vocē." Bella
dropped her arms and glared at her mother. Then she stomped past
the doctor and her parents out the door. Her mother would never be
able to answer why. Growing up her mother made it implicitly
clear Bella could be her own person and she didn't have to be like
anyone, but Bella. She would never be like her mother or anyone
else for that matter.

****

Lunch almost seemed typical, except Amanda had been
unusually quiet sitting next to Vick. Bella stopped talking a few
times to study the two of them. Seating arrangements changed
dramatically over the past few weeks leading her to believe the two
actually were dating on the down low. But if they were she
couldn't imagine why. With about ten minutes left they excused
themselves leaving her and Sarresh at the table, so Bella asked,
"What do you think we should do this weekend?"

"Amanda and I are going to a movie Friday night. You should
join us," she answered.

"No thank you."

"Why?"

Bella sighed. "Because I'm tired of all the dirty looks I get
from Amanda. They've gotten worse since Miah and I broke up."

"Then why do you sit at the same table as her?"

"Will you join me if I move to another table?"

"No."

"That's why. I don't want to ask my friends to choose sides."
Somehow Bella felt eventually it would come down to that.

"I got you."

Sarresh nudged her, which forced Bella to look up from the
muffin she had nibbled on for the past thirty minutes. "What?"

"At your five," her friend muttered.

Glancing in that general direction she saw David approach.

Stopping at her table he leaned down and glanced to Sarresh. "Will you give us a second?"

"Sure." She left the pair alone.

Taking the spot Sarresh had occupied, he dropped next to Bella. "Hey."

"Way to start a conversation after kicking my friend from the table."

"Sorry about that, but I'm not big on an audience."

"I suppose all these people in the cafeteria don't count?"

He grinned. "In this instance, no they do not."

"You were saying."

"You have plans Friday?"

"No." Good thing she declined that movie.

"Will you go out to dinner with me?"

"Yes." *Strange how easy that came when all the other times "no" felt right.* She shook the confusion of her answer from her head. Watching as he gripped the back of his neck her smile faded. "Why do I get the feeling there's a catch?"

"Well, there is a little bit of one I guess."

When he didn't continue, she prompted, "Which is?"

"There's a certain dress code."

Getting a tad annoyed, "Meaning?"

"Will you wear a dress?"

Blinking rapidly she stared at him. Of all the catches, she hadn't expected to have to dress like a lady. Her attack changed the way she dressed completely. Like she did a full three-sixty on clothes. She didn't even own a dress any more. No longer would she be so accessible.

"We can go somewhere else. I just want to take you someplace nice."

For a moment she considered his offer to change venues and nearly accepted it, except the truth hit her in the gut like she'd been tackled to the ground by a lineman. *Modesty didn't stop the attack.* That thought danced all over her brain, but given the *what?* look crossing David's face she must have said it out loud too. Shaking her head she smiled. "No. We'll go where you have planned. I trust you."

"I'm glad you do because I'd never let anything happen to you."

"What time are you picking me up?"

"Seven."

"I look forward to it."

"Me too." He left the table and passed Sarresh.

Bella slid off the bench and looked at her friend. "Either we need to go shopping or I need to borrow a dress."

"We can check out my closet after school. Cheaper and if you don't see something you like, we can still go shopping."

"Sounds like a plan."

"I take it you're going out with him then?"

"Yes." No need to divulge more. Sarresh already knew about the Jeremiah situation. Sunday had been filled with a little bit of drinking and gossiping. One would've happened regardless, but the other because she hadn't planned to go home. Her presence had been requested for Thanksgiving dinner tomorrow night, but in all likelihood she'd go home soon anyways, letting her parents know she still lived. Made more sense for David to pick her up there for their date. He didn't grow up believing in God, he had money and did what he wanted because his parents were never around. Just the prospect made her smile, especially when the idea of torturing her parents with his presence popped into her head.

What fun.

Chapter Ten

David turned into the restaurant parking lot and slowed down as he came to a carpeted entrance. A sign with the word *Cello's* written in excessively neat cursive hung over the canopied walkway. He brought the car to a stop, put it in park and got out. As he rounded the other side of the vehicle a man in black pants and a red jacket greeted him. The guy gave him a ticket and promptly walked around to the driver side. David opened the passenger side door for Bella and offered a hand, which she accepted as she swung her legs out to the side.

Her heels hit the ground first. With one hand in David's she pushed up out of the car and held the small hand-held purse Sarresh let her borrow with the dress. She'd never worn anything this sexy before. Once out of the vehicle she stepped up onto the sidewalk and brushed a hand down the bodice of the single-shoulder strap, satin, honey-colored dress she wore. She hadn't become accustomed to the way it hugged her curves. Even the outfits she had recently purchased didn't compare, but Sarresh commonly wore things like this. According to her friend the dress had been purchased post-baby. Sarresh hadn't even been sure she'd had a chance to wear it and she let Bella borrow it. That was a true friend. Tonight, as suited for the dress, one side of her midnight black hair had been swept up and pinned with a diamond studded hair pin. She completed the outfit with a pair of diamond studs.

"Ready?" David asked.

Bella nodded as he entwined his fingers with hers and escorted her to the restaurant entrance. She could see two sets of doors. The first set had two men on either side that promptly opened them once they were close enough. David opened one of the second set and removed his hand from hers long enough to let her walk in before him.

Once inside he wrapped an arm around her waist and moved forward to the hostess. "We have reservations."

"And the name?"

"Warren."

"Follow me," the hostess said.

She led them up a staircase to a balcony table. Bella looked around and noticed the romantic atmosphere. White lace draped every table with two golden candleholders containing matching lit white votive candles. All the overhead lighting was low. When they got to their table, which happened to be a bit secluded David helped Bella into her seat first then took his own. The hostess placed their menus down in front of them and said their server would be there shortly. Bella completely understood the reason for the dress code. Denim didn't fit this kind of place. "This place is gorgeous."

"Thank you."

Opening the menu her eyes popped wide. *They can't really get away with charging prices like this, can they? Good God, I can buy groceries for a week on what one meal will cost.*

"Pick whatever you want, don't fret over the price."

"But David —"

"No buts. I can afford it."

His parents never kept it a secret how well off they were. To her that didn't matter and somehow he managed to miss her point. Closing her menu she watched as he continued to look over his. "Why did you chose this place?"

Flipping his gaze from the menu to her he sighed. "I wanted to take you someplace nice."

"Why this place? We drove an hour out of town to Carlsbad when we could have easily gone somewhere in town."

He gave her his full attention. "I didn't take you anywhere in town because I wanted to go somewhere we could say was ours. I want you to have a good time. As for this particular restaurant, this has the atmosphere I was looking for. And I happen to know the food is delicious, no matter how much it costs."

His answer had been genuine and heartfelt. She couldn't blame him for wanting something that belonged to only them. She knew all the restaurants in town and had been in each more than once. Smiling she nodded. "I can accept that."

"You're okay eating here then?"

"Yes. I may be a simple girl, but I can't deny a man who goes this far out of his way for me. We'll eat here." She opened the menu again, this time prepared to select an entree.

****

Jeremiah rubbed his brow as he read the same line in his History book for the tenth time. Realizing he would get nowhere he slammed the book shut. While he really wanted to get some school work in before he left for Vick's, that didn't seem to be happening. Bella had been running a marathon in his head all week long. The rumor mill around school didn't help either. People were talking about the fact that he and Bella must have broken up because supposedly she'd started going out with David. They'd seen him at her lunch table the other day. Not to mention he'd been spotted talking to her at her locker multiple times. Jeremiah really didn't like the guy. He sighed, got to his feet and headed out of his bedroom down the hall. Female voices in the kitchen made him stop before he walked into their direct line of sight.

"They're actually going out?" Amanda asked.

"Yes." Sarresh nodded, forking some noodles together and winding them around before stuffing a bite full in her mouth.

"I don't like this. Not one bit."

Sarresh snickered. "You aren't the only one."

"I thought you were okay with the guy."

"I'm impartial. He probably wouldn't be so bad if he didn't have a temper."

"Temper?"

"He went off on this guy last year. Beat the hell out of him. I don't exactly know what started it, but I heard it had something to do with a girl he asked to the dance."

"That's messed up."

"I'm saying. It's not just that though. I wish he would've done some things differently with Bella too."

"Like what?"

"I told you about the tattoo Bella got, right?"

"Yeah. You said he talked her out of the tombstone she wanted."

Sarresh nodded. "Which was a good thing, but then he had to go and ruin it by getting the exact same tattoo."

Amanda bobbed her head from side to side thinking over what had been said. "Weird, but I can't see how that would ruin it."

"His doesn't say 'Deuteronomy.' His has her name."

"What?"

Jeremiah buried his face in his hands because he couldn't stifle the groan that wanted to escape any other way. More and more his brain considered that the guy had stalker potential. But the temper he'd heard about worried him more.

Sarresh nodded. "Oh yeah. Only good thing is Bella's freaked out by it. Except she didn't tell him that."

"Why not?"

"She told me she understood. And when they talked about it his reasoning made complete sense."

"Wait, I'm confused. He talked to her about it beforehand?"

"Nope, after." Sarresh stuffed more noodles in her mouth.

"Damn. If I didn't want to kick his ass before, I really do now."

"Too bad you agreed not to." Sarresh laughed.

"Yeah, me and my big mouth."

"For now, I'm going to choose to view his tattoo as a good sign. But if he hurts Bella, I'm with you. And I didn't tell your brother I wouldn't kick his ass."

"Just promise me one thing."

"What's that?"

"I can watch."

Sarresh laughed again. "Sure."

Great, just what I need. Jeremiah popped back in his room long enough to get his wallet and keys. This time when he stepped out he purposely closed his door loud enough the girls could hear it. Mandy was the only one Sarresh got along with in the house, except for maybe his mother. Then again his mother had more patience than he did. For some reason he had yet to understand why Sarresh got on his nerves. He walked back down the hallway and headed into the kitchen. Politely he nodded to his sister and cousin as he grabbed a bottle of water out of the refrigerator.

"Where you off to?" Amanda asked.

"Vick and I are going to the movies."

"Oh."

He nodded. "I'll see you later Mandy. Sarresh." He turned to leave.

"Hey Jeremy," Sarresh called out.

Rarely did it ever happen. For once he wanted to escape without getting into some kind of scuffle with her. They both knew they didn't get along, but she had to go and stop him anyways. He sighed. "What can I do for you Sarresh?"

"That's a good question," she replied as she set down the noodles. "For starters, you can stop being such an ass. I get that you don't like me, but you don't even know me. I don't know what Aunt Christine has said about my mom, but I'm nothing like her."

He turned to face his cousin. "I don't care to know you. I learned all I need to from Bella. And my Mom hasn't said anything."

"You do realize we were bound to cross paths. I mean come on. We go to the same school. I'm friends with Bella. And what do you mean you learned what you need to from Bella?"

"You two weren't talking while we were dating and she told me why."

"And that changed. Now as the one person who has the inside scoop, don't you think it would be wise to at least try to be nice to me and actually get to know me?"

Mandy shook her head. "I don't know why you even bother, Z."

Jeremiah glared at his sister then returned his attention to Sarresh. "Why so I can find out how much she's being influenced by you? I've seen how she dresses. That isn't her. If you're such good friends, it can only mean it's coming from you. And you got nicknamed a letter. What? People can't say your name?"

Sarresh's lips tightened as her eyes narrowed. "Listen up jackass because I'm going to say this once and only once. My nickname is part of my name. The Z stands for my last name Zirlan. As for how your sweet and innocent Bella is dressing, she did that on her own. But maybe you would know that if you hadn't left her. Then again, you also might realize she thinks she is being punished. You were the one person she needed and you turned your back on her. Now she believes the rest of us have too. Everything you're doing right now, well, you can't blame her for running to the arms of someone who is doing whatever he can to be there for her. Get off your fucking high horse and stop thinking you are above any of this."

Well, okay. Jeremiah turned around and continued out the door. Aside from the fact that he felt like an idiot, he was pretty sure he just got his butt handed to him. *I really am a jackass aren't I?* As much as he thought he should go back and apologize, he didn't. Once he got outside and shut the front door, he went straight to the car and took off. He needed to think before he opened his mouth again to that girl. And a movie sounded like the perfect place to do that.

****

Dinner had come and gone without incident and she only thought about Jeremiah three times. Bella chastised herself every time because of the disrespect she showed to the guy she was on a date with by thinking about her ex-boyfriend. To his credit if David ever suspected anything, it never showed. Afterward he escorted her back downstairs and over to the club. Before going he asked her if she would be okay walking a couple blocks. Sure she had on four-inch heels, but she thought she could make it. The shoes weren't hurting her feet as he suspected they would, but he was kind to ask. Fresco's wasn't like T2. Mostly because there were more bodies and it was on a higher scale. Like the only people there were upper class. David fit in perfectly. She felt like a poser.

They'd hit the dance floor five times and found a table where she'd downed two cokes. Now she understood why her parents never allowed soda in the house, it was addictive. Coming back from the bathroom she brushed her dress down and headed for the high top where he waited. The smile that spread on his face when she came into view was exquisite and she just had to stare at his lips for a moment.

Returning her gaze to his eyes he offered his hand. "Up for another dance?"

"Yes." She nodded. Together they headed to the dance floor just as the song changed. Previously all the songs had been up-beat and fast-paced, but a slow one came on. For a moment she wondered if it had been on purpose. Picking a spot that put them close to the center he spun her around until she came flush against his body. A hand slid to her waist hovering near her butt as she grabbed a firm hold of his shoulders. Even with the heels, he still had a good eight inches on her. Wrapping her arms around his neck couldn't put her close enough to him right now. Staring up into those sparkling blue eyes she felt that moment between them that had appeared a couple of times before. She saw David hesitate and wondered if he felt it too.

Wanting him to know he wouldn't get pushed away this time she ran her hands up his shoulders giving them a good grip pulling him closer. Taking the hint David leaned down toward her slowly and then held perfectly still. Like the first song they sang at karaoke she pushed forward and met him halfway. Her whole body started to tingle the moment their lips touched. Heat crawled up her legs, abdomen, and arms as her heart raced. The kiss began innocent and soft, then became deep and desperate. She thought they may have stopped moving as they kissed and the song may have changed. The hunger they'd found didn't last though.

A flash of cigarette smoke replaced David's woody scent. The arms that held her close weren't his. The club transformed into an alleyway full of dumpsters and the stench of a man ripping her apart. Panic found its way in and before she knew what happened, she'd yanked free from David's arms, shoved him off of her knocking him into the crowd and tore off. Tears streaked her cheeks. The air outside was just as stagnant as the air inside. Needing further away, she started running down the sidewalk. At some point she stopped and pulled her heels off. Frantically she looked around hearing the pounding of shoes behind her, a male voice calling out her name forced her to keep going until she saw a group of taxis lined up along a curb outside some building. She wrenched the door open of the first one she came to and slammed it shut.

"Please drive," she said through heavy breaths.

"Where to?" The cabbie asked.

"I don't care, just drive!"

"I need an address."

"Just drive!" She yelled needing to get out of there. Rocking back and forth she locked her hands behind her head and pleaded with the cabbie. Finally he pulled the taxi onto the road just as she heard her name called out again. Knowing she had to calm down she pressed her head against her knees and tried to release the trembles she'd held on to. With only a little relief she reached over and grabbed her purse. Digging around she asked the driver, "You got a bottle of water?"

"Yeah." He passed her back an unopened one.

"Thanks," she mumbled taking a hold of it. Popping a couple pills in her mouth she took several swigs. With half the bottle gone she went back to her purse and found her driver's license. Still trying to catch her breath she handed it to the cabbie. "Drive me here."

He took the plastic from her hand, glanced at the address and pulled off to the side of the road. Looking back to her as he returned her license. "You realize that's over 50 miles away?"

Taking hold of her license she nodded and wiped her face. "Please, just take me there. I promise you'll get paid."

"Whatever you say."

She returned everything to her purse, then brushed off her feet and slid her shoes back on. She jumped when her phone started to vibrate in her bag. She pulled it out, saw the number, and let David go to voicemail. Then pressed a couple buttons, brought up the messaging feature and texted, *I'm sorry. I'll talk to you tomorrow.* It was all she could say. Maybe she should've told him she was okay, except she wasn't. The text wasn't a real apology, but she could go over to his place tomorrow and do that. Maybe she could explain if she understood herself. Getting comfortable for the drive home, she leaned back against the seat.

Chapter Eleven

Her parents were waiting when she got home the night before around midnight. If they noticed that a cab dropped her off instead of David, nothing got mentioned. Truthfully she figured they were just happy she came home. Somehow she managed to say goodnight, get to her room, out of the dress and to bed. She'd been so out of it from the pills she actually slept in her bed. Up until that point it hadn't mattered that her parents had the bed replaced, she still saw the dead dog every time she looked at it. When she woke up and realized where she ended up, she immediately jumped up and took her first shower. Since then she'd taken three more showers. Dressed and ready to go, she just needed to force her feet out the door. Bella looked at the clock on her nightstand. It read five p.m. She could wait forever and it wouldn't make what she had to do any easier. *Now or never*, she told herself. She could easily attribute her dread to the nausea she'd felt all day long or the low back pain she'd had, but none of it had been bad enough to warrant that kind of blame or excuse. Rising to her feet she stopped in the kitchen, grabbed a bottle of water and took off for David's place.

Thirty minutes later she pulled down his driveway. The house he lived in was expansive, but not nearly as large as the one Sarresh's. It looked to be at least two stories and the driveway circled around a gorgeous fountain. Bella had never been there before and if she hadn't been exposed to something similar she might be in more awe at everything she saw. Climbing out of her car, she headed up the stairs to the door and rang the bell. His ice queen sister answered.

"What do you want?"

Sighing Bella tucked her hands in her jean pockets. "Is your brother here?"

Heather rolled her eyes. "Yep."

Figuring Heather would step aside she waited. When she didn't Bella asked, "Can I come in?"

"What for?"

In no mood to be nice, polite, or anything else she had formally been, she boldly stated, "Let's get something straight Heather. If I start dating your brother, I plan to be around here a lot. Now you have two choices, get the fuck used to it or get shoved on your ass every time I have to walk all over you like a goddamn rug." Bella didn't know what part of that got Heather's attention, but whatever, it worked. Just in time for David to walk up.

"There a problem?" he asked.

Smirking a smile at the shock on Heather's face, Bella looked at David. "None at all. Somewhere we can talk?"

"Yeah. We can go to the library."

Inhaling deeply she nodded and followed after him. Once they were inside he closed the door and she slowly paced the large room. It was big enough she could walk around trying to keep hold of her nerves.

David propped up against the huge oak desk and waited on her.

Rubbing her lower back she gave in and sat down on the chaise lounge. "I'm sorry about last night. I panicked."

"I'm more concerned about what prompted it so we don't go there again."

She sighed. "I don't think it was anything you did. It was just... I don't know." Unable to sit still she stood again and proceeded to walk around. "The smallest thing reminds me of the night I was attacked. You have this woodsy smell and from out of nowhere, I smelled smoke... stale cigarette smoke. Everything changed, I didn't see you, didn't feel you, didn't see the club. All I could think was that I had to get away. I had to run." She felt like she was babbling. David got up and stood in front of her and kept her from pacing.

"Bella..." He placed a finger under her chin and lifted her eyes to his. "You could've told me. We would've left right then. I'm in no hurry for whatever is happening between us. I'll wait as long as

I need to for you to be okay with any kind of intimacy. You need to believe that."

She'd managed to contain the tears through all the pacing and talking, but not now, not after what he said. Blinking tears down her cheeks she stared at him and tried to speak, but she had no clue what to say. She did the only thing she could think of to show him exactly how grateful she was. Wrapping her arms around his neck she placed a tender kiss on his lips and snuggled deep into his arms.

He held her tight. "If that's a thank you, it's the best thank you I've ever gotten. We'll go as slow as you need to. I'm just glad I get to spend time with you."

She didn't deserve him, but God knew she needed him. Sniffling she wiped her face.

"You need a tissue?"

"Yes, please," she replied softly.

"Okay." He kissed her forehead and started for the door. "You eat dinner yet?"

Still wiping at her face she shook her head. She wouldn't tell him she hadn't eaten since dinner last night

"If you don't mind staying, I'll have chef whip up something."

"That sounds good."

"Okay, stay here. I'll be back in a few minutes." He closed the door behind him.

Bella had to wonder what the hell she was doing. She broke up with her boyfriend a week ago and here she encouraged David to something he would never really have from her. Turning back to the chaise lounge she sat. As much as she didn't want to compare herself to David's sister, she could possibly be just as much of a bitch. But she felt alone and he hadn't made her talk about anything she didn't want to. He even tried to get her to only think about happy things. She knew he wouldn't make the loneliness go away, but at least she could have one person on her side.

She rubbed her lower back as pain struck her once again. This could only mean her period was coming, except she didn't think she was due for another week. Hard to say since she hadn't paid much attention to when it came and went since the attack. Bella got back up to her feet determined to walk some of the sensations off, especially when she felt the onslaught of cramping. God, she'd never experienced anything like this before.

The pain slammed at her again, but a lot stronger and much, much harder. Forced to grab onto the desk to keep from falling over, she felt what must have been a thousand needle stings all at once. Almost like someone had just stabbed her uterus with a knife. Unable to handle it any longer she used the furniture as she stumbled to the door. Tears had already started down her cheeks from the amount of pain that racked her body.

Once at the door she fumbled with it as she attempted to get enough control that she could grip the knob and open it. Finally she got the door open and looked out to the two people standing in the open plan foyer. The last thing she recalled was saying David's name before her muscles gave out and she collapsed onto the floor.

****

Slowly Bella's senses returned to life. Something had been clamped on her left forefinger. She could hear a steady beeping off to her side and felt something sticking in her nose. As everything started to make sense her eyes fluttered open. She knew where she ended up without looking. The hospital.

"Welcome back." Chief Jamar Detrone smiled.

"Where's David?" She croaked out.

"Waiting outside."

"Why?" she squeaked. "What happened?"

Jamar sat in silence and hesitated to answer her question. "You should talk to the doctor."

Shaking her head she cleared her throat. "Tell me, please."

Again he hesitated. He rubbed his brow as if he contemplated what or how to say what he needed to. Then he sighed and said, "As far as I know you passed out at David's. He brought you in. When I got here, he was yelling at the nurses and doctors because they wouldn't let him see you. He calmed down and I told him to wait outside until you woke up." He studied her. "Bella, I tried to reach your parents, but I haven't had any luck. Do you have a number where I can get a hold of them?"

Whatever he had to say must be bad. She tried to remember what happened. As the memories flooded her brain, she recalled there was pain, a lot of pain, and she passed out. Maybe she hit the floor and busted her head or something. With the hand attached to the monitor she reached up to the back of her head, but didn't feel anything except for maybe a small bump. "They're out of town, but I don't want them here. Can you just get David?"

"Sure." Jamar got up and stepped outside.

Seconds later the door flew open and David practically ran across the room to her side. "Are you okay?"

Bella smiled and nodded. She watched as he looked over every part of her. "I'm fine."

He settled in the chair by her bed, took her hand in his and sighed. "I'm sorry. I've just been a little worried. They wouldn't tell me anything. They wouldn't let me see you."

"Did you really yell at the doctors?"

"Yes. I wasn't happy they wouldn't let me in. Maybe it was a little much, but their answers just kept pissing me off. Chief Detrone told me if I didn't calm down he'd have me escorted from the building and I wouldn't see you until you got released."

There was a knock on the door and a doctor entered. "How's my patient?"

"Awake. Can you tell me what happened?"

"I can." The doctor looked to David. "Would you excuse us?"

Bella shook her head. "I don't want him to go."

"Are you certain?" The doctor asked.

"Yes. Anything you have to say to me you can say in front of him."

David remained in the chair beside her bed. Needing reassurance he was there, Bella squeezed his hand.

"You were pregnant and had a miscarriage," the doctor answered.

Baby? There had been a baby growing inside of me. Oh God. Her gaze trailed down her body to the flat belly she had. She had dreamed of having children later in life after she graduated. When she met Jeremiah she was positive he would be their father. This was nowhere near what she had planned. Not only would the baby have been a product of her attack, but she lost the baby too. A life she was supposed to protect and she didn't. Tears rolled down her cheeks. She could feel David looking at her, but she didn't care. "What caused it?"

"There's no way to tell," the doctor said. "Sometimes these things just happen."

She wiped at her face and took in a breath to stop the tears from falling any further.

The doctor asked, "How are you feeling?"

"My head hurts a little, but the cramping has died down."

"That's to be expected," he said and stepped around to check the machines and her vital signs. "You suffered a minor concussion when you passed out, which was likely exacerbated by other underlying issues. Any conditions I should be aware of?"

"I haven't eaten in several hours and I'm on painkillers from a broken arm and gunshot wound I suffered a couple months ago."

"Okay, well that would definitely be an underlying issue. You should be eating regularly with the pain medication. Have you suffered any side effects?"

"No," she lied. The pills were why she hadn't eaten as much. True, she'd dropped a few pounds, but not enough to make her change what she did.

The doctor nodded. "Good. What medications are you on?"

"Morphine twice a day and Oxycodone once every six to eight hours as needed."

"Most of the pain from the miscarriage should have passed by now and since you're already on Opioids I won't prescribe anything. Your vital signs are good, so I'll sign off on your discharge. You need to eat something before you leave. Your boyfriend can get you something from the cafeteria downstairs. Do you have any questions for me?"

Boyfriend? Good Lord there were too many words being thrown around for her to deal with another unexpected one. *Deep breath, just take a deep breath. Question, he asked a question.* "No."

Again he nodded and stepped out of the room.

David stood and kissed her on the forehead. "Will you be okay by yourself a moment?"

She nodded.

"Okay. I'll be back with some food." David stepped outside.

She let the tears fall. Her mind hadn't stopped spinning on all the words that were being thrown at her *pregnant, baby, miscarriage, boyfriend*. The last one she simply couldn't touch right now because the other three got all of her attention. She had no clue how to feel. Happy because she wouldn't have to deal with looking at the child's face constantly being reminded of what happened or giving the child up because of how it had been conceived. Sad because even if the baby came from part of her attacker, it also came from her. She didn't see it as a fetus, but a baby. Without knowing about the pregnancy, the moment the doctor told her what occurred with her body, she'd attached to the baby she no longer carried. Her heart broke and she hated herself for simultaneously loving and hating it. Unfortunately the door didn't stay shut long. *Why can't I just cry in peace?* Quickly she wiped her face hoping it was only David, but it wasn't... instead Sarresh and Mandy stepped in. She didn't remember giving permission for visitors. *Oh hell, what does it matter?*

"Hey," Amanda said walking over and sitting in the chair David had occupied. "How are you feeling?"

"Like shit doesn't end," she answered. Her desire to mask her feelings faltered. *God I need some pills.*

Sarresh took up a spot on the other side. "Well you've always got us even when everything sucks."

Bella nodded. "I'm just glad David's here." Her eyes started toward Sarresh, but when she caught a grimace on Amanda's face from her periphery she instantly changed directions. Looking at her friend. "What's with the look?"

"What look?"

"The look on your face, like I just said something terribly wrong."

"Nothing."

"Just say it."

"Is David your boyfriend?" Amanda asked bluntly.

That word again. "I'm not defining our status to you right now. And even if he is that's my choice."

"I don't like it."

"You don't even know him!" Bella barked.

Sarresh pointed to Amanda. "You, stop antagonizing her." Then turned to Bella. "You, relax."

For a moment she thought Mandy would say something else, but she just shut her trap. Apparently it had been timed perfectly because the door opened again except this time it was David.

Amanda didn't move. Sarresh slid down to make room for him. Quickly she found a way to replace her annoyance with a smile and tried to push herself upright so she could eat.

"Hey now," David said as he set the tray down and moved to help her into a sitting position.

"Thanks." She smiled. Once she was up he placed the tray in front of her. He picked out chicken salad on rye, a side of fruit and a cup of soup. Offering him a partial smile when he came around and placed a light kiss on her head Bella asked. "Can I go home soon?"

He nodded. "Yeah. A nurse will come in shortly to disconnect the monitors. Either she or your friends can help you get dressed, but I don't think you should stay at your house tonight." Looking over at Sarresh he said, "I was hoping she could spend the night at your place."

Before Sarresh could answer Bella asked, "Can you guys give me a sec to talk to David alone?"

Both Sarresh and Amanda nodded and stepped outside.

"So. What's so important you had to kick your friends out?"

"I want to stay with you."

David blinked. "What?"

"You heard me." She couldn't define their relationship, but that didn't matter. The last thing she needed was to see Sarresh's baby and be reminded of what she lost.

"Bella, I don't think —"

"Then don't think. Just do. Please. Please, don't make me stay with Sarresh. If you won't let me stay with you then just let me get my car from your place and I'll go home. My parents aren't there anyway." Grateful again they weren't home. She didn't want them to know about this. Would she ever tell them about this? No, not if she could help it.

"But you don't have any clothes at my place."

She didn't get it. She pressed to stay at his place and he continued to find an excuse on why she couldn't. Bella hadn't figured he would fight her on this. "Then we can go by Z's and get my clothes from her place. Or go by my house and I can pack a bag. Or I'll wear what I have on. I don't care. I don't want to be alone and I don't want to stay with Z."

Sighing he rubbed his face. "You said your parents are gone for the weekend?"

"Yes."

"When will they be back?"

"Tomorrow night."

"What if I stayed with you?"

Bella swallowed. They'd have to sleep in her bed. Could she face it without having to scrub her body a thousand times over? She looked to David. If she didn't want to be alone, she'd have to since he refused to let her stay with him. "Okay."

Brushing some of her hair from her face, David said, "Now that that's settled I'll go talk to Sarresh and Amanda."

"Okay." She watched as he got up and left the room. Such a normal conversation, as if nothing drastic had happened. Internal didn't compare to external. Her two sides violently argued and not just about the baby, the miscarriage, but Jeremiah and David. Good thing the doctor released her, it meant she could get out of this hell hole and jump off the bridge. Unfortunately her pills were in her purse, which she left in her car. Since David planned to stay with her, maybe they could go by his place first. She could get her car and her pills all at once. She looked up as the door opened. She thought all three of them would come in, but only Sarresh did. For all the support her friends were freely giving, she wished they would go away. Maybe she should make this easier and end it all. No more shit, no more falsities, no more pretending and no more just getting by. Maybe she could finally find peace. That would be nice. Peace and quiet would be really nice.

"Where's Mandy?" Bella saw Sarresh chew on the inside of her cheek and knew that meant she didn't want to say anything. Her friends were interfering and not in a good way. According to the monitor both her heart rate and blood pressure spiked.

"She stayed to talk with David."

"Porra!" Bella muttered. Annoyed she glared at Sarresh. "What the hell is wrong with her?"

"Mandy's just worried about you."

"And what? She thinks he's bad news or something?"

"No. We just don't want you to change."

"Then I suggest you get with the fucking program!" She yelled and pointed to the door, "Because that guy doesn't have a damn thing to do with me changing! Unlike Jeremiah he has been there for me!"

Sarresh held up her hands. "All right, I'll talk to her. Please, just calm down."

Bella opened her mouth and shut it when the door opened up and David and Amanda walked through. She took a deep breath as David walked around and placed another kiss on her forehead.

"Everything's set," he said.

Bella sighed. This was the longest Saturday she'd ever had. At some point, the day would end, right? Maybe, but her nightmare wouldn't. Not unless she took things into her own hands. No, she couldn't or could she? Shaking the thought away, she wrapped her hands around the sandwich and took a bite making her friends happy.

Chapter Twelve

Hanging on the wall was a sixty-inch, flat screen, HD television. David and Bella were curled up together on his king size bed, on top of a black bedspread. The pillows had matching 100% Egyptian cotton pillow cases. A dresser stood against the left wall with a desk next to it. On the television screen were two teenagers sitting at a classroom desk.

Bella and David were in their nightclothes. Bella wore flannel pants and a tank, while David had on sweats. Since her conversation with the doctor Saturday she had changed her Oxycodone dosage about fifteen times. She went back and forth over the right amount to take - one, two, or three. David didn't help any. She thought he might have been afraid to leave her alone because David hadn't left her by herself at all the past few days. She had spent more time at his house this week than normal. Then this morning he showed up at her house to give her a ride to school. They made a secret plan for her to spend the night, but she told her parents she would be at Sarresh's house. He told her it could be a practice run for Saturday. When she asked what he meant he said they were driving up to enjoy the Electric Light Parade in downtown Roswell. There would be food, singing and celebrating before the parade that night. Something to look forward to.

She dug her hand into the bowl of popcorn between them. She had no idea what the hell they were watching. David told her with as deprived as she'd been over the past few years he picked something that according to his sister girls liked and he could be fairly certain she'd never seen, which was practically everything. She didn't really watch movies until she started dating Jeremiah. The last two movies she watched with him weren't as strange as this one. Talking fish were a little weird, but she loved *Finding*

Nemo. Okay, and a short brown alien called for her to think outside of the box, but she liked *E.T.* This one went beyond the box and left the planet. Something with teenagers and she had no clue what. He told her, but she couldn't remember. "What's this called?"

"Twilight."

Shaking her head she half glanced. "Never let your sister help you pick out movies again."

"What? You don't like it?"

"I just don't get the point. And this Edward guy. Is he supposed to be hot?" She asked a tad sarcastically. Sure he was cute with his mussy hair, but her attraction lied with someone a bit more clean-cut.

David laughed. "I don't know. It's just what Heather recommended."

"Yeah, next time if you need to consult someone, get with Z." She leaned up a little and pressed a gentle kiss on his neck. "I appreciate the effort. But honestly, did you pick this out for me or is there something you like?"

He tried to hide it, but she felt the tiniest shiver escape him. "Truthfully, I think Kristen Stewart's hot."

With a snicker she punched him in the shoulder. "Excuse me?"

"Don't worry, you're the hotter Bella." He laughed and kissed her forehead.

"What? Are you associating me with her?"

"No."

Tilting her head she stared hard at him. "You know, maybe I should go by something different just in case. Maybe Chris? Christa? Maylin? Or what about Nadalia? I have two middle names."

"Don't you dare."

"Why not?"

"Because your nickname is sexy and I like how it rolls off my tongue." With a wide grin he wiggled his brows.

Unable to help herself she leaned up and kissed him. Slowly she felt him open up to her enough that they had a brief make out session. Bella pulled back and took a breath. With a tiny nibble on her lower lip she grinned and turned back to the movie. "He doesn't know how to talk to girls does he? I mean, he really asked her about the weather." Still in shock by the perfectly wonderful kiss they just had David remained stone dead quiet. She munched on a few pieces of popcorn and looked back and forth between him and the movie.

"He's supposed to be like a hundred years old."

"Eww. That's kind of gross."

Snapping back into the movie he chuckled. "Yeah, but he's permanently seventeen."

"I don't know if I would like that."

"I could see it. Lot of chances to fix your mistakes."

Rolling her eyes she dug into the popcorn. And tossed some playfully at him and then in her mouth. "Okay, I really don't get her. Twenty seconds ago he walks away and she's still drooling over him. You ever do that to me and I'll never speak to you again."

Stealing a couple kernels from her hand. "Duly noted. Now, are you going to comment throughout the whole movie?"

"I'll try to shut up." She shrugged snatching a kernel back. "But I make no promises." A few minutes later. "Are guys really that nervous around girls?"

Shaking his head he sighed. "Yes."

"But you aren't with me."

"I just hide it better."

Lifting an eyebrow she studied him for a moment because she didn't believe him. Letting it go. "I'll shut up now."

He grinned. "I don't believe you can."

"Come on, how can you expect me not to comment? Who blurts things out like that?" She laughed when he didn't respond. Either that or he figured he could make her be quiet if he didn't answer. Though really the only way she would understand any of what went on in the movie was if she paid attention. Not to mention it served as a distraction. When he first talked about her spending the night at his house, she panicked. He had spent Saturday night at her house. Like a gentleman he slept on the floor and she slept in the bed. Tonight he planned for them to share a bed. Sleeping in the same bed with Jeremiah felt natural. But with David, she kept going back to the unknown about how she'd handle intimacy. Yeah they shared a good kiss several minutes ago, but would it always be like that? Or would she react the same as she did Friday night?

Tossing a couple more kernels in her mouth she glanced over to David. "Okay. I see why girls would like this. I like the sparkly."

He chuckled and nudged his nose against her neck. "Does that mean you like him better than me?"

"No." She shook her head and teased. "He's too pretty." Bella tightened her lips when David leaned back and stared at her in shock like she said he wasn't pretty. "I didn't say you aren't pretty, just that he's too pretty for my taste." Unable to contain her amusement any longer, she busted out laughing. Eating more popcorn she looked back to the movie. "Okay. Seriously, who stares at each other that long?"

As if he was trying to prove a point, he stared at her, then slowly brushed a hand down her cheek. "I think I could."

Her lips parted slightly as her breath caught in her throat. *Holy shit!* Okay if she would feel like that, he could stare all-he-wanted. Drawing her in he leaned down and gently kissed her. But, man she wished his lips would find hers again and *soon!*

"Now, can we watch the movie?"

She nodded because he had stumped her into silence. No words came from her mouth anytime in the near future. Watching the way Bella and Edward became a couple in the movie reminded her of how quickly she and Jeremiah came together and fell in love. She hated thinking about her ex-boyfriend, except that hadn't been the only thing that crossed her mind. Completely untrue because it hadn't left her mind since the doctor and Mandy referenced David as her boyfriend. But Bella had been reluctant to question him about it. Not because she didn't want an answer or feared what it would be, but because in some insane way she liked the idea of being his girlfriend. She liked it because it would be an acceptable label at school and might get the kids to stop calling her names. Cuddling up to him on his bed like this, she should just take a shot and ask him if she was his girlfriend. And if he rejected her, well, nothing new, right? God she hated where her head went sometimes. Dreadfully she asked, "Can I talk to you about something."

"As long as it's not about the movie, sure."

"It's not." She chewed on the inside of her cheek. "Am I your girlfriend?"

Picking up the remote beside him he paused the movie and turned to her. "Why would you ask me that?"

His question hadn't been harsh, just honest. She felt like such a dork. Sighing she pulled herself up to a sitting position and looked at him. "The doctor called you my boyfriend. And I guess I didn't think much about it until Mandy asked me if you were."

Smiling he tucked a loose lock of hair behind her ear. "I did use the word 'girlfriend.' Mostly because it was easier than saying I was the guy who had taken you on a couple of dates."

She nodded but felt annoyed. "So, I'm not your girlfriend?"

"I'm not labeling anything right now."

"Oh." She dropped her gaze from his.

Gently he slipped a finger beneath her chin and tilted her face to his. "What about that upsets you?"

Damn! She didn't mean for him to hear the disappointment in her voice. Shrugging she sighed. "I guess, I like the idea." Silence. He went still. And at a moment like this, it wasn't golden. Like she'd stolen his ability to breath he remained quiet for what felt like forever. No longer able to take it she blurted, "I mean, only if you want it."

"Why wouldn't I?"

He asked a question she wouldn't answer. *I'm attracted to you but I'll never be able to give you my heart. I want to be your girlfriend because I want to stop getting identified as... take your pick. I'd never be able to live up to your standards. We may never be able to have a normal relationship.* She shrugged and remained silent.

"Bella, that is something I want, but only when you actually want it too."

"I do!" She blurted out again. *Good God almighty! What the hell is wrong with my mouth today? Like I have no control over it.* She really was a selfish bitch. And the look on his face, pure joy.

"Really?"

Smiling she nodded hating herself for it. Knowing damn good and well she would hurt this wonderful, wonderful person sitting before her. And she nodded anyway. With all his happiness he didn't stop himself from leaning forward and kissing her on the lips. Thinking the last time they *really* kissed popped in his head because suddenly he pulled back. No, that wouldn't be acceptable this time. Sliding a hand up around the nape of his neck she grabbed a hold and brought him back to her lips. They forgot all about the movie for a little bit. Although he was a damn good kisser, the heat she felt with him was nothing like Jeremiah. David got closer to her and knocked over the bowl of popcorn still sitting between them. That stopped them and Bella wondered if she could still have another panic attack because when she and Jeremiah had make out sessions, nothing stopped them. Maybe they paused, but nothing that gave them more than a moment of air.

Looking down David laughed and picked up the bowl and tried to get any loose kernels back inside. He set it aside and propped himself back up on his bed. "Come on. Let's finish watching the movie."

Nodding she curled back up to him and physically got comfortable. Mentally wouldn't happen though. Probably a good thing to actually focus on the movie, then she didn't have to think about all the trash collected in her brain. After all, knowing you were damaged was a far, far cry from believing you were ruined.

****

With her hands pressed against the cool marble of the sink, Bella stared in the mirror. The pill bottle had been sitting in the same spot in front of her right hand for ten minutes. After she and David finished watching the move, she excused herself to use the restroom. She planned to wash her face, brush her teeth and take a few pills. She'd gotten through the first two tasks without a problem, but the last had been difficult. This should have been the easiest step ever. This wasn't her first merry go round. They had been steadily getting her through the days, but she'd never taken them around David, even Saturday. That night had been the first and only time in weeks she'd gone to sleep from utter exhaustion. She slept in the bed and he slept on the floor. Now was different. Spending the night in the same bed made it worse. Bella had opened and closed the bottle twice.

She couldn't sleep tonight without the pills. He would know if she never fell asleep, not to mention she had school tomorrow. With a heavy sigh she reached for the bottle again. She could do this. Taking a deep breath she twisted the cap and set it down. Her gaze lifted from the bottle to the mirror again and she stared at her reflection. "Stop being a damn – " The bathroom door swung open and bumped into her and caused her to drop the bottle.

"Bella?" Heather asked.

She paid no attention to the female voice. Instead she frantically started collecting the pills and returned them to their bottle. Reaching around the sink, she muttered, "No, no, no." She couldn't lose any pills!

"What are you doing?" Heather asked as she grabbed a hold of Bella's arm.

Without regard to any pain she yanked her arm away and went back to getting all the pills. She couldn't lose a single one down the drain! Blinking she looked all over and made sure she got every last pill. Satisfied she had, she turned her attention to Heather. "What the hell?"

She crossed her arms and stared at Bella hard. "I should ask you the same thing."

"I don't know what you're talking about."

"You've got to be joking. I'm not blind. I can see the bottle right there in your hands. Are you a fucking junkie?"

Junkie? Where did she get off? Grinding her jaw, Bella pulled herself together. She needed to set Heather straight. Firmly she stated, *"I am not a junkie."*

"You must really think I'm stupid," Heather said and spun around on her heel proceeding to walk away.

"You said it." Bella inhaled a quick breath and lied through her teeth. "I'm still on them for my injuries."

"Then why did you freak out when they spilled everywhere?" Heather turned back to face Bella.

"I don't want to lose any. I can only get so many at a time. I don't want to waste them."

"Whatever." Heather huffed and stormed off.

Bella closed the door and filled a glass with water. With steady hands she shook out three pills and knocked them back. She could do this.

****

"What happened the afternoon of October ninth?" The prosecutor asked.

Their first time going over her testimony and she had no desire to be there. She'd rather be at David's curled up with him on his bed like last night. But nothing could change what she had to do. "I left school around five and started toward the church."

"How did you travel?"

"I walked."

"Did you always walk?"

"Yes."

"So you're comfortable walking?"

"Until that day yes. I've done it my whole life." Bella answered.

"How long does it normally take you to get from the school to the church?"

"About twenty minutes."

"How do you know that?"

Bella unfolded her hands and readjusted in the chair. "I've walked that path enough times to know."

"What path do you usually take?"

"I walk down Main Street until I hit *Italianio's Pizzeria* then I cut through the alley until I hit Thirteenth Street."

"What happened in the alley that day?"

So far she'd managed to get through all the questions, but they were simple. Now they got into the tough questions. Inhaling deeply she looked to the prosecutor. She could do this. "I was walking down the alley when someone grabbed me from behind, bent my arm back and slammed me against the building. I tried to get away, but I got yanked back and thrown on the ground. Then I was pinned." Bella paused and took in another breath. She tried hard to keep it together. She hadn't even gotten to the seriously difficult part and yet she still had issues in repeating everything. Shaking her head, she looked to the prosecutor. "I can't Mr. Perez. I'm sorry, but I can't."

He leaned back against his desk. "Yes you can. I know it's hard, but you can get through the questions Miss Naughton."

"No." Bella rose to her feet. "I'm done."

"But Miss Naughton — "

"'But' nothing. I told you before I didn't want to do this."

"Yet you knew there was a strong possibility you would have to testify."

"No I didn't!" She yelled. "Chief Detrone swore to me I wouldn't have to repeat this nightmare over and over again." Bella shook her head and glared at Mr. Perez. "Forget it. I'm done." She spun on her heel and headed out the door. She was determined to ignore the attack for as long as possible. At no point had she planned to relive that horrible night.

****

Slamming the book shut Bella shoved it aside. For the first time since her miscarriage Saturday she had time to herself. Her parents weren't home. She told David she'd be working on her statement with the prosecutor all afternoon and hadn't called when it ended early. Lying to David had become as easy as lying to everyone else. Now she was alone and she had no clue what to do with herself. Homework couldn't take her mind off anything. One boring subject after another. She had never been this antsy. Sighing she got up from the dining room table and headed over to the refrigerator. Bella opened it and grabbed a bottle of water then walked to her room. Maybe she could clean.

Energy to burn with no way to expend it. Setting the bottle down on her nightstand she looked around trying to decide where to start. Without realizing she had made a decision she headed over to the bookcase. A lot of books and she had read them all at least twenty times or more. Reading over some of the titles she smiled. A lot of good memories. But all that stopped when her hand landed on the Bible. Slowly she pulled it out and turned it over in her hands. Something that contained words of great importance. It had also been the one thing in her bedroom the criminals who vandalized the house left untouched.

Bella couldn't say what came over her, but suddenly all the rage she had repressed blew to the surface. She threw the Bible across the room. Then ripped every book out of the bookcase and flung them at the wall. When she finished she moved on to something else and didn't care what. She needed to destroy it all. Everything had to go. Making it over to the closest she yanked all the clothes off their hangers. With all the anger, frustration, and sadness expended she dropped against the wall and slid to the floor. Settling her breaths she looked over her room and laughed until she cried. She'd made a mess. Matched her life.

Chapter Thirteen

The Friday afternoon bell had rung. Students rushed by the spot Jeremiah had taken against the wall. About fifteen to twenty feet away Bella removed books from her locker and placed them in her backpack. She laughed and talked to a classmate who occupied the locker to her right.

He stood too far away to hear what they talked about, but after overhearing his sister and Sarresh, Jeremiah wondered what her plans for the weekend were. He had spent all week staying out of sight. He avoided the cafeteria. Classes didn't matter because he didn't have any with Bella. Up until now, he'd done a decent job of not seeing her in the halls. *But that won't happen today, will it?* Instead he stood there, and watched his ex-girlfriend. With her focus elsewhere she hadn't spotted him. Then she turned when somebody paused at her locker and said something. As soon as they walked away, her gaze found his.

He considered turning around and heading off, except he couldn't make his legs move. Bella's eyes locked on his freezing him in place as if his feet were glued to the spot he stood. He couldn't explain what held him there. While he claimed insanity, it had to be love. The words Vick said to him over a week ago banged around loudly in his head. Likely because Bella smiled and laughed. She appeared to be genuinely happy. A smile slowly crept onto his face and bloomed. He took one step in her direction when David swept in. He watched as the guy wrapped an arm around Bella's waist, spun her and placed a kiss on her lips. He got a full view of David's hands running through her midnight black tresses while he kissed her like a boyfriend would. Unable to stand still he turned and walked away like he should have a few minutes ago. Unsure he could handle another day of this torture, he knew he needed to talk to his parents about getting out of the city for a week or two. Jeremiah knew he had to leave if he expected to climb out of this hole.

****

At first the kiss was a nice surprise, until it went from a kiss to a *kiss*. Pulling out of his grip, Bella looked at her boyfriend only to realize he hadn't been looking at her. Glancing over her shoulder she followed the hard stare burning in his eyes. She saw Jeremiah walk away from them, when she swore he had started in her direction. Turning her attention back to David she narrowed her gaze. They normally didn't share kisses like that in school. In fact, those were usually done in private. Their kisses were tender and soft, not hot and wild. Shaking her head she really hoped she'd be proved wrong. "What the hell was that?"

"What are you talking about?"

His glare still hadn't moved. "That!" She declared pointing in the direction Jeremiah had just disappeared in.

Finally he looked down at her. "I still don't know what you're talking about."

"Was he the reason you just kissed me?"

"I always kiss you."

"Not like that. At least not here."

"What are you trying to say?"

"You did, didn't you? You wanted to make sure Jeremiah saw us. Were you trying to rub it in his face or something?"

"Bella, I don't —"

"Don't you dare fucking lie to me!"

He sighed. "I'm sorry. I just... I didn't like the way he was looking at you."

"What? Did you expect him to be okay with us overnight?" She shook her head. Reaching into her locker she grabbed the last book she needed and slammed it shut and turned and started toward the exit.

He followed after her. "Bella come on. I wasn't trying to be a jerk."

She spun on her heel and glared at him. "Yes you were. Now, if you're smart, you will *not* follow me."

"But I thought we were going out tonight."

"Well, I guess that depends on how calm I get during my appointment." He called out another apology after her. She shook her head and muttered, "Babaca!" *David is an asshole.*

At least he had enough smarts to heed her warning. David backing off would allow her to calm down. *What the hell makes him think the silent declaration is necessary to begin with? What an ass. Whatever. He needs to get off that macho train and fast. No way in hell I plan to put up with that. He has no reason to feel threatened by Jeremiah. We weren't talking and nothing happened. So I looked, it doesn't mean I'm interested. I'm with David, so he has nothing to worry over. Maybe he just needs more convincing. What is wrong with me? Did I really excuse his behavior? Fuck no! I'm not territory to be marked. I will look and talk to whoever I damn well please! And he can't stop me.*

Standing in front of her car Bella paused and stared at the keys in her hand. She could leave town and just say *fuck it*. Right there sat her getaway ticket. She had a full tank of gas, a credit card, maybe fifty dollars cash in her purse and she didn't need anything else. The idea of leaving it all behind, she toyed with often. Nobody knew how close she'd come to calling it quits. If they suspected, no one ever said anything. Especially considering no one knew how to leave her the hell alone, like she had constantly been on everybody's watch list. But driving away without looking back, it wouldn't last. At least not the way she wanted. Sighing she walked on to the car and climbed in. She started the engine just in time to see Amanda heading her way. God, she had that glint in her eye that meant she wanted to talk; the last thing Bella was in the mood for. As if she hadn't spotted Amanda, Bella buckled in, released the emergency brake, and placed the car in reverse. She didn't move fast enough. Amanda knocked on her window.

Damn. Bella looked up. Rolling down the window, she shifted the gear back into park. "Hey, what's up?"

"Hey. Could you get out of the car? I need to talk to you for a second."

"Is it important? I mean, I'm on my way to an appointment."

Amanda nodded. "Yes. It is."

For a moment she wondered if Amanda would just walk away. Realizing the unlikelihood of that occurring, Bella shut the car off and climbed out. "What is it?" She leaned against the car and watched Amanda nervously rock back and forth on her feet. She'd never been the twitchy type. "Whatever it is, you can tell me."

Loosening up her lips a little. "I know it's none of my business, but I think you should tell Jeremy about the miscarriage."

Okay, maybe that shouldn't have been said, but Bella did tell Amanda she could say whatever. Sometimes the worst words came out of Bella's mouth. Sighing she asked, "Why?" *My patience has been tried once today, why not a second time? Sure, bring it on.*

Amanda didn't hesitate. "I know you're David's… well, whatever you are…"

"Girlfriend," Bella inserted for her. "I'm his girlfriend."

Amanda stopped for a second and stared at her hard. "Yeah, girlfriend. As much as that may be, I know you aren't in love with him."

"For crying out loud Mandy, he and I have been dating a week. It doesn't happen that fast."

"Bull. Shit!"

Two words, but they spoke volumes and Bella had no argument. Afraid she might stick her foot in her mouth more she resigned to remaining quiet. Because she couldn't fight the truth. No matter how many times she tried, she always lost. And there were only so many people she could hide it from.

"You and Jeremy fell in love hard and fast. Don't you dare go spouting that shit off to me. I know how the two of you really feel about each other. You should make sure you understand that because I know it won't change, no matter whose girlfriend you are," Amanda spit out. "Which is exactly why you need to tell him about the miscarriage. Got me?"

Although everything she'd said had been true, it didn't make one bit of difference of what she did or didn't tell her ex-boyfriend. And they would never ever have that conversation. She knew staying silent would only encourage Amanda more, unfortunately it didn't take much time to get her up to boiling again. Everyone always wanted her to do something - her parents wanted her to see the counselor, the prosecutor wanted her to testify, Jeremiah, hell she didn't know what he wanted, she wasn't even sure he knew. And now this, now Amanda wanted her to tell him about something he had no right to know, forget it! Pushing off the car she stepped in toward her friend. "Fuck off!" Bella took a deep breath. "I don't care what you think you know. He left. He made that choice. He has no reason to know anything about the miscarriage."

"If you won't tell him, I will."

"I doubt that. You promised you wouldn't and of all the things you do, going back on your word isn't one of them. Now, if you'll excuse me, I have an appointment." With that she spun around and moved back for her car.

"We're not finished!" Amanda exclaimed as she grabbed onto Bella's arm and turned her around so they were facing each other.

Sick and tired of people grabbing her like she was a ragged doll, the moment she felt Amanda's hand on her arm, Bella balled up her other hand and using the momentum punched Amanda hard in the face. Figuring Bella stunned her friend into silence, she took the opportunity. "Leave me the hell alone!" With nothing else to say, Bella climbed back into her car, reignited the engine, backed up and sped off.

As she pushed the speed limit without caring her doctor's office was only ten minutes from the school, Bella took several deep breaths. Every part of her burned with fury. Too many things triggered her anger lately - therapy, Jeremiah's faulty attempt to fix things, the miscarriage, Heather's discovery (Bella still waited to see if that bomb would drop), David's reaction, and now Amanda. What came next? She heaved a sigh and automatically slowed as the road she needed approached. A few turns and the doctor's office came into view. She turned right into the parking lot and found a spot.

Bella put the car in park and shut the ignition off. She glanced over to the passenger seat where her purse and backpack were. Gathering her purse into her lap she swallowed and opened it up, then pulled out the pills that had steadily become her best friend. When she felt how light the bottle had become she turned it around and blinked. She didn't remember going through so many pills. *How can it be that low already?* She started the week with a hundred pills and had half a bottle left two days ago. And now there were roughly twenty remaining. *That can't be possible.* She tossed the bottle back into her purse and zipped it shut. More annoyed than before she yanked the keys out of the ignition, got out of the car, and slammed the door shut. The next ten minutes were a complete blur as she checked in and got escorted to the room with the couch.

Silently Bella walked to the large window of her psychiatrist's office and stared. She stood there for maybe ten or twenty minutes. It made no difference. The same things still cycled through her head. Her mind hadn't left the pregnancy in over a week. Then the word *girlfriend* got thrown in a time or two. Her failure at everything. That moment of a look with Jeremiah earlier. Chewing David out over his reaction. The fight with Amanda. But of all of these things, they weren't what caused her to stand at the doctor's window and watch the world below as if it held some secret key to a puzzle she needed to solve. No, that came from Heather calling her a junkie. She wasn't a drug addict. She could quit. Yeah, that's what she had to do. Monday, she would tell Tommy no more.

With that decided she felt a slight weight lift. Unfortunately, that allowed her to focus on the fight she had before she left school. She punched one of her friends. It didn't matter if arguing with everything Mandy said had been futile. Didn't make a difference she was right. Or that her heart belonged to Jeremiah and always had. Telling him about the miscarriage made perfect sense. Which made her despise logic. And yet she worried if she told him about the baby he would be disgusted further. Would he feel sorry for her? His reaction scared her more than the idea of telling him did. Feeling the urge to actually talk to her psychiatrist about something other than her parents or what currently ran a five mile course in her mind was extremely unnerving. Out of nowhere she said, "I was pregnant."

"Was?"

"I lost the baby," she answered candidly. Compelled she continued, "The doctor said 'Sometimes these things just happen.' The ease in which he said it was like we were talking about a lost dollar, not a baby. A baby." Was she crying? Realizing those were in fact tears she wiped at her face.

"What are you feeling?"

"A lot of things." Bella didn't know how to explain her emotions so she talked about her actions. "I cried the first few days. Yesterday I threw things and screamed. Then I cried some more. The worse part, I don't know if it's because I lost my baby or from the attack." She stared out the window. "I feel like screaming again."

"Do you know why?"

"Yes. I feel like a part of me died and somewhere deep inside, I'm happy about it. And I'm angry because I feel like I was robbed. And I don't have anyone who understands that."

"How so?"

"More than one thing has been ripped from me. My friends treat me like I'll crack at any moment. They don't know how to talk to me anymore than my parents do. And all I can ask is why. Because I don't know what I did to deserve any of this." Silence filled the room. She knew the doctor couldn't answer why. No, only one person could answer and she hadn't been talking to *Him*. Proof that God hated her - for the first time she'd been honest with the doctor and she didn't feel like it did a damn bit of good. If talking about losing the baby didn't make her feel better, then what the hell would make her think talking about the attack would make a difference?

"Do you think you would feel differently if you hadn't miscarried?"

"I've wondered that myself."

"And did you come up with an answer?"

"Sometimes I think I have. Part of me thinks I would be happy, but then I wonder if I would be able to look at the child at all. Would I be able to love it? Would I hate it almost as much as I hate myself? I don't even know what I should be allowed to feel."

"Anything. You have a right to be angry at everything that has happened. And you can be sad at the loss of a child, no matter how the baby was conceived."

Turning from the window she looked at Dr. Filmore. "And if I'm relieved?"

"That's okay too."

"Then why do I feel like shit for being relieved?"

"Because despite the relief, you loved that baby. And the loss saddens you."

True. Returning her stare back out the window she thought about all these different emotions. Silence found its way into the room again.

"Was anyone there when it happened?"

"Yeah. I was at David's when it started. He's been there since, doing whatever he can to make me feel better. Some days it works and others it's all I can think about."

"It's good that he's there for you. Thoughts are going to vary from day to day."

She nodded. "Yeah."

"What I want you to think about are things you can tell to or do for yourself that will help you get through the day. We'll work on that more next time."

Bella's gaze snapped over to the clock. *How can our time already be over?* Usually she looked forward to the end of these sessions, but today she needed it.

Chapter Fourteen

Jeremiah walked along the street and looked around checking out the variety of aliens depicted over multitudes of stores. Lights were strung up all over the store fronts. The smaller shops had Christmas trees in their windows decorated with several different ornaments. Some of the aliens wore Santa Claus hats. As he continued on he saw multiple advertisements for the Electric Light Parade. He slowed his pace when he came upon a diner in the heart of downtown Roswell. His stomach rumbled convincing him this was the place to eat. He opened the door and stepped in.

    After being forced to watch the display of affection between his Bell and David he approached his parents about taking off for a week. He'd been extremely thankful they agreed without argument. When he arrived yesterday afternoon he chose to fast and stay in the hotel so he could pray and read the Bible. He'd showered and changed clothes earlier. Now he felt free to get some food. Settling down on a stool at the countertop he snaked a menu and looked over it. When a server came over he ordered a glass of water and a turkey BLT sandwich on whole grain with a side of fries. Reaching into his pocket he pulled out his cell phone and accessed the camera, where he could flip through all the pictures he'd taken of Bella including a few of the two of them together. Then he found the one he'd been searching for, his favorite. She'd worn her hair down and she had on a white tank top underneath a white lace short sleeve button up with a knee length denim skirt and a pair of sandals. She'd been laughing at some joke he'd cracked. Her smile brightly lit up the grass and sky around her giving off a halo effect.
    "She's beautiful," someone next to him said.
    He half glanced to the person. "That she is."
    "Mind if I ask who she is?"

Good question. He didn't quite know how to answer. He could easily say her name, or that she was his ex-girlfriend, but neither truly justified just how much she meant to him. Even if they were both technically true, she would always be more. Looking from the man sitting next to him back to the picture he stared at, he smiled when it suddenly occurred to him on how to respond. "This is my angel."

"Explains why you look at her picture the way you do. You must really love her."

"That I do."

"Is she here with you?"

"No." He had no idea why he spoke openly to this man. Except the man was comfortable to be around. Like he'd found a long lost friend he hadn't seen in quite a while. Maybe it had to do with the fraying gray hair or the wrinkles lining his face revealing wisdom or it could be the warmth in his eyes. Understanding why didn't seem as important as the topic they currently talked over.

"How come?"

This old man definitely asked the hard questions. Again there were a few different answers: he didn't believe to be the man she needed, she broke up with him, or he was a coward. All three were true. At the same time, he knew those weren't the only reasons, but they were a part of the main one. "She got hurt and ended up in the hospital. I couldn't handle the devastation and ran away. I've been here for a day and a half trying to pull it together and overcome my fear."

The old man nodded. "It must have been extremely hard on you."

"But it was harder on her and I can't stand the fact that I hurt her more when she needed me the most."

"Sometimes in life, we come across things we don't initially know how to handle. But we always have someone to turn to who will help us through. Just have to talk to *Him* and He'll answer."

"That's why I came. I think I lost sight of that. I was different when she and I met. I was confident I could protect her. Then she got attacked and I knew I failed to keep her safe. I figured if I couldn't stop someone from hurting her, then I wouldn't be able to protect her at all. Since I've been here I've learned I didn't have the right understanding. I thought to protect her, I had to do it physically. I never considered emotional protection."

"Good. Sounds like you're on the right road."

Jeremiah turned his attention from the old man to the server as she set a plate of food in front of him. He smiled. "Thank you." Turning back to the old man he blinked when he realized he was gone. *When did he get up? I didn't hear him leave.* No, he hadn't heard a sound. The old man just disappeared. Okay, a little strange. Pulling his head together he picked up one half of the sandwich and took a bite. Thinking back over the conversation he recalled the last thing the old man said. "Right road." They were words of encouragement. And he couldn't have asked for them at a better time. He'd begun to wonder if he'd done the right thing by leaving. When he talked to his father, he hadn't really been sure what he needed. But maybe the old man had the answer he'd been praying about. He wouldn't stay any longer than a week. Then he could start fighting for what he really wanted.

A half hour later he stepped out of the diner and into the warm December sun. Taking a left, Jeremiah shoved his hands in his pockets and started walking. While going back to the hotel sounded like a good idea, he realized he needed to be outside for a little while. It would help him think on how to start getting his Bell back. Calling up the vision of her the day before he knew if he could get David out of the picture, it wouldn't be too hard. She still cared, but that wouldn't be enough. He needed to be able to show her he wouldn't go anywhere. But the only way to prove that would be if David didn't try to pull her away every chance he got. Unfortunately they'd gotten closer in the past couple of weeks than he hoped possible.

He paused when he came across a small novelty store. In the window hung an ornament that caught his attention. From the string dangled a woman from the old country hovering over a child sitting at a desk with a book open. This would've been their first Christmas together and he hadn't much thought about it. But that ornament, it was one hundred percent Bella. He smiled and decided to go inside.

Five minutes later he stepped outside with his purchase and spotted something across the street he prayed to be a mirage. Jeremiah shut his eyes and rubbed them. Looking again, he knew without a doubt what he saw to be real. Bella and David were standing in front of a shop window talking about something. For a split second Jeremiah thought this could be an opportunity, except David caught his gaze the moment he went to open the door for Bella. Something flared in the guy's eyes, which made Jeremiah reconsider walking across the street. He wasn't afraid of this guy, was he? No. Deciding he wouldn't go down without a fight, he took a step in their direction.

Unfortunately David seemed to think quick on his feet too. A couple of horse drawn carriages lined the side of the cobblestone street. Without wasting a second David grabbed Bella's hand, escorted her away from the store and helped her up into a carriage. By the time Jeremiah got through the crowd and across the street where they had been, the carriage had already gone half a mile away and turned the corner. Thinking fast he walked over to a carriage that hadn't left. "Excuse me. Do all these carriages take the same route?"

"No señor, we each have our own."

Brushing a hand through his hair he nodded. "Thanks." No way he'd catch them on foot and he could end up walking around for hours without knowing which route their buggy went. Sighing he started toward his hotel.

****

Bella had to be seeing things. It didn't seem possible Jeremiah would be in downtown Roswell. Except she hadn't been able to confirm anything for sure. The moment David got her in the carriage he all but practically made sure she didn't look back. He managed to keep her eyes forward. She could make a couple guesses as to why, but it wouldn't make them true. Besides, what would Jeremiah be doing there? Unless he came up with his family for the festival too. They hadn't been together long enough for her to know how they spent the holidays. Shaking her thoughts away she looked up to David only to see him staring off behind them. Turning around she followed his gaze and saw a whole lot of nothing. Crossing her arms she smirked and returned face forward. "Good to know whatever's back there really has your attention."

Looking back at her, David sighed. "I'm sorry, babe. If I promise you have all of my attention for the rest of the day, will you forgive me?"

Tilting her head she lifted a brow. "I suppose."

"What would it take to put a smile on your pretty face?"

A smile, he wanted a smile. She could easily give him one, but that didn't mean she shouldn't have to make him work for it. "Ice cream and a kiss."

"Things I absolutely love," he stated as a wide grin spread across his lips.

She gave him a tiny smile. At least until he leaned down, took her into his arms and pressed his lips to hers. She might never get enough of kissing him. It hadn't been passionate, but she still enjoyed it. The carriage slowed for another turn as his lips left hers. As he relaxed against the seat, she caught sight of a caricature artist on one side of an alleyway and a small ice cream shop on the other. It took up the corner and even had a window to order from, so she asked, "Think we could stop?"

David simply quirked a brow.

"You haven't fulfilled my demands and I do believe that was an ice cream parlor I just spotted."

He glanced back over his shoulder, then turned his attention to the driver. Leaning forward he said something to him and the driver pulled over to the side of the road. With a smile David offered her his hand. "Shall we?"

She nodded as he hopped down first and then helped her. Hand in hand they walked back to the ice cream parlor she saw. A short line had already formed, which gave them both time to look over the menu. Nothing immediately struck her as "forgive me" food until her eyes landed on the *Oh, Fudge split*. It sure sounded like chocolate heaven she could roll around in - Fudge Me Chocolate ice cream served with frozen chocolate covered bananas, covered with a ladle of hot fudge, capped with towers of chocolate whipped cream and topped with a chocolate covered cherry. *Holy shit! This will probably be better than the introduction of soda or the ChocoMel Volcano I shared with David on our first date.* And if this wasn't "forgive me" food, then she didn't know what would be. She must've been salivating pretty badly because when she looked over to David he held a tissue out to her.

"Guess that means you know what you want," he said as she accepted the offered tissue.

With a faint smile her cheeks flushed and she nodded. "The *Oh, Fudge Split*."

"Okay."

Needing a moment to gather herself she said, "I'm going to go check out the caricature artist, okay?"

"Sure." He flashed her a devilish grin. "I'll be over once I get our orders."

God, help her. She felt like she would be in trouble if he gave her anymore of those bright eat-you-up smiles. She walked away while he went up to the window.

As she stepped off the lip of the sidewalk she glanced down the alleyway and could have sworn she saw Jeremiah at the other end. Unsure if her mind played a trick on her she started in that direction. Strongly compelled to find out if she imagined him there in Roswell, she didn't pay much attention to the fact she walked down an alleyway. Halfway down she spotted the dumpsters and slowed her pace. She shivered as goose bumps crawled up her arms and the hairs on the back of her neck prickled. Her eyes bounced back and forth between the brick walls, then quickly glanced over her shoulder with a sudden sense she wasn't alone. As she closed in from one dumpster to another the scents of rancid milk, spoiled meat, and aged cheese hit her like a full-to-the-hilt dump truck. She blinked and tried to block out the smells that began to overwhelm her nostrils, but she couldn't. Everything about the alley had been too strong.

The two o'clock afternoon lights faded to dark and she didn't just smell the milk, meat, and cheese, but five day old anchovies. A deli didn't come up on her right, instead a pizza parlor did. Seconds later with no time to react her right arm got bent back and someone slammed her against the wall. Then a large man whose face she couldn't see yanked her back against his body. She screamed at the pain that radiated up her arm to her shoulder. Releasing her arm he spun her around and threw her down on the ground. He straddled her and pressed her arms above her head against a mound of garbage bags. Bella cried out trying to fight back when he punched her and said, "Be a good girl honey bear and this will go easy."

Tears formed in her eyes and she pleaded as another guy wearing a dark gray hoody stopped next to them. His hands replaced the man's who already had her pinned down. Attempting to use the switch to her advantage she popped up and tried to shove the one on top of her off. But she didn't move fast enough because she only got slapped. The one that joined the party took a firm hold of her arm and slammed it so hard it went through the garbage bags and cracked against the concrete. Her forearm snapped and she screamed at the agony that pierced her body. Someone punched at her again and ripped her skirt clean up the middle. Sobbing through heavy breaths she shut her eyes.

One of the men slapped her and then grabbed her by the chin. "Look at me."

Bella refused to open her eyes, instead she squeezed them tighter.

Someone slapped her again, then got in so close to her face she could smell the remnants of a cigarette on his breath as he stated in a coarse voice. "Don't make me hit you again. Be a good girl and look at me."

As much as she didn't want to look and desperately wanted to float away to anywhere but where she had to be at that moment, she opened her eyes. Her face hurt so bad that a logical sense to protect herself in any way possible overrode any fear she felt. All she could think about was doing what he wanted in order to survive. So she looked. His face flared with a wide sadistic grin as she noted the scar that ran down the right side of his face. The hoody she recalled being over his head had gotten flung back.

He brushed his gloved hands over her hair. "Good. Honey bear, tell me, are you going to be a good girl?"

She nodded.

"Say it!"

"I'll be a good girl," Bella whimpered.

He nodded to the man holding her arms still. Slowly they were released as the man on top of her yanked her top apart. She turned her face away as she continued to sob. She cried out when one of the men punched her again. Another ripped her panties and she no longer cared about surviving as she felt rough hands over her body.

All she wanted was to die. Bella covered her eyes with her one good arm trying to block everything out.

With her face covered and eyes squeezed shut, she hadn't heard anyone else approach. Nor did she hear the sound of her own name being called. The tears hadn't stopped and her breaths were rapid. She hesitated to open her eyes afraid she really had gone back to that alleyway. Suddenly someone tried to pry her arm open. Oh God! It hadn't been a dream! "Please, please, I'll be a good girl," she pleaded.

"Bella..." a soft voice said.

That voice - it didn't belong to her attackers', but sounded familiar. She knew that voice.

"Come on, Bella..." the voice repeated.

Slowly she allowed her arm to be gently moved away from her face as she opened her eyes. Blinking she whipped her head back and forth and looked from one open-end of the alleyway to the other. Her gaze shifted to the person in front of her and she blinked down more tears. Seeing David in front of her she threw her arms around his neck, nearly collapsing against his chest as she sobbed.

Holding her in his arms he tried to quiet her. "Ssshh. It's okay. You're safe."

Impossible to tell how long they stood there. No matter how hard she cried or shook, David remained calm, comforted and consistently reassured her she was safe. After some time the shakes finally stopped and the tears slowed. With a couple of deep breaths she pulled herself somewhat together.

"You okay?"

She nodded.

He pressed a feather kiss in her hair. "You sure?"

Again she nodded.

"Can you talk?"

Sniffling she wiped at her face and nodded again. "What happened to my ice cream?"

David laughed and pressed another kiss in her hair. "I tossed them the moment I saw you. I'll get replacements."

Wiping at her face a bit more she pulled back from him, pausing to look for her phone. She crouched down, picked it up and looked up to David. "I think it's broken. I must have stepped on it."

He kissed her forehead and took her hand within his own. "Come on."

They walked back down the alleyway toward the ice cream parlor and the caricature artist. On the other side of the artist there were a couple of tables. David escorted her over to one and helped her sit in a chair. "What about my phone?"

With her settled, he crouched down, held out his hand and took her phone. After looking it over he returned it to her. "It looks dead, but we'll go by a store tomorrow and get another one. Okay?"

She nodded.

Brushing a hand over her head down her hair he studied her for a moment. "You going to be okay by yourself?"

"Yeah."

"Okay." He rose to his feet.

She watched him walk away and stop by the artist. With a short distance between them she easily heard him ask the man to keep an eye on her. Embarrassed by the fact she needed a babysitter she had to turn away. Bella couldn't remember what led her to walk down the alleyway to begin with. She knew better, having avoided the whole downtown area back home since the attack. What the hell had she been thinking? Still a little shocked from what went on she stared off until David returned with their ice cream. He set her *Oh, Fudge Split* in front of her. Relieved by the quiet that followed she dug in and hoped it would remain silent.

"Do you want to tell me what happened?"

She should've known it wouldn't last, but she had no desire to talk about it with him anymore than she did her psychiatrist. "No."

"Bella —"

"I said I don't want to talk about it."

"Okay."

God she hoped it would be that easy and he would just drop it. "What do you want to do next?"

She stopped mid-bite and looked up at him in surprise. One, she couldn't believe he didn't try pushing her into saying something about what happened back in the alleyway. Two, he didn't say two words about leaving, which meant he still planned to stay for the festival. Staring at him she waited for him to change his mind, but he didn't. He just kept right on eating like everything was perfectly fine. She didn't know why, but tears streaked her cheeks again.

David sat up, set his ice cream down and leaned forward. "You okay?"

Snickering she wiped at her face and nodded. "Yeah. I'm good." When it didn't seem like he believed her she squeezed his hand. "They're good tears." For the first time in weeks she felt a weight lift from her shoulders. He wouldn't make her talk about something she didn't want to. And she did want that, for somebody to think about her.

Lifting her hand to his mouth he kissed her fingers. "Okay. So, what do you want to do?"

Smiling at him she glanced over her shoulder. "Some caricature artwork."

He nodded. "Yeah."

****

Eight hours had passed since Jeremiah had seen Bella and David downtown. When it turned out following them hadn't been possible, he couldn't help but try to figure out another way to find them. First he thought he'd try calling Bella. He considered the likelihood she wouldn't answer, but decided to take a chance anyway. Except when she did answer he heard screaming and pleading and something about being a good girl with a lot of sobbing. Jeremiah had no clue what brought on the screams, but he could only think about finding her. He didn't know what happened, but at some point the line dropped. Since then he'd repeatedly called her phone, probably a good thirty times or more by now. But she never answered. His next idea had been to drive around the city searching for them. Now back at the hotel, worried sick because he never found them. *Think, Jeremiah. Think. What can I do? How can find out if she's all right? I don't know David's number and even if I did, no way in hell I'd call the guy.* He had one other option, he could call his sister. Bella might answer her call. Sarresh would've been better, but he didn't know her number either. Pacing the room he pulled out his cell phone and dialed his sister.

Two rings later. "What's up bro?"

"I need a favor."

"Do you ever need anything else?"

"Stop it! I'm serious! I saw Bella and David here in Roswell. I called her earlier and I don't know, she was having a panic attack or was being attacked. And I can't find them!"

Silence.

"Mandy?"

She sighed. "What do you need me to do?"

"Try calling her."

"I don't know she'll answer me."

"What are you talking about? Why wouldn't she?" he exclaimed.

"We got into an argument yesterday after school."

"And?"

"She hit me."

He groaned and rubbed his face. "Then call Sarresh and have her call!"

"All right, all right. Chill. Give me a minute."

"I will not chill! This is my girlfriend we're talking about!"

"Your what?"

"Never mind! Just get to dialing." Jeremiah heard his sister grumble underneath her breath and he didn't care. There were some other noises - chair scraping, socks shuffling against the hard wood floor, then the beautiful beeping sounds of numbers being dialed. *Girlfriend?* Wow, he really called Bella his girlfriend. He could explain the term with a moment of insanity, but that wouldn't be accurate. No, his mind had switched to autopilot and that popped out.

A few minutes later his sister said, "Bella didn't answer her either. Sarresh is going to call David."

"Great," he mumbled. He didn't know what he hated more - the waiting or the fact that the only way to find out if Bella was alive and well had to be through David. He did the only thing he could - he paced the room.

Finally his sister came back on the line. "He says she had a panic attack earlier. She wouldn't give him the details, but he was able to calm her down."

"Are they still in Roswell?" His sister repeated his question to Sarresh.

"No, they're back in town. They left early because she got sick."

"Is she okay? Really okay?" For a second he thought she sighed in frustration, but he couldn't be sure.

"Yes. He says she stopped throwing up after they got back and she's been asleep since."

Feeling his body relax he dropped down on the bed. "Thank God! What about her phone?"

"He says it broke, but he isn't sure how. They're getting her a new one tomorrow."

"Okay. Thanks sis."

"Yeah."

She didn't even say goodbye before hanging up, but Jeremiah guessed he deserved that. Thankful Bella was okay, he hung up the phone. His one concern was her. His angel was alive and as well as she could be. He'd never been so stressed out. Sighing he knew what he had to do.

Chapter Fifteen

Friday afternoon, Bella clutched her books tight against her chest as she walked down the hall. Several of the students murmured as they glanced her way. Some of them spoke loud enough she could hear them. One called her a *hypocrite*. Another called her a *liar*. Someone else said she was a *slut*. Like she'd heard all week long another person said she *faked it*. It was bad enough she had to hear all this crap at school, but since Sunday people had been calling and texting her phone with the same things. Now if she just didn't have to walk these halls and hear all the horrible things people said about her.

When she saw David waiting for her at her locker she forced a smile. They exchanged a brief tender kiss before she proceeded to put in the combination and open her locker.

"You all right?"

"Yeah." As good as she could be. She focused on gathering the books she needed for the weekend and loaded up her backpack, instead of giving too much attention to her boyfriend.

"You sure? That bug isn't coming back is it?"

"No. It's not coming back." Not if she had her way. After she got sick Saturday she decided stopping the pills had been idiotic. *No way in hell I'm doing that again.*

"Maybe you should just skip your appointment. We could go do something fun. You look like you're a little stressed out."

Bella sighed. He could be observant enough to see she was bothered, but she didn't really want to tell him what caused it. When he called the house the first time this week she told him her phone was acting up and she'd have it looked at. She had no desire to tell David the truth about all the phone calls. She didn't want to tell him she had to turn her cell phone off for hours at a time. Or that people were blowing up her phone with text messages telling her she was a lying, cheating whore and she should do the world a favor and end it. She didn't want to tell him two days ago she started getting messages calling her a murderer. That one she still couldn't figure out, but maybe it had something to do with her attacker sitting in jail. But she had to say something, didn't she? Because he wouldn't keep accepting her crappy answers. She sucked in the corner of her lips and chewed on the inside of her cheek for a moment. With another sigh she glanced to David. "You know how I told you I've been having issues with my phone and that's why you've had to call the house?"

He nodded.

"That isn't entirely true. I've been getting weird phone calls since we got back."

"How weird?"

"Heavy breathing. Whoever it is never says anything and hangs up shortly after I answer."

"Why didn't you tell me sooner? Have you told the police about them?"

"I didn't want to worry you. And what would I tell them? I'm getting unidentified hang ups on my cell phone. There isn't going to be anything they can do. No way to identify who they're coming from. It could be anybody." She closed her locker. He took her hand in his as they started walking toward the doors that led to the parking lot.

"You need to tell the police. They may find something. You don't know they won't if you don't give them the opportunity."

"Yeah, because they've done such a bang up job already," she sneered. Stopping mid-stride she turned to him. "I'm sorry David. It's not your fault. I guess I'm just irritated with the entire case. I just… I wish it was over already." *Then maybe people will stop calling me names. Except if being David's girlfriend hasn't stopped the ridicule, nothing will.*

Tucking a lock of hair behind her ear, he pressed a tender kiss to her lips. "I know babe. Come on, let's go. Since you insist on going, you need to get your appointment over with, so I can have time with you."

She smiled and curled her fingers in his. "Sometimes I think you're too good to me."

"Nah."

Happily disagreeing she bumped into him, which they both laughed at. He was right about one thing, she couldn't wait for the appointment to be over with so she could go over to his place. Good food, horrible movies, and great company that sometimes included a nice make out session. Okay, maybe he was right about the calls, except all the ones she'd received she'd been fairly certain were from classmates. He worried her attacker made the calls, but that didn't make sense to her. Then her car came into sight. She was used to being called a *whore* and a *slut*. And when she heard the word *murderer* for the first time two days ago she hadn't related it to the miscarriage. She didn't know who, but someone had to tell. Unless the destruction on her car hadn't been by anyone at school and those calls were from someone close to her attacker.

That had to be it. *Murderer* and *baby killer* - those words couldn't be linked to anyone at school. Right? Only four people knew about the miscarriage. But those words, they didn't indicate that, they made it sound like she had an abortion. She could only stand and gawk with the rest of her peers while she struggled not to cry. Why did she always feel like something else shouldn't be happening? That for some god forsaken reason she had been stuck in an endless nightmare. She might have been strong enough to handle it, if a crowd hadn't formed and turned all their attention to her the moment she and David walked up. Unable to contain the tears any longer, she turned and buried her face in his chest letting his arms wrap tightly around her body.

"Come on, let's get out of here. You can cancel your appointment today." With her in his arms he led her over to his car. He held her until she calmed down enough to get in. Once he was in and they were heading away from the school he took a firm hold of her hand and lifted it to his lips. Placing a kiss on her fingers, he stole a quick glance. "Have you gotten away from any of this since it all happened?"

"No," she sniffled. "There was so much to do with the Fall Harvest Production and then I needed to heal. The trip we made to Carlsbad and Roswell, that's the furthest I've been."

"Then that's what we need to do. We'll go by your place and you can pack a bag. I'll go by my place, pack one and then we can go wherever you want to go."

"What are you talking about?"

"We're going to get away from here. You need to escape all this and we can leave for the weekend. Be on a plane in a couple of hours to anywhere you want."

She blinked at him. He couldn't be serious, yet the look on his face said nothing else. *Get away from Rescate County? Where will we go?* She shook her head. Her parents would never go for that. "Are you for real?"

"Yes! Absolutely!"

Good God! A weekend, in a hotel, with him - no friends, no judgment, no pity, no family, no one who knows me or what's going on in my life. It'll be heaven. She looked to him again. "Anywhere?" Could she do it? Could she convince her parents? Would she have to mention the car? The miscarriage? Or could she leave without them noticing?

"Anywhere."

"A beach?" Bella answered still unsure how any of this would work.

"Okay, so we could go out west to California or east to Florida."

"How long will it take to get there?"

"Five to seven hours for either."

"Where will we go? Wait. Can I even get on a plane?"

"In Florida we can go to Orlando, Miami, or Daytona Beach. California we can go to Los Angeles or San Francisco." He quickly glanced to Bella. "Yes. You're sixteen and considered a young adult. Besides I'm 18 and I would be accompanying you." David grinned.

She nodded. "What's the difference between those places?"

"Well, Orlando has theme parks like Universal and Disneyworld, Daytona is racing, and Miami I think its clubs. Los Angeles is mostly Hollywood. Good place to go for home of the stars and they're close to Disneyland. As for San Fran, I don't think it would be a good choice, at least not for us."

"Theme parks?"

"Yeah, rides and things like that."

"That sounds fun." She smiled.

"Orlando is better than LA so we'll go there." He said pulling into her driveway.

She wouldn't care if her parents were home, but she was extremely glad they weren't. Bella headed straight back to her room and quickly pulled a bag together making preparations for good and bad weather. David collected things out of her bathroom and when they were set to go he took her bag in one hand and one of her hands in the other and tugged her along down the hall.

They got back into the car and David placed her bag in the trunk. Once he was in the car, they hit the road for his place. She couldn't believe they were actually leaving the state. "I'm going to call Sarresh and let her know what's up."

"Good idea. And make sure you call the police about your car."

"All right." She agreed not because she wanted to, but because it made sense. Reaching into her purse she pulled out her phone and dialed up her friend. She would also call her parents and tell them she planned to crash at Sarresh's for the weekend and she'd be back Sunday.

****

Jeremiah sighed as he flipped through the channels eagerly trying to find anything good to watch for a Saturday. Uninterested in anything on the television, he considered doing something else when a knock called his attention to the door. Only his family knew where he had gone and if they needed to contact him, they would've called. The second knock had him up out of the chair and traipsing across the floor. Unfortunately with no peep hole he had no choice but to open the door. And the last thing he expected had been the person on the other side.

Sarresh stood there tapping her foot with her arms crossed. "You going to invite me in?"

"Umm, yeah, sorry. Come on in," he said to his cousin.

"Thanks," she said walking into his room. Taking everything in she glanced back to him. "It's nice. Almost a step up from a shithole."

"What are you doing here Sarresh?"

"I needed to talk to you."

"How did you even find me?"

She grinned. "I pulled your sister's teeth out."

"I highly doubt that."

"Close enough."

He rubbed his face squeezing tight with a groan. "Please just talk or get out." No idea why she annoyed him, but she did. Could be the attitude she exuded, like men were all royal jackasses and they only deserved to be treated like dirt. His mother raised him to be a gentleman, but sometimes Sarresh tried his patience. Good thing he rarely dealt with her.

"Let me start first by asking when you plan on coming home?" Sarresh relaxed her body, uncrossed her arms and dropped them to her side.

"Tomorrow," he replied. *God, why did she come here? Sure she was family, but I can only take so much of her.*

"Good because right now Bella is spending the weekend in a hotel with David. And I know you guys broke up, but you need to get off your ass and start working on getting her back."

"Hotel?" That certainly got his attention. "Why is she in a hotel?"

"First, I need you to understand at no time are you to mention where this information came from. When you do talk to her you need to make sure you don't mention any of what I'm about to tell you. Promise me."

"I'll do my best."

"That's not good enough. Promise me."

He sighed. "Fine, I promise."

"Two weeks ago she went on a date with David. I don't know the specifics, but something happened and they went home separately. The next night she went to apologize and passed out while she was there and ended up in the hospital. She got released after a few hours. Yesterday her car was tagged with 'whore,' 'slut,' 'murderer' and 'baby killer.' Add to that the letter, her freak out in Roswell, and you get a trip to Florida with David."

As he listened to everything she told him, he could tell there were holes. People had been calling her a whore and slut since the rape, but the other two words didn't make any sense. Frowning he glared. "What aren't you telling me?" He waited and waited some more. Perfect way to try his patience. Still waiting he churned everything over in his head. Baby killer and murderer - Bella would never do that. She'd never have an abortion, not mention to do that she'd have to be... *oh God!* His eyes widened with a curt stare at his cousin. "Please don't... she wasn't..."

Sarresh nodded and remained silent for a while longer. Talking about this seemed to burden her greatly as if she were betraying someone who trusted her. Finally she spoke, "Her rapist, he got her pregnant."

Pregnant? Jeremiah stumbled over to the chair he'd been sitting in and dropped back into it. The rape had been unbearable and now this? *God, how the hell did Bella handle this? A baby... she's going to have a baby? No, wait...* "You said she went to the hospital? Is she okay?"

"Jeremy..." Sarresh paused either lingering for full effect or struggling to say it. "She had a miscarriage. Amanda and I saw her while she was in the hospital. She seemed fine, but I just don't know where her head is anymore."

My sister? She was there? Why the hell hadn't she said anything? I would've gone to see her! He yelled. "Amanda knew? She knew? And didn't tell me?"

"Before you get upset with your sister, Bella asked her not to. Mandy tried to convince Bella otherwise, but couldn't."

"So why are you telling me?"

"One, I'm worried about her. Two, I didn't promise I wouldn't and I don't think she'll tell you herself."

"What do you mean?"

"Before the miscarriage she spent a lot of time at my place. But after it happened, she stopped staying with me. I see her at school. And with all the time she's spending with David, I don't know what's going on with her. I knew things were bad from everything I saw while she was with me, but now I don't know."

Clenching his teeth he forced his hands together because he wanted to strangle her right now. What was it with the women in his family waiting to tell people stuff? "Define 'bad.'"

Backing up a step she crossed her arms and gave him a look that had been an attempt to calm him down before she spoke. "First I thought it was just drinking, but I found pills in her purse. I don't know how many she's taking or if she still needs them. When she stopped hanging around, I figured it was because of the baby issue."

"Pills? Drinking? What the hell Sarresh?" He jumped up. "I thought it was just the tattoo! But this, this is worse!"

"Hey! Don't go jumping down my throat! The pills are prescribed, so I don't know how often she's taking them or if she's even taking them! And the drinking she only did on the weekends with me. But you need to know everything because when you walked away you really fucked her up! Do you hear me? You only added to the damage her rapist did. So don't you go pulling that shit on me!"

He could feel the room closing in on him. He needed to walk and she had to go. "I need some air," he said shoving past her. Snagging his room key along the way, he paused after opening the door and glanced over his shoulder. "You can show yourself out." He didn't hear whatever she called out after him. Right now, he needed to be alone. Did Vick know about any of this? What about his sister? And why did Sarresh just sit back and let it happen? He needed to get out of his own head, but that wasn't possible. He wasn't sure if Sarresh did the right thing telling him now. He tried to figure out how he would look at Bella with all this enlightenment. Her parents had no clue. If she'd been drinking, the psychiatry visits couldn't be doing any good. Not if she was self-medicating. None of what happened sounded like her. He didn't even know her anymore, but maybe that had become the point. God, what could he do?

****

Bella stared at the phone. She didn't care about stopping the tears that started a few minutes ago. She could only think about how she needed to get the information she had just received from Chief Detrone out of her head. When the doctor told her she had a miscarriage she believed everything happened on its own. Her body had gone through all the physical motions, but that hadn't been the case. Apparently he helped it along after being presented a court order requesting the *products of conception* as the Chief put it. Suddenly the term *baby killer* made so much more sense. Even if she didn't remember any of it.

She'd been in the room getting dressed while David got a beach bag ready for them. They'd been invited to a bonfire. She heard him call out, "Babe, you about ready? We need to head out."

His voice pulled her gaze from the phone to the hallway. For a moment she wondered if he knew what happened. Then she remembered he had been stuck waiting. David wouldn't have known anything. Maybe he could have overheard? No, not likely.

"Babe?" David had come down the hall and stood in the doorway looking at her.

"They took the baby."

"What are you talking about?"

She got up off the bed and paced the room. "They got a court order for DNA testing. And the doctor helped my miscarriage along to provide what was needed."

"Oh." He placed his hands on her shoulders and stopped her from pacing. "How are you doing?"

"I don't know. I don't know what to think. When the doctor said I miscarried, I just... I thought it all happened naturally."

He nodded. "I don't get why the doctor didn't tell you."

She shrugged. "Maybe because I didn't ask."

"Maybe. Bella, can I ask you a question?"

"I guess."

"Didn't you know before the miscarriage you were pregnant? I mean, wouldn't they have tested for that when you were raped. Or given you some kind of pill or something."

"I declined to take the morning-after pill. The doctor said I could have my blood tested for the pregnancy hormone and to come back after a few days. I didn't want to know. So I didn't go back and have it done."

"I see."

"Do you?"

David sighed and sat on the bed. "You've had a lot to deal with. I know the rape hasn't been easy for you. So it makes sense not wanting to know a fetus was growing as a result of the rape."

"It's not a fetus. It was a baby." Bella didn't feel she should have to correct him, but she was raised to believe life started at conception.

He quirked a brow. "But you wouldn't have even been able to hear the heartbeat."

"That doesn't mean shit." She left the bedroom and started for the front door. The room had suddenly gotten too small for the two of them.

"Bella, I'm sorry." David followed after her.

"Leave me alone."

He grabbed her arm. "Bella come on. I didn't mean anything by it."

"Yes you did!" She slapped him. Her hand stung. She would gladly take the physical pain over the emotional anguish she felt. Her heart broke in ways she didn't know were possible.

The slap barely phased David as he stepped closer and tried to wrap his arms around her. "I'm sorry."

"Get the hell away from me!" Bella shoved him. She walked closer to the door. "You don't get it! You think it wasn't a baby just because the heartbeat couldn't be heard? That's bullshit! Maybe you don't believe life begins at conception, but I do!"

She walked out the door and toward the boardwalk. No matter how many times she said "baby," David just kept referring to it as a fetus like it hadn't been a life-form at all. So what if it hadn't been that far developed? She didn't care if she hated the baby's father. Part of it belonged to her and she loved that baby even if she didn't know about it until it was already gone. Jeremiah would understand. He saw things the way she did, but not David.

Looking up for a moment she continued down to the boardwalk then to the beach itself. At least she had this wondrous view to accompany her as she walked because she needed to get as far away as her feet would let her. *This isn't happening* had become a new catch phrase in her life. She didn't know how much more she could take. It hadn't been enough that she had been hurt physically, that *that* had been done to her, or that her baby died. Now she had to deal with them using the baby's DNA and for what? The prosecutor told the chief it only proved she had sex with the defendant. Like she chose to! If it was still her word against his, then what the hell did they take her baby for? On top of which, the information had to be disclosed to the defendant's attorney. *Bunch of bull shit!*

Bad enough everyone at school now knew she'd been pregnant. Now her attacker would know too. One punishment hadn't been enough. No. Instead she had to suffer three or four times. Why did God hate her? Hadn't she praised Him? Spread His Word? Believed in Him? Prayed to Him? Read the Bible? Respected her parents? Didn't she do everything He ever asked of her? So why in the hell did He hurt her so much? Why had *she* been put in this awful situation? Separated from the man she loved, angry at her boyfriend, upset at losing a baby she didn't want, always hurting, so alone and constantly wishing she were dead, hoping for a way out.

Stopping she looked around. The place was empty. Somehow she managed to find a spot at the beach where she could be by herself. December in Florida was nothing like December in New Mexico. She wasn't sure it would be warm enough to go in the water. Cool air typically meant cold water. And she didn't care. With no one around she fearlessly stripped the t-shirt and shorts she'd thrown on over the midnight blue bikini David insisted she get. Tossing the clothes to the side she started in toward the water. Maybe if she waded in far enough the tide would carry her away. Maybe she would struggle against the water or waves would crash down on her and she would drown. Inevitably the fight would be over. Deep down that was all she wanted - to stop fighting. She'd become so tired.

The cold water came up to her waist now and she could feel the shivers crawl up and down her body as her teeth chattered. She stopped treading out further when she heard someone scream her name from behind. She didn't need to look. She knew it was David. Pushing harder she trekked on through water until it came up to her chest. Her temperature must've been dropping because she was freezing. Again her name had been yelled out, except this time it had gotten closer. She glanced back. He'd started in the water after her. She blinked and for the first time questioned how much she cared. Even when he got her attention David didn't stop. It was one thing to risk her own life, but was she be prepared to endanger his as well? Had she become that detached?

The water already came up to his knees. Not much space between them now. As a foot taller than her, he had longer strides. In a matter of seconds he would be right there with her. She had two choices: go back or continue forward. As badly as she wanted to end it all, she didn't want to be the cause for anything happening to him or anyone else. Turning around she headed in his direction.

She didn't know what she'd say if he asked her about this, but she'd figure something out.

Except she didn't get a chance to say anything when they came together, water to her waist and the top of his thighs. Without hesitation he reached down, lifted her up and hugged her tightly to him. Wrapping her arms around him she buried her face in his neck. There were things he couldn't make go away, but sometimes the smallest bit of affection relieved some of the pain.

"I'm sorry," she whispered.

"You don't need to apologize."

"I was just upset."

"I know." He walked them out of the water. When he got close enough he slid his arms under her knees and carried her out the rest of the way. Once they were back on the beach he kissed her and nuzzled her before setting her down. "Why were you out there?"

She opened her mouth to lie, but nothing came out. There'd been no issues lying to him thus far. Why couldn't she lie now? Except would she really be lying? She wanted to escape, just on a permanent basis. Would it be lying if she didn't include the last part? *Shit.* The answer was simple, maybe she could be a little honest. "I knew the water would be cold and I just, I didn't want to feel for a little while."

"Were you planning on coming back? You kept going."

"I'm sorry. I'm... I'm on overload. I don't know if I'm strong enough to handle any more bad news."

"Is that what happened?"

She nodded. No point in hiding what she'd been told. "The DNA only proves we had sex."

"What?"

"I still have to testify. That and the photos they took of me." She looked down at the sand and rubbed her arms. "Either way the Chief still says the other guy can be blamed."

"Other guy? What are you talking about?"

"I was attacked by two men. Only one has been arrested. They still haven't found the other guy."

"Two guys? Bella, I'm so —"

"Stop that statement right now! I do not need any fucking pity! You're the only one that hasn't, so don't start now."

Gripping the back of his neck, he shut his eyes tightly and nodded. Blinking them open he gazed down to Bella and sighed. "You're right. We came here to have a good time and get away from everything. Come on, that bonfire sounds pretty good right about now."

"Yeah. It does. I'm kind of cold."

He wrapped his arms around her and rubbed her back. "Put your clothes on. That will help."

Quickly she found her clothes and tugged them on so they could head off. "How far is this party anyways?"

"Not far." He slipped his hand in hers. The two started walking in the direction of the beach party.

They were quiet as they went along, which could be dangerous - gave her time to think over everything. Making out with David was distinctive from making out with Jeremiah. In all likelihood it could be because she felt quite different about each of them. Jeremiah - he had her heart and soul and being apart from him shredded it. For the longest time she tried to deny her feelings for David. She liked him, but she'd never love him. Her attraction to him was mostly physical. Maybe because she didn't have to think around him, even though she did. Staring out at the ocean as they continued to walk she felt a brief squeeze of her hand. Cracking a smile she glanced momentarily in David's direction before turning back to watch the waves. Being out there under the cold water had been bliss. She wondered if she could find that same bliss with David. Could she be that care free? Sometimes she wanted badly to let go, except then she'd think about how empty it would be on her side and how much she would hurt him if he ever found out. If it ever went that far, she could never let him know what it wouldn't mean to her.

Chapter Sixteen

"Did you think about what that would do to her before getting the warrant?" Jeremiah asked his father. He'd arrived home less than fifteen minutes ago and already he'd gotten an earful of what had gone on with the case. His hands balled into fists the moment his father told him what happened with the baby and about the DNA.

Squeezing tightly had been the only way he could stop himself from throwing or breaking anything nearby. Yet he still had the urge to punch the hell out of his father, the one man he had always respected and counted on. If anybody would do the right thing, he figured it would've been his dad. He had raised Jeremiah the same way he had been. And there he stood telling him they collected the products of the unborn baby and used it in an attempt to solidify their case.

"I know you're upset and I understand she might be to, but I want to do anything I can to make sure she doesn't have to get on the stand."

"Then you sure as hell didn't think, did you? Because it didn't do shit!" Cuss words weren't something he normally used, but he was beyond livid and could care less about what came out of his mouth.

"Watch your language young man!" His father scolded.

Jeremy dismissed his father's statement with utter annoyance. "Why? You're standing there trying to tell me you're looking out for her and I can't see it!" Shaking his head he inhaled deeply attempting to calm down. "Come on Dad. You can't honestly tell me you seriously thought DNA would prove anything aside from them having sex. A baby doesn't prove rape."

"I know son," Jamar replied. "I'm sorry for that. I really hoped it would make a difference and I can't change what happened. I would do anything to get this guy to take a deal and deliver up his accomplice."

"And we're still in the same spot we were before. Only this time a lot of fucking people are going to know she was pregnant! Did you think about what that would do to her?" He exclaimed as he stormed out of the kitchen.

Jamar stepped in front of Jeremiah's way and stopped him from moving forward. "I don't care how angry you are. You are in my house and you will follow my rules and watch your language. Keep trying me."

Sixteen years and he'd rarely been punished. Maybe when he'd been younger and first learning, but not in quite a while. He'd learned early on to respect and listen to his parents and yet there he stood purposely defying his father. He always believed his father put the victim first. Praying his father could prove otherwise, Jeremiah said, "Just answer me one thing. At any point did you get her permission or talk to her?"

He sighed. "No. I told the prosecutor and he got a court order."

"And who served it?"

"Myself and another officer."

"And she was awake?"

"No."

"So who was there? Her parents? A friend?"

"I couldn't reach her parents. David Warren was waiting to see her, but nothing was disclosed to him." Jamar told his son.

"I'm going to go unpack." Jeremiah rubbed his eyes and pinched his nose. He walked around his father and to his room. Three weeks ago, when his world fell apart, Bella didn't out right confirm she was spending time with David, but Sarresh did in everything she told him the day before. Still he hoped at least Amanda or Sarresh had been at the hospital when the police collected the baby. Even if David only waited outside, it still sucked. Shutting the door behind him he hefted his suitcase on his bed and stared at her side for a minute before shoving the bag aside. He dug his phone out of his pocket and climbed onto the bed. Calling her had to be nuts, but he needed to hear her voice. Hell, he wanted to comfort her, but he would settle for a conversation. Or at least her hearing him out. Taking a deep breath he pulled up her number, hit dial and pressed the phone to his ear.

****

Popping one last pill in her mouth she drank a bit of water and swallowed. She couldn't afford more than three pills. When Tommy gave her another bottle a few days ago, he'd only given her about thirty pills, which wasn't the usual. And ever since yesterday's episode she'd started taking more than the norm and now she only had twelve left. She needed to go up another level on the pills. But she didn't want to think too much on that. She turned the hotel faucet on and washed her hands. Her phone started ringing as she dried them, so she reached into her back pocket and pulled it out to see who called. She'd told Sarresh they were leaving in a few hours to head to the airport and she would text her when they got back, except her friend's face hadn't been the one that popped up. Closing her eyes and reopening them she hoped maybe she imagined things, but she hadn't. Knowing it to be Jeremiah made her pause, unsure if she should answer, especially since the last time they fought and broke up. But if she waited too much longer it would go to voicemail and she wouldn't get to hear his voice. Her heart made a decision without a chance for her mind to catch up. "Hello?"

Silence. Surely if she hadn't been in the bathroom she might hear the crash of ocean waves with as quiet as the other side remained. Maybe he didn't hear her, "Miah?" *Fuck!* She should've used his full name, not the nickname she gave him. She'd gotten accustomed to using it, she didn't think twice.

Just when she thought he'd hung up she heard, "Hi Bell."

As upset as she should be at him, she was currently calm - likely because of the pills. Her smile brightened at his use of those two words. God she missed him. "Hi." Silence returned to the line as if he didn't quite know what to say to her. They'd never had this problem before. She could ask *why now*, but she knew why.

"How are you?" They asked simultaneously.

She laughed. "I'm all right."

"That's good. Look, I hope I'm not interrupting anything."

Glancing back to the bathroom door she considered the meaning of the word. Funny, if she took it literally he could be, but David had gone to get drinks and ice. "No, you're not. What made you call?"

"I just wanted to check on you."

"Why?" There'd been no hesitation on her end, but there had on his. When he didn't answer the question right away the reason became abundantly clear. "Who told you?"

"Does it matter?"

"It was Amanda wasn't it?"

"Bell, it's not important."

"Bull shit! I told her not to tell you. I'm the one who should've told you."

"No one thought you would."

"It was my place to tell you about the miscarriage. Not hers!"

"Amanda didn't tell me anything."

"She didn't?"

"No."

"Then who told you?"

"I told you, it doesn't matter. I was told. I also know about the car and what they did with the baby."

No, she would not cry. Quietly she bit the inside of her cheek to try and prevent the tears. Too many had been spilled already and she refused to waste anymore. Desperate to know how he found out, she swallowed and asked, "Your dad?"

"Yeah."

"He *doesn't* have that right," she said through tight lips. She *hated* that his father had to be involved. How she wished she could shut off all of her emotions, but she couldn't. She didn't have that kind of strength.

"I'm sorry. I didn't give him much of a choice."

"Then you had no right to ask."

He sighed. "Bell, I just wanted to know what was going on."

"Then you should've asked me."

"Would you have told me?"

Her emotions swiftly overwhelmed her and she lost control of the tears she'd achingly clung to. Quickly she wiped the ones she blinked free and tried to find a path away from herself. "I don't know," she whispered. "Maybe."

After all he had been the one person who knew everything. After the home invasion she talked to him about the nightmares. When she spent the night at his house and they fell asleep on the couch, she expressed all the concern she felt over the vandalism and the worry she had for her parents. When they walked from the church to the hotel Bella and her parents stayed at while their house was repaired, Bella and Jeremiah talked about when David asked her out, how much she wanted to say yes, she even told him about David's predecessor. Jeremiah knew that she had said yes to Jake Riley, David's best friend, and shown up to the winter formal only to find him kissing Heather. Nothing had been kept from Jeremiah, but they were dating. This was different. Jeremiah stopped being her boyfriend even before the official split. David was her boyfriend now and that meant she should be talking to him. Except she didn't fully trust him, no matter how well he treated her. But she didn't trust Jeremiah either.

"Have you told your parents?"

"No." She paced the bathroom. She had to walk some of her thoughts out. Even if it was a small space.

"Are you going to?"

"No."

"Bell, you should tell them."

"Like I should've told them about the nightmares? Because that went well!" *Jeremiah is out of his frigging mind.* She'd followed his suggestion once before and told her parents about them a couple days before the attack. And look what that got her, therapy.

"They're just worried about you."

She narrowed her eyes. "Did someone tell you about that too? Because I sure as hell didn't!"

"Mandy told me and your mom confirmed it." He sighed like he regretted saying it.

Clutching the phone tighter she paced the narrow space. "You're talking to people behind my back. You walk away. You leave. And this is how you check on me? You have no *right!* You are not my boyfriend, so stop acting like it and leave me the hell alone!"

"Bell, I'm sorry. I just wanted —"

"It's all about what you want. You wanted to leave. You wanted to stop talking to me. Now you want to try and fix things."

"I'm not trying to make things right. I know you're with David. But that doesn't mean I don't care about you. I want you to be happy."

"I don't believe you," she choked out through trembling lips and shaky breaths.

"Bella, that's all I want."

"I don't believe you!" She screamed out and angrily threw her phone across the room at the door. Sobbing hard she dropped to her knees and buried her face in her hands.

****

"Bella?" The line had gone dead. Taking the phone from his ear Jeremiah looked down at it to confirm she had been cut off. She had valid reasons not to believe him, but he wished she did trust him. He pulled up her contact information and redialed, but it just rang and went to voicemail. "Bella, it's me. Please call me back." Pushing the end button on his phone he thought about trying again. Would she answer or let it go to voicemail again? Could she answer? Rubbing his eyes he decided to try anyways. He'd finally talked to her, even if it ended in an argument, they'd talked. It had to be a step in the right direction, sort of. Voicemail. "Bella. I'm sorry. You're right I shouldn't have asked, but I need you to believe I did it only because I care. Please, please call me back." Disconnecting he tossed the phone aside as someone knocked on his door. "Come in."

Mandy cracked the door. "Is it safe?"

"Yeah," he murmured.

She closed the door behind her before she took up a spot next to him on the bed. "Z talk to you?"

"Yes, Sarresh found me."

"And Bella?"

"For a little while." Steepling his fingers together he placed them beneath his chin and pressed his elbows into his knees.

"Guess it didn't go well."

"We got into a fight."

"I'm sorry. You want to talk about it?"

He snickered. "Why not, I seem to be good at it."

"What are you talking about?"

Dropping his head he gripped the back of his neck. Slowly he slid his hooked fingers apart and let one fall to the side while he rubbed his hair with his other. "She got upset with me because I was asking and talking to everyone about her instead of going to her."

"I'm sorry. I should've tried harder to convince Sarresh not to tell you."

He shook his head. "I'm glad she did, but it wasn't just that. It's me. I asked Dad about the case when I got back and talked to her mom."

"You talked to Dad?"

"More like yelled at him."

"Why?"

"I wanted to know if he knew about the miscarriage and what happened to her car."

"I saw that. Did they get anything?"

"Yeah, but nothing linked to her rapist."

"What about the DNA? Isn't that going to help?" Mandy inquired.

He shook his head. *No* seemed redundant at this point. He wondered if all rape cases were like this - the victim's word against their rapist. God, he hoped not.

"Damn."

He huffed in agreement. Inevitably Bella would have to testify. The only thing he could do would be to get her to listen to him. With only two weeks until the trial started he'd begun to feel the pressure. If he couldn't get her to listen to him now, how in the hell would he get her to hear him out in such a short time frame? He sighed because he had no clue. Although the argument remained fresh in his mind and he really shouldn't want to know more, he did. Jeremiah turned to his sister. "Can I ask you something?"

"Shoot."

"How did you find out about the miscarriage?"

"David's sister called Sarresh when Bella passed out. Z called the house, talked to Dad then me. Dad called the hospital, then called the prosecutor and left. Since Dad took the car, Z came and got me."

"Was David still there?"

"Yeah. He was in the room with Bella and the doctor, so we had to wait until the doctor left."

"So he was treating her right?" He didn't want to hear any of this but he needed to know she would be in good hands. It wouldn't stop him from talking to her, even if he couldn't be sure as to the reason why.

"As much as I hate to say it, yeah. He's protective of her."

"So it seems."

Mandy tilted her head at her brother. "You don't sound so happy about that."

"He has a reputation of having a temper. I worry if he's protective of her, his temper could become an issue."

"Certainly not toward her."

He shook his head. "If she pushed his buttons it could. He's more likely to react to those around her."

"Well, we'll just have to keep an eye on her then."

"Yeah." Jeremiah half nodded then pushed up off his bed. "I need to go apologize to Dad."

"You apologize? That's a first." Amanda got up as well.

"Yeah, yeah."

"I'm just saying." She grinned as she walked out past him.

"You going to ride me for this?"

"Yes, quite enjoyably, I might add."

"Great," he muttered. "My luck."

****

Bella didn't bother to look up when the bathroom door flew open. Nor did she say anything when David said her name or walked over and sat down beside her. She didn't care about him being there, not even when he gently pulled her into his lap and wrapped his arms around her. As much as he tried to calm her down by stroking her hair and rubbing circles on her back, she didn't care. She'd just gotten into another fight with Jeremiah and she couldn't understand why. She wanted to believe he cared, but if he did then why had he always pushed her further away? Why hadn't he talked to her like he used to? Why did he leave her hospital room? Why did he stop talking to her? There were so many unanswered questions and the only person who could answer them hadn't been around. Thinking maybe she could call him she looked for her phone and discovered it split into about three pieces.

The cover had gotten cracked. As her labored breathing eased up she tried to recall what happened.

David glanced down to her and wiped what remained of the tears on her cheeks.

"Sorry about that."

"Hey, you don't need to apologize for anything. A lot's going on right now."

"Why are you so good to me?"

He smiled, placed a finger beneath her chin and tilted her face up. "Because I care about you and all I want is to be the one putting a smile on these lips." Leaning down he tenderly pressed his lips to hers.

Softly she rested a hand on his cheek and stared into his eyes. "Well you're very good at it."

"I'm glad. Do you want to talk about what upset you?"

Turning her face from him, she stared at the floor for a moment. "Jeremiah called."

"Oh."

David's one word response didn't surprise her. If she had no clue what to make of it all, then how could he? Thinking over the phone call, she went back to the one thing Jeremiah actually asked. Would she tell him about all that happened? Her response still didn't change, but God knew she wanted to. She wanted to be as open to Jeremiah as she had once been. But how could she open up to Jeremiah when he had worked so hard to shut her out? She didn't know how to get past that. Gazing back up to David, she didn't have to ask to know she would never be that open with him. David couldn't be faulted with any of her reasons. She just knew they wouldn't have that type of relationship. Even if she had steadily convinced him otherwise.

"What did he want?"

She pushed up out his arms, got to her feet and started pacing around the bathroom. "To see how I was doing. He knows everything. I don't know who told him what, but he knows about the miscarriage. He knows about the DNA results. Everything."

"What?" He exclaimed rising to his feet.

David became quiet for a long while.

"Was it his dad?"

"At least on the DNA. I don't know about the rest," Bella replied.

"I'm sorry babe. He shouldn't have done that. You're the only person who has any right to tell anyone about what's going on."

Stopping mid-pace they locked eyes and she smiled. "Thank you."

"For what?"

"Being on my side," she said closing the distance between them. Pushing up on her toes she leaned in and kissed him gently.

"Come on. Let's get out of the bathroom." David picked up her dead phone and draped an arm around her shoulder as he escorted her into the bedroom. "So what happened to this?" He shook the phone.

"I threw it."

He nodded. "Maybe we should just get two or three, you know, as back-ups."

She sighed and climbed on the bed. David followed after her. Settled on the bed she curled up to him. "My emotions got to me."

"Okay, so if extra phones aren't the answer. How about yoga? Or meditation?"

Bella punched him in the gut. There wasn't a lot of strength behind that fist, but he still gave an "Umph." Slightly pleased by his reaction she smiled. Then she thought about their return home. Her parents had made random calls to check on her, but still believed she was at Sarresh's. Unfortunately she had to explain about the car, conveniently leaving out a couple of key words, and why she didn't tell them about it Friday. Turned out to be nothing but a big joke. According to Chief Detrone fingerprints had been located on the car. None of them matched any of the prints on file for Quincy's known associates. He didn't explain the details on how, but the prints were matched to a few of her classmates. David had someone pick up her car when it was released this morning so she didn't have to report it to insurance. And she begged Chief Detrone not to disclose any information on her car to her parents. She convinced the Chief she would tell her parents about her car. At least her parents wouldn't see the words *baby killer* and *murderer*. Even though she would never have an abortion, she suspected if her parents ever saw or heard those words, they might think otherwise right now. Hadn't her parents said in their last therapy session they didn't know her anymore? They were right. No one knew her anymore.

"What's going on in that head of yours?"

"Hmm?"

David turned her face toward him with a finger on her chin. "You look like you're thinking too much."

She looked up to him. "I'm always thinking."

"Then maybe I should turn on the T.V. We could use the distraction."

She shrugged. Television shows never really interested her. She only watched movies when she spent time at his parents' house. Or when they went out to the movies. But she never watched the television. David turned it on anyway and found something. She had no clue what and didn't care enough to pay attention. She snuggled deeper in his arms. While he watched whatever she lifted her hand and started tracing the design on his shirt. After a couple minutes he pressed her hand flat with his. She frowned and wiggled her hand free and started tracing again.

Again he flattened her hand with his. "Stop."

"Why?"

"Because it tickles."

"Really?" She sat up and grinned.

"Yes."

Bella straddled David and started tracing the lines with both hands.

He gripped both of her hands tightly. "Why are you intent on torturing me?"

She laughed and pressed a quick kiss to his lips. "Because it's better than being in my head."

"And you can't think of anything else to do?"

"We could make out."

He quirked a brow.

"Are you telling me that you don't want to?"

"I like kissing you, but not as a distraction."

I guess he'd hate to learn that's all he is. She sighed and slowly sat up. "I don't want to think about anything. Not home, not my parents, not my car, not the miscarriage, and especially not..." She bit her tongue. She almost said Jeremiah.

"Bella —"

"Forget it." She climbed off of him and headed out of the bedroom. She'd gotten to the living room when David appeared in front of her, picked her up, and tossed her over his shoulder.

"David!"

He didn't say two words as he dropped her on the bed. He climbed on the bed and hovered over her. He brushed her hair aside. "Walking away isn't the answer."

She blinked at him. "Then what is? All I want is to do something enjoyable."

"You want to make out so you don't have to think about everything going on in your life right now."

"Yes." Bella smiled glad he caught on. She pressed a soft kiss to his cheek then his lips and settled back down.

"You are absolutely evil."

"I have no idea what you're talking about." Whatever. His lips came down on hers and she knew she'd won. They could kiss and she could not think. Too bad her brain had other ideas.

****

"What do you mean the situation hasn't been dealt with?" Quincy slammed his fist on his side of the table. "Exactly what has been done?"

"The letter was delivered as you asked, sir. When that didn't work I went to school and dropped some information. Rumors generated and a car was tagged."

"Then why are you here in front of me?"

"I'm sorry, sir. Lieutenant felt it wiser that I maintained contact. The messenger remains unknown."

Rubbing his chin Quincy nodded. He dropped his hand and glared at Swifty. "Change your strategy. Get creative. Resolve it."

"How sir?"

"How do you think?" He snarled.

Swifty swallowed. "But sir, isn't that extreme?"

"You must be prepared when the waves come crashing down. If you cannot frighten the sea into silence, then it must be imposed. Do you understand?"

"Yes, sir."

"Good. You may go."

Chapter Seventeen

"What's really bothering you?"

Chewing on the inside of her cheek, Bella stared at Dr. Filmore. For the past forty-five minutes she had talked about anything and everything before Jeremiah came into the picture. She told her psychiatrist about how she stopped her dad from cutting down the tree outside of her window. The good doctor got an earful on when she met Vick and how they became best friends. She mentioned how her parents started the teen Bible study sessions because of a boy who beat her up when she was younger. Bella even discussed Sarresh a little, but she didn't tell her about her baby girl or how Bella had been avoiding anymore sleepovers with her friend or how they took a hiatus from their friendship for a year. Jeremiah hadn't been talked about. And even though the doctor asked, she refused to talk about David too.

On their trip back, David reassured Bella it was okay. But it didn't matter how many times he said it or how he said it, she was embarrassed. Especially when she didn't even realize another panic attack happened. It didn't matter he said he would wait as long as needed. She hated that the attack hindered her trust, made her afraid to be alone, forced her to fret over what people thought, physically subdued her, and put her in the position of questioning her beliefs for the first time in her life. On top of that she feared intimate touch; just when she thought things couldn't get worse, they did.

Deep down it had been more than all that. The closer she got to David, the more she needed her pills. Looking at her doctor she reached over and rested her hand on her purse. When they came home Sunday she had twelve pills, now she had two. Except she would be meeting Tommy later for a delivery. Then maybe she could stop avoiding David, which she'd done for the past two days. She skipped lunch so she wouldn't have to face him let alone anyone else at school. God, they hadn't even slept together and all she could think about was what people would say. They'd be able to see it on her face, she knew it and if they didn't see it in hers, surely they would see it when she was around David. For once in her life, she couldn't figure out what could be worse, being called a prude, a slut, or... broken. Because that was exactly how she felt. Pieces of her were all over the place like a shattered mirror and she had no clue if she could even pick them up. Forget about trying to put them back together.

"What are you avoiding?"

She'd managed to stay quiet for another five minutes. She only needed to make it through ten more minutes then she could escape. "Nothing," she finally answered the doctor then glanced to the clock. Five minutes left before she found sweet freedom.

"Bella, I know you don't think you're getting anything out of these sessions. And maybe that's true, but if you asked yourself 'Am I really trying?' do you think you would say 'yes'?"

"You're right, I'm not getting anything out of these sessions. And yeah, maybe I'm not trying, but it's not as simple as you'd like to make it sound."

"Why's that?"

"Because I'm not here for myself. I didn't chose to come. I had no say in the matter. My parents made that decision. I'm here because they'll take my car away if I don't."

"Have you talked to them about that?"

She shook her head. "No. What would be the point? Why would they start listening now?" Pushing up off the couch she stared coldly at the good doctor. "I believe we're finished for the day."

Doctor Filmore sighed. "Yes. We are."

Bella didn't wait for a dismissal. Taking her life into her own hands she walked out the door and headed downstairs.

****

Normally Bella would sing loudly along with the songs on the radio, except the first song she heard when she got into her car was *Only Hope* by Mandy Moore. A song from her favorite movie *A Walk to Remember*. Afraid of what would come on next she turned off the radio. As she approached the driveway to her house, she wished to see either of her parents' cars rather than the one that currently sat there. With no other choice she pulled in and parked behind David's BMW. She watched him as he opened the door and climbed out. Although she placed the car in park, she didn't bother shutting off the ignition. *I can run, but where?* Her heart raced with indecision as he stood there. Bella had no clue what to do. Facing him would be the logical thing to do, but would be contradictory to avoiding him. If she'd given his response much thought she'd have realized this was bound to happen.

He shut the driver side door and walked toward her. Pausing just outside her car door he looked down. "Are you coming out?"

It seemed pointless to roll up the open car window now. Blinking she stared at him because she wanted him to go away. *Great, I'm starting to feel about him the way I feel about all my other friends.* Her chest rose and fell rapidly. She had to do something. Taking a deep breath, she asked, "What are you doing here?"

"I figured it was the only way to talk to you."

She couldn't deny that. With a heavy sigh she pushed the automated button to return the window to its rightful state, then shut off the car and climbed out. "You could've called or caught up with me at school."

"Except you haven't been taking my calls and you hide from me at school."

Walking past him to the walkway she headed toward the front door. "I don't know what you're talking about."

"Bella..." David sighed running a hand through his hair before gripping the back of his neck. "I know that's a lie and you do too. We both know what's going on here. I don't want to fight. I just want to talk about it."

He hadn't yelled, but God she wished he would. She deserved it for more reasons than he knew. Being a selfish bitch hadn't even made the top of the list. *User* would be. That would be exactly what she was - a horrible, self-centered user. Drugs weren't the only thing she used. Which would be why she refused to accept he would ever be okay with what happened Sunday. One minute they were having an intense make out session and the next she came around to him rocking her like a baby. She hated herself and he should too.

"Talk is cheap." Unlocking the front door she half glanced over her shoulder.

"That depends on who you're talking to. And I hope you aren't comparing me to your psychiatrist."

Heaving a deep breath she turned around and looked at him. "You're not going away, are you?"

"No. Not until we talk."

Squeezing her eyes shut a moment she shifted her gaze to the ground, then sighed in defeat as she turned and opened the door. "Fine. Come on in."

Following her in he shoved his hands in his pockets and found a spot to stand out of the way.

You'd think he's never been here before by the way he acts. Then again I'm treating him as an unwelcomed guest, aren't I? How else should he act? Bitch. I've become a heartless bitch. "I'll be right back. You can sit on the couch in the den." She gestured, then dropped her purse on a small end table by the door before disappearing to her bedroom. She opened her bedroom door and stepped in long enough to put her keys and the wad of cash in her back pocket in her desk drawer. With her stuff put away, she leaned on the desk wondering what the hell she would do. She didn't have the energy to talk. Seemed like she'd been doing it her whole life. Except this time her parents, friends and her psychiatrist didn't want her to talk about being bullied or her opinion of various Bible passages. They wanted her to talk about her feelings and she just couldn't. Now David did too.

What happened Sunday embarrassed her. But *that... that night* she never wanted to relive again and talking would only accomplish that. She looked to her bedroom doorway. He came here about Sunday and no matter how she felt, for once he deserved some truth. Pushing off the desk she headed out of her room. Stopping in the entrance way of the den Bella stared at David for a moment. "You're right. I have been avoiding you. I know what you said before we left and on the plane, but it hasn't kept me from feeling crippled."

"What are you talking about?"

She shrugged. "I don't know. I hate that I keep freaking out on you. It's like this attack has damaged me or something."

"You are not damaged. Do you hear me? You are *not* damaged. Something was taken from you and no one has the right to do that. But that doesn't mean you're broken."

She still hadn't moved from the spot she'd taken up in front of him. "How do you know?"

"Because I do."

"But how?" Unless he could give her a good explanation, the only thing that made sense was that she had in fact been broken.

David patted the cushion next to him. "Come on."

Bella hesitated, but after a couple of minutes she approached the couch and took a seat.

"You remember a few months ago when we were sitting at the piano? We talked about why you said no, but you never asked me why I wanted to go out with you."

She nodded. "I remember."

"I wanted to go out with you then because you were stronger and smarter than any girl I'd ever met. No matter how hard people tried to put you down, you always remained standing. And when you stood up to my sister, man, Bella I can't begin to tell you how that made me feel! I got a rush of excitement because I knew for certain you were special. After you got attacked, you came back to school within a week. Not a lot of people have the courage to do that. Even now when someone is trying to keep you from testifying, you're taking it head on. And that is how I know you're not damaged. Because you're still standing." He reached over and tucked a lock of hair behind her ear.

Nothing about what he said confused her, but he certainly didn't understand why she did those things. Staring at him she considered the possibility that if he knew the real reason why, then he wouldn't look at her the same. His face wouldn't be shining with respect or love. She blinked a couple of tears down her cheeks because she had no doubt in her mind. Knowing exactly what she would do to him, she said, "I really don't deserve you."

"We'll just have to agree to disagree on that. Because I'll always think it should be the other way around."

She really had become a horrible person. She deserved every word people said about her, all the rude comments, all these little unwanted gifts. But she couldn't let him know that. With a small smile she leaned up and kissed his lips. "I'm okay with that."

He grinned. "Good. Now, does this mean I get my girlfriend back?"

"Yeah." She nodded and pressed another kiss to his lips. The deep kiss they'd only begun to enjoy parted seconds later as soon as they both heard the front door open.

David addressed her parents the moment they paused in the very entry way Bella occupied not more than ten minutes ago. "Afternoon Mr. and Mrs. Naughton."

"David," her father stated.

It was only his name, but it had been enough to say he wasn't welcome. David looked over to Bella. "You going to be okay if I head off?"

"Yeah." She nodded. "I'll walk you out."

Offering her his hand as he rose to his feet he helped her up. She couldn't help but smile as David shrugged off the annoyed glare he received from her father by draping an arm around her shoulders and pulling her flush against him. Comfortably she hooked an arm around his waist and leaned her head against his chest. Out of her periphery she watched her parents head into the kitchen without caring about her father's obvious disappointment by her apparent lack of respect.

Like a gentleman, David reached for the knob when they got to the door. "What do you say to dinner and a movie Friday night?"

"I'd like that." She smiled.

"Then it's a date," David said then leaned down and pressed a soft kiss on Bella's lips. Happily he opened the door. A medium size, long brown unlabeled box with Bella's name scrawled across the top sat just outside. "What's that?"

She shrugged. It looked like a plain old regular box, but that didn't mean anything. Not with the way her life went. She could pretend she believed it contained nothing of importance, but she knew that to be as unlikely as chocolate without cocoa. Glancing from David to the box, she had one of two options: forget all about it or open it and find out what surprise awaited her this time.

Chapter Eighteen

She stepped out, leaned down and picked the box up. "I don't know."

"Maybe you shouldn't open it."

"Do you think there's something dangerous in there?"

"I don't know, but it would be safer if you took it to the police and let them handle it."

She rolled her eyes and snickered. "Yeah right." *Like I'm going to do that.* They'd failed to stop these things from coming and if anything like a bomb happened to be in there, well at least it would all be over.

"All right, but I'm not leaving."

"Fine." She shrugged and proceeded to open the flaps. She felt David hover over her shoulder. He was more afraid of what she would find than she had been. If it was a bomb, maybe he shouldn't be standing so close. As she worked on the box she took a few steps forward in a small attempt to protect him. The box didn't blow up, but it definitely contained a message. Long-stemmed black roses were a little cliché, but she suspected the note meant more than anything else. Picking up the small sheet of paper she stared at it. She spoke Portuguese, but some Spanish words were similar enough for her to get the gist. *Muerte.* They wanted her dead. *Take a number.* They weren't the only ones. She blinked when the box began to move in her arms. Dropping the box she screamed as a pair of rats crawled out of it.

Wrapping an arm around her, David pulled her close.

Her father stepped out of the kitchen. "What's going on? I thought you were leaving."

"Yeah, then *that* showed up." David pointed at the box on the floor. Holding Bella in his arms, he kept her tucked against his body. Glaring at her father David snapped out, "Did you see it when you came in?"

"What? No."

"You sure? You going to tell me in the five minutes you've been home someone dropped that off?" David exclaimed a little aggressively.

"Are you trying to imply we just ignored it and left it there for her?"

"If the shoe fits."

"I wouldn't do anything to intentionally harm my daughter."

"And you aren't doing anything to protect her either! She's the one that suffers every time something like this happens."

"I am doing things to keep her safe. And this is the first time this has occurred."

"Bull shit! Have you not been paying any fucking attention?"

"I am well aware of what goes on in my house!" Her father yelled.

"Stop it! Both of you stop it!" Bella screamed through tears as she moved away from the two of them.

Simultaneously both David and her father said, "Bella –"

"No!" She cried out and yanked her arm away from the hands that grabbed at her. "Leave me alone!" With that she turned and ran to her bedroom.

David flinched when he heard the door slam shut.

"Amahl, what is wrong with you?" Bella's mother hollered at her husband then switched her attention to David. "And you, don't think you're completely blameless. You may be her boyfriend, but you will give my husband and I the respect we deserve. We can't do anything to help if we don't know what's going on. Do you understand me?"

He sighed and nodded. "Yes ma'am."

"Behira—"

"Don't start, Amahl!" She shook her head. With a deep breath in her best motherly tone she said, "Now, the two of you go sit down in the den. I'll go see if I can get her to come out."

The moment she disappeared down the hall, both David and Bella's father exchanged a look they each seemed to comprehend. And they took up a spot on opposite sides of the den.

****

For once not caring about the memory of the dead dog she flopped down on her bed and cried. *I can't find peace anywhere!* Not from the people who were supposed to love her and not from all the escalating threats. Even her weekend escape didn't work. The feeling of being carefree lasted one day, then she got slammed back into reality. She couldn't just walk into it, she had to be thrown in. "Nightmare" didn't begin to describe her life. Her entire world had been falling apart. Jeremiah was ashamed of her, maybe even hated her. David desperately tried to hold on to her, no matter how far away she always was. She couldn't be sure what her parents were doing, she hardly talked to them anymore. Between the blame she placed on her father for bringing those men into her life and the issues she had with her parents pushing her to see a therapist. Not to mention she started turning on her friends, yelling at them, hitting them - all worse than a cold shoulder. She hated what she'd become. She hated her life. She hated being here. She hated herself.

The knock on her door told her no one really understood what *leave me alone* truly meant. She figured it had to be either David or her father coming to apologize, but her mother's voice came from the other side of the door. "Bella?"

"Và embora!" *Why can't she go away?*

"Só quero falar."

She just wants to talk? No. "Và embora!" David was right, maybe if they paid enough attention they would see how much she hated going to that psychiatrist. They would figure out conversation hadn't really been on her mind these days. Only one thing had been. Wiping away some of her tears she looked around her room, she knew what she needed.

"Eu posso entrar?" Her mother wiggled the doorknob.

I'm not letting her in. I just want to be left alone. "Nao! Deixe me em paz!" She yelled out climbing off the bed. *What did I do with the pills?* Thinking the bottle had to be somewhere in her room she started at the desk. Opening the drawers she began flipping through and looking under papers. When she didn't find it there she pulled out her big drawer and shoved its contents around. Still nothing, she glanced back to the room and moved over to her dresser. Quickly growing impatient by the time she got to the second drawer she began yanking clothes out and tossed them over her shoulder. Four drawers later and still nothing. Closet - maybe she put it there. Going through the boxes that were there she started dumping them out on the floor. Nothing. *Shit! It's in my purse! Where did I leave my purse?* Frantically she went back from her closest to her dresser to her desk to her nightstand and still came up empty. Where was it? She ran back to her closet, nothing. She repeated the closest, desk, dresser, nightstand cycle three more times all the while mumbling, "Where is it?" Then it finally hit her - she left her purse on the table by the door. *Shit!*

Looking back to her bedroom door she paused realizing it had become a little too quiet. Calming her frantic breaths she listened.

Outside her door she heard her mother say, "No, it's locked."

"We could pick it," David said.

No! They can't break into my room! Her eyes quickly flipped from one side of the room to the other as rapid breaths escaped her mouth. She had to get out of there. But even if she did, how would she get away from the house? Think, think. She closed her eyes and recalled her first steps when she got home. She left her purse on the table and came back to her room where she put her keys and money in her desk drawer. *That's it!* Without a second thought she headed for the window pausing at her desk long enough to grab keys and cash. She pushed the window open and climbed out the sill. Let them worry about how to get into her room while she ran around the front, hopped in her car, and backed out the driveway. Getting away over-flooded her brain as she put the car in gear and pressed the gas pedal to the floor.

****

"Did you hear that?" Amahl asked.

"Hear what?" David questioned.

"I thought I heard a car door."

David and Amahl looked at each other. Simultaneously they said, "Shit."

"Her purse is by the door." Behira stated and walked past them. They both followed after her and walked from the entranceway to the bay window while Bella's mother dug around her daughter's purse.

Amahl looked over to Behira. "She's left. Her car's gone."

Behira stepped over to them. She held out the near empty bottle of pills toward David. "Do you know anything about these?"

"They're painkillers. I think she still takes them on occasion for her ribs and arm. Why?"

"There's no label."

Shocked by the obvious, David looked to Bella's mother. "You can't think Bella is using them recreationally."

She shook her head. "No. I'm just concerned."

David nodded and glanced back out the window and stared for a moment, before he turned back to her parents. "I'm going to take off. Can you have her call me when she gets home?"

Her mother nodded. "Sure."

Without another word he left the house.

****

For the first three hours Bella had driven around because it would be less likely they would find her if she didn't stay put in one place. During this time she realized she didn't have her phone - that she *also* left in her purse. Unfortunately since she left her pills there too, she would have to deal until she got her new bottle. Now there she waited for her *date* to show up. They'd agreed on nine and she'd arrived an hour ago when food began calling her name. Whether he ate or not she didn't care, she happily worked on another piece of dessert. The sugar had been the only thing that kept the twitching under wraps. Her knee shook like crazy and she felt like she had hives all over, but if she did something to keep busy she could pretty much ignore it. Then her savior stepped through the door and walked her way.

"I see you ate without me," Tommy said.

"Sorry, I was hungry."

He nodded. "It's okay." Picking up a menu he waved over a waitress. When she got there he rattled off, "Bacon Cheeseburger, medium well, side of fries and a coke."

"And let me get another slice of chocolate cream pie," Bella chimed in.

Once the waitress had taken off Tommy raised a brow at her. "How many pieces have you had?"

She shrugged. "I don't know... four... maybe five."

"And you're going for another one?"

"Don't judge. If you had my day you'd be doing the same thing."

He held up his hands to fend her off. "All right, deep breath."

With a shake of her head she rolled her eyes. "I'm not in a good place. Orders will not help you."

"You can't be out already," Tommy said more than questioned.

"Not completely, but I had a little spat with people and I haven't had any in like eight hours."

"Christ," he groaned.

"Hey!"

"Yeah, yeah. I'm sorry, but you know you can't go that long." He shook his head. "You want to tell me about this spat?"

"No. We'll just say I had to sneak out of my house and I left my purse with all the good stuff by the front door."

He grinned. "What would you do if you didn't have me?"

"To be honest, I have no idea." That wasn't true, she would die because she would never be able to climb out of the rabbit hole. They both remained silent when the waitress showed up with their food and patiently waited as she set the plates down. Bella immediately forked a bite of the pie into her mouth and waited for the woman to leave.

"It's a shame you're David Warren's girlfriend."

"I thought you said that was a good thing. Meant I got treated like a friend."

"Yes, that's true. I was saying it was a shame because I wouldn't mind having a girl like you on my arm."

"I'm no trophy."

"On the contrary —"

She snapped a hand up when she spotted William, one of her friends from church, walk in the diner because she quickly needed Tommy to shut up. Slouching Bella whispered angrily to Tommy, "I thought you said no one comes here."

He nodded. "No one from your school does."

Exasperated by his previous lack of detailed information she exclaimed, "What about the other schools?"

"Some do."

From her periphery she checked to see where her friend was. If anyone from Blanding Wood knew Tommy, then it would be gravely possible her friend did too. Her luck William chose that moment to look in her direction. *Shit!* And with a brief wave he started her way.

Chapter Nineteen

Not calmed by Tommy's prior response she tried to get more specific. "Does anyone from Blanding Wood know what you do?"

"Yes. I'm not an exclusive business —"

Quickly she motioned for Tommy to zip his lips as she bolted upright. With her best fake smile she looked up as her friend stopped. "Hey William."

"Hey Bella. Long time no see."

"Yeah. I've been really busy."

"I see." He faltered at hiding the frown on his face. "Where's Jeremiah?"

This was not turning into the hello/goodbye she hoped for. Based on his question, apparently he hadn't heard. Irritated by her lack of options, she stated the obvious. "Not here."

Crossing his arms William scrutinized her. "Uh huh. So, who's your friend?"

Afraid he would recognize the name even if he didn't know the face, Bella avoided his question. She needed to divert his attention, but how? Her gaze shifted to the girl who stood beside him. Before she stopped going to the teen Bible study she recalled something about a girl in his life. *Perfect!* "Is this your girlfriend?"

He nodded. "This is Natasha."

After she and his girlfriend were formally introduced she heard Natasha say something about eating.

"Sure thing," William said and briefly returned his focus to Bella. "It was good to see you."

"Yeah, you too." Thankfully the two departed; which gave her the opportunity to breathe.

"Care to explain?" Tommy questioned.

"Not really."

"Whatever," he muttered.

Just the answer she was looking for. She was glad he planned to drop it. Trying to be sly she turned her head a little and glanced over her shoulder to see where William sat. Bella cursed under her breath as she returned her attention to her "date." Next to Vick, William was one of the few friends that could read her. If his girlfriend hadn't said something he would probably still be there berating her with questions. She sighed and took a huge bite of pie. "Everything like we agreed?" Her coat was on his side of the booth. The way it worked, he put her merchandise in the pocket of her coat in exchange for the cash that was in the same place.

"Yeah." Tommy finished the rest of his burger and slid out of the booth. "I'll be back."

They always left together. Why was he leaving without her? "No! Wait! Don't leave me here by myself!"

"Why? Afraid the big bad wolf will find you?"

She crossed her arms innately offended by the humor he found in her concern. Defensively she muttered, "No."

"Then you'll survive." He grinned and headed for the bathroom.

Bella slumped down thinking maybe if she hid then being alone for a minute or two wouldn't be all that bad. Funny, for weeks all she wanted was for people to leave her alone and yet there she was afraid to be alone. Of course, that was only because she didn't want her friend to - *Shit!* - too late.

"Where'd your friend go?" William asked as he slid in across from her.

Unable to hide, she slowly pushed herself back to an upright position. "Bathroom."

He nodded. "Now who is this guy?"

"Like you said, he's a friend."

"I'm not stupid Bella. So stop dodging the question. What's his name?"

"Why does it matter?"

"Because you're hiding something and I think it has to do with him."

"I'm not hiding anything!" She snapped with as much force as she could muster.

"Don't lie to me."

"I'm not lying."

"Bull! I've know you long enough to tell when you're lying. Your face scrunches and your shoulders tense."

Dammit! Goading him wouldn't do any good. She already knew what he could see no matter how hard she tried to hide it. Backed in a corner there was only one other option. She narrowed her gaze on her friend and firmly stated, "It doesn't matter because it's none of your damn business. Now, you can leave."

"Not until you tell me what is going on."

Bella crossed her arms. "Then I suggest you get used to silence." He could bait her all he wanted, she wasn't biting. With as many reticent therapy sessions she'd had, uncommunicative was something she was quite accustomed to.

"You're really not going to talk to me?"

Keeping her lips still she refused to answer him.

"Bella, come on. This isn't you."

Damn, he almost got her on that one. She could easily claim he didn't know her anymore. None of them did. How could they? The Bella they remembered was gone and the person sitting across from him was all that was left.

"Bella —"

"Am I interrupting something?" Tommy asked.

William's gaze softened and it was enough to break her heart if it hadn't been so empty.

"No," William said and slid out of the booth. He paused one last time by her, and then walked away.

Tommy quirked a brow as he reclaimed his seat. "You okay?"

"Can we go?"

"Yes."

She watched as he dropped a couple of twenties on the table while she climbed out. Tommy stood up with her coat in his hand and helped her into it. He draped an arm over her shoulder and escorted her to her car. Unlocking the driver side door she asked, "We all good?"

"Right pocket. Call when you need me again."

"Thanks." Bella got in her car and took off.

****

Jeremiah stared at the book in his hands. The lines had started to blur together. Frustrated with having to reread the same passage four times already he shut the book. He rubbed his face because as much as he wanted to get through the thing, Bella had weighed so heavily on his mind he wasn't getting much done. He'd tried calling and texting, but hadn't gotten anywhere. Trying to catch her at school had been about as bad as what people were saying about her. When the rape first occurred most of their classmates empathized with her, now they thought she deserved it. And even though school records indicated she hadn't skipped, he hadn't come across her at all. If they were playing a game of dodge ball, she'd be winning. He slid out of the breakfast nook and stretched a bit as he rose to his feet. With a quick neck pop he decided to grab a soda then attempt to tackle *The Scarlet Letter* again.

About halfway to the refrigerator, he heard a knock at the door. *Who can that be at this time of night?* He glanced at the clock in the kitchen and confirmed it was 11:32 p.m. Afraid whoever it was would wake the rest of his family he stepped out of the kitchen and headed to the door. He opened the door and glared at David hard. "What do you want?"

David took a deep breath. "I need your help."

"You've got to be kidding," Jeremiah snorted and proceeded to close the door in his face.

Quickly David grabbed a hold of the door jam and stopped the door with his other hand. "I'm not joking. Bella's missing."

Jeremiah snapped the door back open. "What are you talking about?"

David glanced over his shoulder for a second, then returned his attention to Jeremiah. "Can we discuss this inside?"

"Why? Are you afraid your people will catch you associating with me?"

"Do you think if I gave a shit about what people thought or said I would be dating Bella?" David snarled.

"Are you saying she's beneath you?" Jeremiah growled.

"No! I'm not saying that at all. For Christ's sake —"

"Excuse me!"

David shook his head and mumbled, "This was a bad idea."

Jeremiah crossed his arms and stared trying to figure out what to do next. He didn't want to help the douche bag, but Bella's safety mattered more than any distrust he felt toward the guy. So he stated, "If she's really missing, I'll help find her. But it would do you well to remember who you're talking to."

"I wouldn't be here otherwise." As patiently as possible David waited until the door opened enough he could step inside. With another calming breath he rubbed the back of his neck, then started to explain. "I was leaving Bella's house when she found a package on the doorstep addressed to her. Inside were black roses and a couple of rats. Her dad and I got into an argument, which upset her more. So she locked herself in her room. At some point she climbed out her window, got in her car and took off. That was seven hours ago. Before I left I told her parents to have her call me as soon as she got home. I started to panic when I hadn't heard anything by eleven, so I called the house. They told me she still hadn't come back."

"Did you try her cell phone?"

"It's at the house."

"What about GPS on the car?"

"I asked. She requested the car without a locating device."

Jeremiah sighed. "Have you tried Sarresh?"

"That's how I got your address."

"She hasn't heard from her either?"

"No."

"What about Vick?"

"I don't have his number and neither did Sarresh."

Jeremiah shook his head in utter disappointment. "I'll be right back. Stay here." He half glanced at David as he turned and disappeared down the hall. The guy didn't want to be there anymore than he wanted him there, but he could tell desperation forced his hand. Refusing to talk to Vick around David, Jeremiah headed to his room and closed the door in hope of privacy. Then dialed.

"Hey man. What's up?"

"Have you heard from Bella?"

"You're the second person to ask me that," Vick replied.

"Who else called?"

"Her parents. A few hours ago."

Jeremiah rubbed his brow. *Guess the dipstick didn't lie.* "Did they ask if you'd heard from her or did they ask something else?"

"They asked me to check my parents' summer house up by Lake McMillan. She goes there sometimes when she needs to be alone."

"Did you find her?"

"No," Vick answered.

"Is it possible she's shown up since it was checked?"

"I suppose so."

"Can you send me the address and directions?" Jeremiah asked as he pulled on a pair of sneakers.

"Yeah."

"Thanks man. I'll let you know if I find her."

"Sure. Call if you get lost."

"All right," he replied then disconnected. Jeremiah stepped out of his room and paused at his sister's. With a quick rap he cracked the door and popped his head in. "Hey sis..." He spotted her sitting at her desk making his question redundant.

"What's up?" Amanda asked without looking up from the book in front of her.

"Bella's missing. She ran away from home earlier and hasn't shown back up. Vick says she likes to go out to his folks' summer home so he's sending me directions. If mom or dad wake up and I'm not back, can you tell them?"

Her gaze lifted to his. "Yeah, sure. But do you think you'll be gone that long?"

"I don't know. I'm not sure how far away this place is or if she's even there."

"Okay. Be safe."

"I will," he replied and half closed the door behind him.

"What did you find out?" David asked as he approached.

"Vick's parents have a summer home she frequents. He's sending me the directions."

"Okay. I'll give you my number and you can send them to me."

"Why?" Jeremiah questioned.

"How else will I know where to go?"

"Maybe I wasn't clear enough. He's sending them to me. I'll drive out there. You can go home," Jeremiah declared.

"You seem to have forgotten something. You *aren't* her boyfriend."

"And your point is..."

"You don't have any right to go after her."

"Says who? She's my friend and I happen to care about her. I have as much right as you do." He watched David take a couple of deep breaths as he squeezed his fist. Jeremiah repositioned his feet and planted his stance and prepared himself for a swing.

"Last I checked, boyfriends have more rights than friends. See, since *I'm* her boyfriend that makes me more important. Make this simple," David snorted and closed some of the space between them. "Send me the directions."

"Not on your fucking life."

Grinding his teeth David said, "That only leaves one other option. And I'm sure neither of us wants that."

"Then I suggest you give up," Jeremiah stated flatly and stepped in closer to David's personal space.

"Not happening. Now back off." David growled.

"Forget it."

He hadn't heard his sister come up until she had shoved her way in between the two of them. She pushed them apart. "Each of you in your own corners."

Neither Jeremiah nor David wanted to move. Each determined to face the other down.

"Now!"

For once in his life Jeremiah hated being the bigger man, but he did what he should and stepped back. Then David followed Amanda's instruction.

"Good. Now listen up jackasses. The two of you will stop acting like self-involved dicks and remember this is about Bella. You both need to stop fighting over her. As for tonight, this is how it's going to go. Since the two of you can't compromise, Vick is going back to the summer house. You," she pointed to Jeremiah, "will go back to your room. And you," she pointed to David, "will go home."

"Not unless I have information."

"Fine. Give me your phone." He handed it to her. She pulled up a couple screens and punched a few keys, then returned it to him. "There, now you have my number and I have yours. I'll text you when Vick gets there. Now, go home."

"I have your word?"

"Yes."

"Fine," he said. David grinded his jaw back and forth as he glared at Jeremiah before he turned and headed out of the house.

Once he departed she spun around to her brother, crossed her arms and shook her head. "What the hell is the matter with you?"

"Excuse me?"

"If I didn't know any better, I could've sworn you were goading him, trying to start a fight."

Jeremiah groaned and dropped back against the wall. "I wasn't trying to push him. I just wanted to make sure he knew I wasn't backing down."

"Yeah, well great way to think about Bella." She snickered and rolled her eyes. Obviously annoyed with him she turned around and headed down the hall.

"Hey," he called after her. "You going to tell me what he finds out?"

She paused at her bedroom door. "As much as I don't think I should, I will." She said nothing further as she disappeared into her room and shut the door.

Based on everything that happened over the past few weeks, Jeremiah knew he would have to play dirty to get Bella alone. He needed to talk to her. He sighed as an idea popped into his head. Lord, he hoped this would work. God, he needed it to work.

****

Jeremiah stood outside the corner of a school building. He watched as students left. Two days ago David had shown up on his doorstep about Bella. Turned out she hadn't been missing, she spent the night at Vick's parents' summer home. She returned home the morning after. The little bits of information he'd gotten yesterday hadn't been enough. He needed more and considered calling, but they hadn't had a great record over the past few weeks and he wasn't positive on how angry her parents were. Instead he texted her last night. He thought over their conversation.

Jeremiah: Hi.
Bella: Hi.
Jeremiah: How r u? R u ok?
Bella: I'm okay. Why?

Jeremiah: I heard u had a situation yesterday.

Bella: A minor disagreement. I needed some space, but I'm back home.

Jeremiah: How did your 'rents react?

Bella: Furious. Got into a fight for climbing out the window with no way to be reached. Then for my room.

Jeremiah: Ur room?

Bella: I had a fight with the room and the room won. But it has been returned to normal.

Jeremiah: Y did u fight with the room?

Bella: I have to go. Talk to you later.

She never answered his last question. Now it was Thursday and Jeremiah needed to physically talk to her, so he waited outside the school. He planned to catch up with her on her way to the parking lot. Hopefully she would be alone. Then he could set something up so they could actually hang out. So much inside of his own head, he hadn't realized she'd walked past him until she made it halfway to her car.

Quickly he made his way into the crowd and started in her direction. Everything that happened next went so fast he had no clue what initiated her ear-piercing scream freezing his heart. To top it off everyone proceeded to run around hysterically. By the time he got to her she lay sprawled out on the ground. He moved to her side and brushed her cheek. "Bella?" When nothing happened he turned his gaze from her to the open car door. There was nothing. Everything appeared normal. Turning back to her he tapped her cheek lightly. "Come on honey. Wake up Bell." She remained still and that worried him. Trying not to panic he checked for a pulse and discovered one. Satisfied she was alive, he checked to see if there were any wounds but didn't get very far.

"What the hell happened?" David yelled as he skidded to a stop.

Without looking up Jeremiah said, "I don't know."

"You can go now. I've got it." David maneuvered himself to pry Bella away.

Refusing to be shoved aside Jeremiah intercepted the movement. "Back the fuck off! I told you I don't know what happened. We shouldn't move her until we know."

"And I don't believe you. I know what you're up to."

"Oh yeah? What's that?"

"You're trying to get her back."

Overall, he had spoken truth, but right now it had nothing to do with why he stayed put. He shook his head, looked around and noticed how empty the parking lot had managed to get in such a short period of time. "Leave her alone." Jeremiah rose to his feet. Hoping Vick hadn't left Jeremiah pulled out his phone and made a quick call. Once Jeremiah knew Vick was on his way, he returned his attention to the jackass and realized David had gotten up to his feet too. The two stood face to face with Bella on the ground between them. "Check her car. I'm going to see if I can find any wounds on her."

"Forget it!" David growled. He pushed at one of Jeremiah's shoulders to shove him back. "You get the car!"

His fist clenched and released as his jaw worked back and forth. "I know it's hard with all of mommy and daddy's money, but you really need to learn to leave your pedestal at home. Bella doesn't need it."

David stepped in and closed the space between them. "What did you say to me?"

"Did I stutter?" Amanda warned him about goading the guy, but Jeremiah couldn't help it. Every time the asshole opened his mouth Jeremiah got more and more pissed off. And with no one around, the hook to his jaw David threw didn't surprise him. He ducked, dropped his right shoulder and launched right into the guy's gut. They both landed on the ground with Jeremiah on top, but it didn't last long. After he punched David, the guy head butted him and knocked him on his ass.

Chapter Twenty

Slowly her eyes fluttered open. With the sun shining brightly on her face she had no clue what happened or why she could feel the hot concrete against her flesh. The background noise didn't help either. All she really knew, her right ankle throbbed and her head pounded like she'd been hit by a ball-peen hammer or something. Bella glanced around as much as her body would allow as she tried to recall her last steps. Then three familiar faces popped up in front of her. Vick, Sarresh, and Amanda all dropped down to their knees beside Bella.

"Bella! You okay?" Vick asked.

"No," she answered truthfully and muttered, "my ankle."

She watched as he studied it, then said to her, "Looks like a snake bite." His gaze shifted to Amanda. "Call 9-1-1. She needs to get to the hospital." Vick looked at Sarresh. "I need you to help me sit her up." When his face returned to Bella she could see how in control he seemed. Then he asked, "Do you remember a snake?"

The fog slowly cleared from her muddled brain. She nodded. She felt two sets of arms reach under and lift her.

"Describe what you saw," Vick said.

"Small, brown... and I think it had spots."

Vick looked at Sarresh as she helped him get Bella in a sitting position. "Could be a Diamondback or a Massasauga."

"The ambulance is on their way," Amanda said.

He nodded. "Good. Now I need you to go to my car and get my green knapsack out."

Bella barely realized they managed to get her partially up. Then she felt Sarresh readjust and move behind her to support her upright position.

Vick snapped a finger in front of her face. "I need you to pay attention to me. I'm going to remove your shoe. Your ankle has already swelled."

"Okay." She looked to her right ankle. He was right. Her ankle had quickly ballooned to the thickness of a small book. "I think I'm going to be sick." A pair of arms helped her shift to the side as she dry heaved. Beads of sweat streaked her face. Despite how much her ankle throbbed Bella continued to dry heave. The nauseated sensation finally subsided. Slightly dizzy she tried to sit against the body behind her. Before she passed out again she spotted the commotion causing all the noise around her. Across the quad, her ex-boyfriend and boyfriend were beating the hell out of each other. "God just let me die," Bella mumbled then she lost consciousness.

****

"Bella?" Vick snapped his fingers.

"I think she passed out," Sarresh said.

Amanda jogged up to them with a green knapsack in her hands. "I've got it.

Vick nodded. "This bite looks venomous." The sound of sirens could be heard coming down the road leading to the school parking lot. "Sarresh, gently lay Bella down and head over there to direct them here."

"Okay." She laid Bella down, then sprinted toward the ambulance.

Amanda smiled at Vick. "I know this is a bad time, but I have to say you're kind of hot when you're in control."

Vick shook his head. He pulled a couple of items out of the knapsack and quickly wrapped Bella's ankle.

"What are you doing?" Amanda asked.

"This will help slow the venom from spreading."

Amanda nodded. "Where did you learn to do that?"

"My Dad. You spend as much time outdoors as we do and you have to learn things like this."

"Maybe you can show me some day."

Vick smiled. "I'd like that." As he finished with the wrap, he looked across the quad where Jeremiah and David had been. A teacher escorted both guys into the school. He returned his attention to Amanda. "You may want to call your dad."

"Do we need to report this?"

"Yes, but I was thinking more about your brother."

Amanda sighed. "I warned him."

"Warned who?" Sarresh asked as she approached with the EMTs. Vick stood then he took Amanda's hand, helped her up and they both stepped out of the way.

"My brother," Amanda replied. "If he gets suspended, he deserves it."

Sarresh shrugged. "Do we know anything about what happened?"

"Aside from a snake bite? No." Vick said. He watched as the EMTs got Bella up on a stretcher. He stepped away from the girls for a moment and exchanged a few brief words with the EMTs before they took off. He pulled his phone from his pocket and called Bella's father.

"Hey Mr. Naughton. It's Vick."

"What can I do for you son?"

"Bella is being taken to the hospital. She was bitten by a snake."

"How is she?"

"She's passed out. I would say based on her body's response the snake was venomous. Likely a Massasauga from her description. I'm sure the hospital will call when she gets there, but I thought I'd give you a heads up."

"I'll call Behira and head that way. Thank you."

"Sure." Vick disconnected and returned the phone to his back pocket. Amanda and Sarresh had moved over to Bella's car. He approached them.

"Everything okay?" Amanda asked.

"Yeah. I just called Bella's father. Did you call yours?"

"Yeah," Amanda replied. "But only after Z and I found this. He's in the area so it shouldn't be long." She handed him a piece of paper.

"Where was it?"

"Under a windshield wiper on Bella's car. I don't know what it means though," Amanda told him.

Vick studied the sheet of paper. It had one word - *Muerte*. He looked to Amanda and Sarresh. "I do. It means 'death.'"

Sarresh crossed her arms. "I don't like this. Do you think this was on purpose?"

"It could be," Vick answered. "But if it was a Massasauga snake, why? It's venomous, but not deadly."

"Because then it couldn't look like an accident." Chief Detrone suggested as he walked up to the trio gathered around Bella's car.

****

After Bella got home from the hospital Thursday evening she texted David and Jeremiah not to contact her. Then David blasted her phone all Friday night with texts. When she didn't respond, he played the call-a-gazillion-times game. Annoyed by the incessant ringing she finally answered. Somehow he got her to agree to dinner at his place tonight. There she stood wearing the so called Christmas attire she purchased: mini black denim skirt, a red semi-cropped v-cut cashmere sweater and a pair of black heeled ankle boots. While she suspected he would like it, in all likelihood he wouldn't get to see it anytime soon. Instead, she stood in front of a door that didn't belong to him.

Bella believed God hated her.

Her best friend Vick called a couple of hours ago and said he needed a ride from his parents' summer home before the storm hit because his car died and he couldn't reach his parents. Her mother worried about Bella's quick departure, but Bella hadn't hesitated to leave, and believed she could beat the onslaught of wind and rain. Except Vick didn't stand on the other side of the door, nope not even close. Jeremiah, stood in front of her. They hadn't really spoken since he walked out of her hospital room. She didn't count the arguments or texts. Her stomach churned all the emotional ramifications she'd worked to bury over the past few months. Yep, God really hated her. She crossed her arms over her chest, and spun around on the porch and moved toward the steps.

"Bella, where do you think you're going?" Jeremiah followed after her.

"Home!"

He pulled her arm and she almost toppled into him. "Absolutely not! No way you'll make it back before this thing hits."

"Not if you stop me from leaving!" She yanked free of his grip with a sudden sense of de ja vu.

"Are you insane? Look at the sky! I know you're not stupid. You're smart enough to know you'll get stuck and being in a car in a storm is suicide. Come on, there's a storm cellar over there. We should head that way."

She snickered. "You must think I'm crazy if you believe for one second I am going to get holed up in a shelter with you to wait out this damn storm!" *No way in hell is he getting me in there!* Her plan for the day did not include her ex-boyfriend. She'd spent two and a half months away from Jeremiah, which included a month with someone else, and it had been good for her soul or so she'd tried to convince herself. Realistically she couldn't avoid him. She and Jeremiah went to the same school and church. She no longer attended the Tuesday night Bible study group her parents hosted since... Unfortunately in a small town, every godforsaken person knew what happened to her. She couldn't stand the look of pity a lot of the people wore on their faces around her. Few people forgot that night ever happened and treated her normal, the two things she wanted. She'd kill to beat the vivid memory into submission and bury it six feet underground.

"No! But I will think you're crazy if you keep pushing to drive in this storm," Jeremiah quipped.

She crossed her arms over her chest again and looked at the sky beyond him. As much as she refused to admit it, she knew she wouldn't make it back before the storm.

"You have two choices. One, you walk nicely with me to the storm cellar or two, I toss you over my shoulder and carry you."

She maintained her stance and narrowed her eyes. "You wouldn't dare!"

He grabbed her by the waist and threw her over his shoulder.

"Jeremiah! Put me down!" She hit him on the back and kicked her feet doing whatever she could to get out of his grip. Angrier than before she yelled again, "Put me down!"

Jeremiah remained silent as he carried her into the storm cellar. Once inside he placed her on her feet and put some space between them. He walked over and locked the door, then found a spot at the end of the stairwell, leaned against the wall, crossed his arms and ankles and dropped his gaze.

Too angry for words, she started to pace the shelter. She couldn't walk out the front entrance because Jeremiah strategically perched himself between her and the door. *What the hell is he thinking? What is wrong with him?*

While she huffed and puffed around the room, he just watched her beneath hooded eyes. "Bella, talk to me."

With a brief pause, Bella scowled at him. It didn't matter how many times she walked this cellar, they wouldn't have a real conversation. They managed civilized text three nights ago. All of their previous physical conversations turned into arguments. Her soul didn't want to fight anymore. The fake happiness exhausted her. She only felt numbness. Even the anger and frustration that crawled through her body barely blipped on her radar anymore. *God, this sucks. How long will I be stuck down here?*

"Please Bell, talk to me."

"What part of 'no' are you not comprehending?"

"Oh, I understand. I simply refuse to accept that answer."

"Excuse me."

"I'm taking a page out of my sister's book." Jeremiah grinned.

Bella's mouth dropped open and her eyes bugged out as a sarcastic grin crawled on his mug. She swept shock under the rug. Enraged she glared at him. "Why do you fucking care? You spent weeks ignoring me! And now you think because we are stuck in here together you can get me to talk? Well, screw you!" Heated with an immense amount of anger she struggled to control her tears, so she turned away. *Why the hell am I crying?* As good as she'd gotten at lying to everyone else, she couldn't lie to herself. She cried because the anger did nothing to mask the hurt. She hated both God and Jeremiah for it.

Jeremiah pushed off the wall and closed the space between them. "I'm not trying to make you talk. I'm not expecting anything. I just want a chance."

She wiped her face and inhaled deeply. Even though she calmed down she didn't turn around. "A chance for what?"

"For me to explain and apologize."

She'd been unprepared for his answer. She spun around to face him and didn't bother to hide the tears that streaked her cheeks. "What?"

"I'm sorry. I shouldn't have left the hospital the way I did. I had no desire to hurt you."

"Then why did you?"

Chapter Twenty-One

Jeremiah started out okay. The moment Bella asked him why, his mind shut down. His brain refused to route the words to his mouth. For weeks he'd wanted the opportunity to tell her what happened and let her know why he walked away. Now he had his chance. Nothing came out. God he missed her. He desperately wanted to touch her, but hesitated to do so. She asked him a question and he needed to answer.

"Why?"

Jeremiah sighed and stared. Although the mini-skirt enticed him, he didn't stare because of it. He stared at her face and how she wore her hair down. If he could get close enough he'd run his fingers through it. Instead of a response to her question, the tears she cried danced around his mind.

"Would you answer me? *Why?*"

He didn't know how the night would end or how she would react to what he had to say. If she hated him now, she could hate him more by the time he finished and see him as a coward who couldn't provide for her. He would take the moment he had and remember all the little nuances of her features: the way her right temple dimpled, the natural bronze of her skin, how her lips plumped out when she smiled, and the lilt of her laughter. He sighed. There were a lot of things to remember and the one he wanted the most he had no right to ask for.

"*Damn it! Why?*"

"I want to tell you, but..."

"But what?"

"Bell, I don't want this to turn into a fight. Every time we talk that's where it always goes. And before I take a chance in going there again…" He wasn't sure how to tell her what he wanted. "I just don't want to fight."

She scrutinized him. "There's more. Why won't you tell me?"

"Because it wouldn't be right."

"Don't you think I should be the judge of that?"

"No. We were both raised right and it's wrong."

"Then you should ask."

Surprised by her response, he shook his head. "I can't."

"I don't care what the Bible says. God has punished me enough for a lifetime, but if you would fall with me, then you're right. You shouldn't."

"What are you talking about?"

"That's why all these things have happened. I don't know what, but I did something wrong. Something I wasn't supposed to and I'm being punished."

"You think God got you raped? Caused your miscarriage?"

"It's the only 'why' that makes sense."

"Did you ever think there isn't an answer to 'why?'"

"Besides the no fighting, you wanted something. What is it?"

Still as stubborn as the day they met, despite all the other changes. "The day you showed up to my house with the note from…the day we..." He couldn't quite get the words out, but he hoped she remembered the day they broke up. He hoped she remembered that one exquisite moment between them. "Before you left, I kissed you. For a second, I thought you kissed me back. It was the first moment we'd had in weeks. That's what I want."

She blinked and dropped her gaze to the ground. Kicking at the sand she glanced around the cellar before returning to him. "I have a boyfriend."

"That's why I didn't want to ask. I don't want to put you in an awkward position."

****

Awkward? Not in the least. She'd kiss him without remorse and wouldn't think twice about David. *I can't believe I'm using David as a reason not to kiss you.* It wasn't the nicest thing to flood her mind, but she wanted to go for it. Jeremiah hadn't been wrong in his thinking, she had kissed him back. Then she remembered all the anger and hurt. Now he asked her to rewind the past three months like they never happened. Dear God, she wanted to. Would she be able to drop it that easily afterward? She had a dinner planned with her boyfriend later. Bella stepped around Jeremiah because she needed to breath. Her chest tightened with such little space between them. She walked to the other side and down an isle of shelves mixed with various dry food items, blankets, pillows, books and a few other things in preparation of a storm. Unsurprised by her thoughts she asked what made the most sense. "Why do you want that?"

"Because I don't think you'll look at me the same after I answer."

She didn't understand how she'd see him any differently. She couldn't think less of him than she did already. She saw him the way she did when they dated, except anger replaced most of her love. None of that showed right now because his request confused the hell out of her. As she considered what he wanted, she realized she had a lot of other questions. "Can you answer me something?"

"I can try."

"Why were you fighting David the other day?"

He sighed and crossed his arms. "I was willing to accept the two of you dating, as long as I didn't have to play witness to it. Except every time I turned around he made sure I knew it. When you passed out, the only thing I could think about was getting to you. Then he showed up exuding this possessiveness that pissed me off. He did the same thing Tuesday night and Amanda split us up before a fight started then. But when you got bit by the snake Thursday, he threw the first punch and I responded."

"Tuesday night?"

"Didn't Vick tell you?"

"Tell me what?"

"Wasn't Vick here when you woke up Wednesday morning?"

"No." Then she held up her hand before he proceeded any further. True, she'd spent Tuesday night there then went home Wednesday morning, but she thought only her parents knew. "Wait. How did you know I was here?"

Jeremiah rubbed the back of his head. "When you weren't home by eleven Tuesday, David panicked. So he came over to my house thinking we would know how to find you. Vick told me you like to come out here when you're stressed. I had planned to make the drive, but David argued with me over it so Amanda got Vick to go instead. He told us you were here sleeping and that he would crash on the couch. I figured he told you everything the next day."

"He didn't," she mumbled. Though it explained why the pillows looked out of place when she came down to leave. He probably saw her car and checked the guest bedroom. The pills had knocked her out so sweetly nothing could've woke her up. She walked back over to where Jeremiah stood and stopped in front of him. His face still wore all the signs of a brawl. Cautiously she reached up and tenderly pressed a finger close to the corner of his mouth. "Does this hurt?"

"Not so much."

She lifted her gaze and stared into his emerald green eyes. She wanted badly to kiss him. She feared if she did he'd feel how much she missed him. Sensing her own weakness she looked away and crossed the cellar again. She could lie and tell him she refused to cheat on David, except she didn't care. Or she could be honest and tell him she wanted to, but dragging him down the landslide with her went against her nature.

Jeremiah sighed. "I'm sorry. I shouldn't have asked. I just..." He rubbed his face and sat down on the bench that had been placed against the wall.

"You 'just' what?"

"Nothing," he said and leaned forward on his knees.

Chewing on the inside of her cheek she glanced over her shoulder to him. Something bounced around in his brain. She wanted to know, but how could she expect him to be honest when she hadn't been. "You said you would tell me why. Is that true?"

"Yes. I've held things in for too long." He looked up to her. "But I need to apologize first."

"You already did."

"This isn't for leaving the hospital. I don't want you to think Vick is the one that tricked you. He was only helping me."

"The phone call wasn't real, but why?"

"I didn't think I'd get to talk to you unless I could get you alone. Practically impossible at school since David's always intervening."

"I'm sorry for that."

Jeremiah popped up to his feet. "Do not apologize for him."

She didn't know how to respond because she couldn't argue the truth. Slowly she turned around to fully face him. Did he intend this when he set this up? They hadn't so much talked, but they hadn't argued either. She didn't know how to define what they were doing, but she liked it. God how she missed him.

"I told you I would explain. And as much as I want a moment to have us back, I want you to know everything more."

She turned around and inhaled a couple of breaths. The tears threatened to spill again as his words hit a place she believed dead. The physical relationship she had with David couldn't compare to the emotions she had with Jeremiah. A tie she knew hadn't been broken, just severely knotted.

"While you were giving my dad your statement, the only thing I could do was take in all the damage you'd suffered. I was so angry. But not at the men who raped you. At myself because I let it happen. I felt like I failed to protect you because I didn't try harder to stop you from leaving when you came by rehearsal when I knew it could've gone longer than five minutes. After you kicked me out a few days later, I started going by that spot regularly. For the life of me I tried to figure out a way I could have changed what happened. That maybe if I had been there it would have gone differently. I'm sorry I failed you."

Unable to stop herself Bella blinked and tears trickled down her cheeks. She covered her mouth and tried to hold back the sob caught in her throat.

She hadn't heard him move as he talked to her back. She jumped when his hand landed on her shoulder.

"Bella..."

She hadn't been able to choke it back this time. Jeremiah spun her around and tucked her in his arms. With no will to fight she allowed him and accepted the comfort he offered. She couldn't remember the last time they'd been like this. Not since before the assault. At the time she needed him so bad and the day he showed back up in her hospital room she couldn't even look at him. She believed he walked away because he'd been ashamed of her. Instead of the pure angel he'd once seen her as, only the dirt that clouded every part of her could be seen. Taking a couple of deep breaths she pulled back and looked up at him.

He continued, "I'm sorry I didn't tell you sooner. I was afraid I would fail you again. And I couldn't bare not being able to protect you, so I stayed away. I thought you were better off without me."

She sniffled. "You're wrong. I wasn't better without you."

"You seemed like it."

"Because I don't want to talk about it. If I look okay, nobody makes me talk." She hadn't been this honest in months. Jeremiah had been the one person she wanted to talk to. She wondered if she could tell him more.

"We all just worry about you."

"I know, but not talking is the only way to forget."

He brushed back some of her hair. "I don't think it's that easy."

She closed her eyes the moment his hand touched her head. Gently she reached up and placed her hand on his. Softly Bella whispered, "I want to... but I couldn't live with myself if I brought you down with me."

"Bell... that couldn't happen. You're the only one I've ever wanted to be with."

Curling her fingers in his she lifted her gaze to his. This couldn't be real. As she stared into those exquisite emerald eyes of his she saw the truth. With a desire to return that honesty, she swallowed and spoke, "I miss you."

"What?"

She could tell him exactly what she meant, but why do that when she could show him. Without hesitation she pushed up on her toes, leaned up and kissed him. His hot mouth melded to hers as she wrapped her arms around his neck. She loved him.

****

If he questioned what Vick told him a month ago about Bella loving him, he believed it now. He didn't know what to think when she said she missed him. But the moment her lips met his and she kissed him like she had before the rape, he completely understood. Jeremiah wrapped his arms around her and held her against him. It felt wonderful to have her like this. God, he missed her. Kissing her deeply, he shifted his arms, swept one beneath her knees and scooped her up. Without breaking the link they currently shared he carried her over to the bench and sat with her settled in his lap. They used to make out in the back seat of his dad's car like this. Although he didn't know what would happen afterward, he happily accepted the here and now. Once they were comfortable he rested one hand on the small of her back so he could feel the heat pour off her skin as the other dove into her black silky tresses. He loved how soft her hair always felt. Not once had he ever remembered the smell of her shampoo, but the way his fingers swam through her locks he could never forget. Her lips tasted as sweet as he recalled almost like he engulfed pure sugar.

Normally as their breathing got heavier they would take a moment, but not this time. They consumed each other as if they hadn't seen one another in years and planned to get reacquainted. Except their kissing didn't last. A phone started ringing, which caused Bella to pull back.

She leaned her forehead against his as she dug her phone out of a back pocket. When she brought it around, she stared at it before she looked at Jeremiah. Chewing on the inside of her cheek she waited until her breathing had relaxed a bit more then answered the phone, "Hello?"

Jeremiah refused to move the hand that hovered near the top of her skirt. He slid his other through her hair and simply played with the ends as he leaned against the back of the bench and listened.

"Sorry, I meant to call. Vick was at his parents' lake house and his car died, so I came to pick him up, but we got stuck in the storm. We're waiting it out in the shelter."

He figured it had to be David on the other end. He didn't think she'd need to lie to her parents about being with him. Although he had no clue how the guy would react if he knew the truth, as long as David didn't take anything out on Bella, Jeremiah didn't care.

"As soon as the storm is over, I'll head that way."

He probably wouldn't have much more alone time with her. If that was the case, he needed to tell her everything. Not just about why he left or stayed away, but what he planned to do going forward. Also something he had no clue how it would play out.

"Yeah, I'll text you before I leave."

Definitely had to be David. Her parents didn't have cell phones or last he knew they didn't. Not to mention he didn't think they knew how to text.

"I promise. I'll see you then. Bye." With that she hung up and returned her phone to her pocket.

"David?"

"Yeah." She nodded chewing on the inside of her cheek again. "I told him earlier I'd go to his place for dinner. When Vick called me I forgot all about saying something to him."

"I see. Do you go to his place often?"

"No. He usually takes me out."

"Oh." He paused and fretted about asking his next question. Carefully he posed, "How come he invited you over tonight?"

She grinned. "It's likely his way of apologizing for getting into a fight with you. I mean, it wasn't like you were the only one I wasn't talking to."

Her answer pleased him more than it should. Glad she ignored the bastard. But she planned to go.

Curiously he asked, "Does he cook?"

Bella laughed. "No. He has a chef to do that. I must say though, his cook makes a mean omelet."

"And you would know this how?"

"I've been there for breakfast a couple times."

"As in you had a late breakfast?"

"No. As in I've spent a night or two there."

Not good information, but he needed to keep his cool so she continued to talk. "Where did you sleep?"

Bella quirked a brow like she couldn't believe he asked such a stupid question. "Where do you think?"

Also not something he wanted to hear. He sighed and stated more than questioned, "You slept in his bed..."

"Of course," she responded gingerly as if it happened every day. As she regarded him she hesitated until she seemed certain of what she intended to say. "I could tell you that you don't have a right to be bothered or get upset, but I would be idiotic if I didn't acknowledge that I partially understand why. I know you don't like him, except you need to deal with him. And before you ask, no, I haven't slept with him."

Jeremiah released a breath of relief. "I'm sorry Bell, I just don't trust him."

"I can accept that."

His gaze shifted from her face to the hair he still played with. The hand that rested on her back he squeezed shut as he considered what to say. Instead of a statement, he inquired, "Where does this leave us?"

She shrugged. "I don't know."

He nodded and lifted his eyes to hers so he could look her straight in the face as he said, "I want you back."

Bella blinked at him. Her mouth didn't drop open so maybe some part of her expected what he told her, but it didn't make the silence any easier to bare. She opened her mouth and nothing came out. Again she tried, but her voice remained inactive.

"Will you please say something?"

As much as he wanted her to stay put she pushed up out of his lap and crossed the cellar then turned back and walked his way. "What do you want me to say? Do you want me to jump for joy? I mean, yeah, you explained everything, but I'm not in the best of places right now. I can't take the chance you'll run again. I wouldn't be able to handle it."

"Bell, I promise you I won't. I'm here for good. I'm not going anywhere."

"How am I supposed to trust that? And what about David? Am I just supposed to tell him I'm sorry, Miah's back? I don't want to make him feel like a placeholder. I can't hurt him like that."

He sighed and rose to his feet as he brushed a hand through his hair. This was the part where things got tough. Sure he could tell her he loved her. And when he thought about telling her what he wanted, he couldn't anticipate anything. He hoped she would tell him she wanted him back too and she'd break up with David. Jeremiah didn't care one bit if the douche-bag got hurt, even if she cared. Not to mention he couldn't imagine sharing her. "I get that you care about him, but don't you think eventually he may feel like that anyhow? What happens when you do trust me enough to take me back?"

No words. Instead she glanced over her shoulder to the door. Outside the storm had either settled or had already passed over them. The quiet magnified Bella's silence. She shook her head. "I can't do this with you right now." Without any real answer she bolted for the door and pushed her way out.

He chased after her. When he caught up with her he grabbed a hold of her arm. "Bell please..."

"Let me go."

This time she didn't yank or pull free. He knew an immediate answer unlikely, so he released his grip. What else could he do?

On impulse he followed her to her car and leaned on the door so she couldn't open it. "Would you please turn around?"

She did as he asked and faced him. "Miah..."

He brushed the side of her cheek and stared in those beautiful hazel eyes. "I..." He started to tell her, but couldn't make himself finish what he really wanted to say. "I want to spend time with you. Please, please say you will."

Chapter Twenty-Two

"Tell me what I need to do for you to trust me," Jeremiah said.

Monday afternoon and the last bell hadn't rung yet. Her professor allowed Bella to leave class early. Jeremiah had been waiting at her locker when she got there. She sighed. "I don't know. Try being my friend again. Be nice to David. I know you don't like him, but I'd prefer not to hurt him."

"I get it. You care about him, but I'm sure you're already aware that's going to happen regardless. And the longer you wait, the harder it'll be and the more it'll hurt."

"I'll hurt him no matter how long I wait. You aren't giving his feelings their due credit."

"Are you saying he's in love with you?"

She chewed on the inside of her cheek because no one except Sarresh knew about his tattoo. Mentioning it to Jeremiah wouldn't be awesomely brilliant, but he needed to know how serious David felt. She glanced around and saw the hall remained empty. "You remember how we were texting about my tattoo yesterday?"

"Yeah."

"He has the same thing."

"Okay, so?"

"David doesn't have Deuteronomy like I do."

"What does he have?"

"My name."

Jeremiah stood there. He didn't look surprised, but he didn't look happy either. "Do you feel for him like you do for me?"

"I can't answer that."

"Can't or won't?"

"Miah..." Bella had no clue what to say. She very much could, but wouldn't. Like never compared to love and she loved Jeremiah. She'd known for a while now. Still she despised the fact no matter what she'd end up hurting David.

"Have you even told him about Saturday?"

"No."

"Are you going to?"

"No."

"Why?"

"Did you like it when he rubbed our relationship in your face?"

He shook his head and cupped her jawbone as he brushed his thumb along her cheek. "I just want to spend time with you."

She leaned into his hand. "I know. I do too, just not this afternoon."

"Why not?"

"David is taking me Christmas shopping. A little over a week to go and I haven't bought anything." She stepped back the moment the bell rung indicating the end of the school day. She and Jeremiah weren't as close as they had been Saturday, but they were close enough they could have kissed again. And her boyfriend didn't need to walk in on it. In an attempt to distract herself she turned toward her locker and pulled out a book she couldn't recall she needed.

"I know the trial starts Thursday, so how about Saturday night. Seven at the lake house?" Jeremiah asked as he backed away from her.

Out of her periphery she watched him walk away. She inhaled deeply then nodded. If she didn't know any better she'd swear she switched roles with a player. Had she begun to live up to the names whispered in the hall? At least as a geek her name wasn't tarnished. She did get one thing she wanted; kids at school stopped feeling sorry for her. Now some of them called her *phony*, that she only pretended to be a *good girl*. Others called her *hypocritical* over how she belittled Heather and her goons for sleeping around when in reality she did too. Did she want Jeremiah back? Despite everything they had been through, yes, but she wanted to refute the slutty depiction more. Going from David back to him would only reinforce the image, not dismantle it.

"Hey babe," David said as he wrapped an arm around her waist and placed a chaste kiss on her cheek.

Startled by his approach, she shivered when he took a firm hold of her.

"Hey, you okay?"

Unwilling to make him think otherwise she nodded. "Yeah. Just too much in my own head."

He took her hand in his and lifted her fingers to his lips. "Well you can tell me all about it on the way to the mall."

Not really. So many times she claimed she didn't deserve him. He could argue all he wanted, but it still wouldn't change the truth. She refused to show him that. Bella forced a faint smile and nodded. Unaware if she had the right books she shut her locker and zipped her backpack before she slipped it on one shoulder.

"You ready?"

"Yeah."

"Do you know what you're getting everyone?"

She nodded grateful for shop talk. "There's a watch my dad wants. And I thought I'd get my mom a silk scarf. A pair of shoes for Sarresh and some slogan t-shirts for Vick." She'd also thought about buying something for Amanda and Jeremiah, but she didn't think that would go over well with David.

"Sounds like you got it all covered."

"Except you," she said.

"You don't have to get me anything."

"But I'm your girlfriend. I should."

"I promise you don't have to. But if you absolutely insist on it, how about dinner with me on Christmas Eve."

"I can't. We start Christmas early in my family and I've already been told I'm expected to be there." Bella sighed. Her parents gave her no choice. If she didn't make an appearance they would take her car away. The only claim to safety she had and she refused to take a chance she'd lose it.

"You sure you're okay?"

"I'm just stressed about having to testify Thursday."

"When are you supposed to go over your testimony with the prosecutor?"

"We've talked a few times, but we have to cover the whole thing Wednesday afternoon."

"You want me to come with you?"

"No."

"You sure?"

"I'm positive. I don't want those images in your head. I don't want you at the trial either."

A few feet from his car, David stopped walking. "Are you serious? You know I want to support you."

"Then just be there afterward. If you hear about everything that happened, I can't undo that. I don't want them in my head, let alone anyone else's."

"Has Jeremiah heard the details?"

Why did the conversation always come back to him? David knew better. Ignorance only carried a person so far. And she could stand there like she had before and lie or she could be honest or plead. "David. Please. Just do this for me."

"Bella, answer the question. Has Jeremiah heard?"

"This isn't about him."

"Damn it! Answer the question!" David yelled.

She jumped because he had never once gotten angry with her. Even though he'd never used this tone with her before, clearly he meant business. She couldn't lie her way out of this one. Bella's gaze shifted to the ground because she couldn't look at him when she answered. "Yes."

"Then I will be there."

Shaking her head she didn't bother to fight the tears as her gaze snapped back up to his. "David, please. I am begging you."

"If he knows, then I have a right to be there. I'm your boyfriend."

"Which is why I don't want you to know!"

"What?" he asked in confusion.

"I don't want you to look at me any differently. And if you hear about all of it, you will."

David shook his head. "That doesn't make any sense."

"Yes, it does," Bella said. "I'm not the girl you think you know."

"Are you trying to tell me I don't know the girl I'm..." he paused as if he caught himself before he said something stupid.

"Yes. You don't know me and neither does anyone else," she said as she backed away.

He rubbed his forehead and dropped his hands to his sides. "Where are you going?"

"Anywhere but here."

"Bella, come on." David sighed. "I'll drop it. If you don't want me there, then I'll man up and I won't go. We'll just go shopping like we planned and I won't say anything more."

Now the idea had been planted in his head. Could she go on pretending it hadn't? Could he? She suspected not and truthfully, neither could she. But she refused to be the person who didn't get something for her loved ones, even if Christmas meant something else entirely. "You promise?" She asked, though she couldn't be certain about his honesty.

"Yes."

She sighed because she didn't want to give in. Even the importance of needing to shop for her loved ones didn't help his case much. They may not talk about it, but he would think about it. She shook her head. "I can't."

"Bella, please. I'm sorry. I shouldn't have brought it up. Just, everything about that guy gets under my skin. I know what he's doing and the position you've been put in, but please, please let me do something."

If he thought Jeremiah bugged him now, how would David react if he knew she and Jeremiah made out a few days ago? Or that she agreed to spend time with Jeremiah at the end of the week. God, she didn't want to know. In spite of her selfishness, she tried to spare David as much heartache as possible. He wouldn't accept that. Pushing him away only drove him closer. Like all her choices had the opposite reaction than what she shot for. "I don't want you to do anything for me." *I don't deserve it.*

"But I want to. And if you let me do this, then we can go shopping and I won't bring the trial up again. I won't attend. I'll wait outside the courthouse for you. You have my word."

Why couldn't she pick a guy that simply took "no" for an answer? Because she didn't take it either. Her luck, she found guys just as stubborn as her. She sighed. "What do you want to do?"

"Spend the next two nights with me."

Bella blinked because of all the request David could make, staying with him hadn't crossed her mind.

Chapter Twenty-Three

Bella still couldn't figure out how David convinced her to stay with him over the next two nights. Yesterday when he asked, she couldn't immediately give him an answer. She told him they should do the shopping as planned, which would allow her time to think over his proposition. By the end of the night she said yes. She looked around to make sure she had the last of everything she needed. Two days didn't require a lot of clothing, but she wanted to make sure she had options. She packed four days' worth plus all of her personal items. Satisfied she had everything she zipped her bag and hefted it off the bed. She pulled the handle up and started for her bedroom door snagging her purse and keys along the way. *Time to break out of one hell hole and fly into another. Joy.*

She should've known she wouldn't get out of the house unscathed. Both of her parents stepped out of the kitchen as she approached the front door.

"Where are you going?" her father asked.

"I'm spending the next couple of nights at Sarresh's."

"But the trial starts in two days," her mother said.

Like she could forget. She turned around, narrowed her gaze and sarcastically said, "Really?"

"Then why are you leaving?" her father inquired.

"Because I have no intention of being around either of you when I leave for the courthouse."

"Why wouldn't you want to go with us?"

"Because I don't want you there!" Bella proclaimed loudly, spun on her heel without a care that her mother remained silent while her father addressed the issue. She opened the door and started down the walkway toward her car. *Let them try and take it away now.*

Her father followed after her. "Where do you get off talking like that to us young lady?"

She placed her suitcase in the backseat, shut the door and moved for the driver side door. Pausing she glared at her father as she spoke, "Because you're the reason those assholes are in my life to begin with. The one that was arrested, he made me look at him because he wanted me to see. He wanted me to know so you could suffer with the knowledge your only daughter got... You sat on those threats because you didn't take them seriously! You are the one that waited until the house was destroyed!"

"I did what I thought was right! I'm sorry you were raped, you were shot, but that doesn't mean any of the rules around here have changed."

"So what? I'm supposed to treat you the same when you let that monster into my life? That I will forever be ruined? Should I be thanking you? Because God knows you've moped around here taking the blame for months. So why is now different?"

"Because you're different and it scares us."

She nodded. "You're right, Dad. I am different. I'm not stupid. I'm not some naive child you can convince God makes the world right."

"Bella, you can't honestly believe that?"

"Why? Because it doesn't make sense I would think He failed to protect me when you couldn't. That no matter how much I fought, I was still attacked. I was still beaten. I was still left for dead wishing for just that. Doesn't the Bible say He loves His children? Doesn't the Bible say He will punish His children when they act out?" The tears had started and she didn't dare stop them. At some point her and her parents were bound to have at it.

"He does love you. And He still loves you even though you've turned your back on Him, that you disrespect us."

"I only returned the favor."

"What are you talking about? God hasn't turned His back on you."

"Yes He has! Just like everyone else! You, Mom, Jeremiah, Amanda, Sarresh, Vick - all of you have. Otherwise you would see what is going on right in front of you."

"We all love you."

"Sure Dad. Let's investigate, shall we? How long did it take you to realize I was missing?"

"This isn't about me or my actions. This is about you and your actions."

"How long?" She screamed.

He sighed with so much frustration at her insolence he could have blown a tree down. "A while."

"Right. You didn't even notice I wasn't there until Jeremiah showed up at the Bible study session without me. Great parenting Dad. I want to be just like you when I grow up. Shall we move to point number two?"

"Bella —"

"How many people did you initially want looking for me?" This time she didn't wait for an answer. "Just you, the police, and Jeremiah. If the other attendees hadn't pulled the information out of you and volunteered I could have been dead by the time someone found me. Shall we move on to point three? Yeah, I think so. Even with everyone looking, all these people who supposedly know me so well including you and Mom, how long did it take for you to find me?"

"A while."

"So seems to be the theme. As a rough timeframe, it took you all an hour and a half. And last, but not least. How do I know all of this?"

Her father didn't shrug, he just stood there.

"From Vick. He had all these great stories to tell me since I saw him more while I was in the hospital than everyone else combined. You and Mom had to work. Great way to show how much you love me. Now, if you'll excuse me I'm going to my boyfriend's."

"That's not what you said before."

"Newsflash, I lied."

"Maylin Nadalia Christabel Naughton!"

"Scream it all you want Dad! I stopped following your rules two months ago when I realized you cared more about your reputation than you did your only daughter. The Juvenile Youth Pastor can't get dirty or mislabeled." Later, when time and fresh eyes allowed proper perspective she would come to regret her words. They were so busy arguing, neither Bella nor her father saw or heard the car come down the street. Neither realized the car slowed as it approached their house. Neither saw the windows roll down or the guns pop out until suddenly several shots had gone off and their voices no longer permeated the air.

The moment recognition hit, her father moved quick as lightning. He grabbed her and they both dropped to the ground. Except he hadn't moved fast enough. She cried out as something pierced her flesh and barreled its way into her body. Her mother ran out screaming as the car peeled off. She looked around and saw her mother frantically yelling into a phone as she hovered over her father who laid motionless in the grass. Her mind didn't fully grasp what happened as she faded into the blackness.

****

Amanda wheeled her mother toward the hospital check-in station. Amazing how many births Jeremiah witnessed his mother go through and the blood-curdling scream still freaked him out.

He stood to the side and said into his cell phone, "Dad? What's going on? Why aren't you here?"

"I'm at a crime scene. I'll be there as soon as I can."

"You're saying a crime scene is more important than Mom going into labor?"

"No, but this one is just as important."

"Is everything okay?"

"No."

"Will you tell me what's happening?"

"Bella and Amahl were shot a few hours ago. They should both be there in the hospital. Last I was told Amahl is still in surgery, but Bella only took a slug in the arm. She's in room 304."

He glanced over as his mother got wheeled away and his sister walked back toward the waiting room. "I'll check on her. What about Amahl? Is he going to make it?"

"I don't know son. It's touch and go at the moment." Chief Detrone sighed. "Tell your sister to stay with your mother and I'll be there soon."

"Sure." Jeremiah disconnected. He stopped on his way to the elevator and quickly recapped everything to his sister. Then told her their father asked she stay with their mother. If the situation hadn't been dire, he might have laughed at her cringe. With that complete he took off and headed to the third floor.

****

Bella blinked. "Mom, you can't be serious?"

"Yes, Bella. I am."

"What if I don't want to stay with Vick and his parents?"

"Then you can choose somewhere else to stay. Either way, you will be out of the house by the time your father and I return."

Bella heard the words, but it didn't make sense. "Mom, please..." The door opened, but she focused on her mother and refused to see who stepped in.

"No. No more. I am finished with these antics of yours." Behira turned and headed for the door.

"Mom!"

Behira continued without looking back to her daughter.

"Mãe!" Bella called for her mother again. Her mother paused at the door. Jeremiah stood in the doorway. For a moment she believed her mother would turn around, but she didn't. She couldn't be sure if her mother said something to Jeremiah or not. She couldn't hear anything. Then her mother walked out the door. Bella got off the bed and ran after her. "Mãe!"

Jeremiah caught Bella in his arms before she got out the door. "Let her go, Bell."

Tears started down her face. She looked to him. "Did she say something to you?"

"Only that she would give them permission for me to be in here."

She shook her head and turned back for the bed. *I am ruined.*

"Are you okay?"

Climbing back on the bed she focused on Jeremiah. "She kicked me out."

"I'm sure she doesn't mean that."

"She does. I have to go somewhere else." Bella wiped at her face. She wouldn't let this get her down. She couldn't. "I need to get out of here. Can you take me away from here?"

He nodded. "Yeah. If you've been discharged."

"I have. My Mom told me."

"All right. Let me go tell my sister and I'll be back."

"Okay."

He placed a quick kiss on her lips, then her forehead and left the room.

****

Bella didn't remember falling asleep, but she must have. Slowly her eyes adjusted and she looked around to gather her bearings and figure out where she ended up. White walls, posters of Kirk Franklin, Diverse City Band, and Toby Mac. Dark blue snuggly cotton comforter with baby blue sheets that smelled like fresh rain. *I know this room.* She smiled. Scooting back a little she reached over and felt the warm body beside her. She felt a hand grab hers as the body pressed in tighter. How long had it been since she felt this? Months. She really missed Jeremiah.

She rolled over flattening her back against the mattress and looked at him. Unlike Saturday when she hesitated on every move she made, this time she simply went for it. Lifting a hand she stroked his brown hair. When his eyes opened and those green eyes met hers she leaned forward and kissed his lips. And he didn't hold back. Suffering a second gunshot wound and her father's life on the line and getting kicked out had put things into perspective. She needed him in more ways than she could count. She wanted him to know not only had she forgiven him, but she needed and wanted him. Only him. It had only ever been Jeremiah in her heart.

His hand reached up and found its way to her hair. To encourage him she kissed him deeper and harder. Their breathing became erratic, but they pushed on and got as close to one another as their bodies allowed. Her legs tangled up in his, his in hers. One hand pressed heavily against her back and the other played with her hair.

She felt him pull away and press his forehead against hers. Her heart pounded. Bella placed her hand on Jeremiah's cheek. "I'm sorry about all the fighting."

"You don't need to apologize."

"Yes I do. I was angry. My life has become crap, except for you. You're the only good thing I have."

"Bella, you don't mean that. You have friends and your family."

"And I've pushed them both away. I tried to push you away, but you wouldn't let me."

"Why would you push me away?"

"Because I wanted to deny my feelings. I didn't think I had any right to them. If I was being punished, who was I to feel the way I do."

"What are you talking about?"

She paused and looked him straight in the face. "I love you."

"I love you too." He pressed his lips to hers again.

All the emotions, all the things they felt for each other engulfed them as she wrapped her arms around his neck. Something seemed off. Bella didn't want him to stop, but Jeremiah acted like he didn't either. Usually he stopped before they got to this point. She wanted him like she'd never wanted him before, but she needed to know if he felt the same way. She pulled back. Bella looked up to him. Afraid he would say no she considered another question. "I need to you ask you something. Will you be there with me Thursday?"

"Are you sure?"

"Yes. I need you there. I can't get through my testimony without you."

"Then I'll be there. I'd do anything for you."

She chewed on her bottom lip. "I need to ask you something else."

"Okay."

"Since my mom wants me out of the house, do you think your parents would let me stay here? I would feel safer here than anywhere else. I would feel safer with you."

"I'll talk to them."

The brief conversation gave them a moment to catch their breath. With a handful of hair Bella pulled Jeremiah back down to her lips. Slowly they devoured each other. She desired him more now than she did Saturday. She didn't want to stop. For the first time, she truly wanted to fully give herself to someone. With everything he knew, she could feel how much he still desired her. She pulled back because she wanted to know if he was ready too. Bella was ready to tell him. She stared into those emerald green eyes of his and softly said, "I want to be with you, but I need to know you want to be with me too."

"I do."

Something about his answer bothered her. She didn't know what. She needed to know more. "Why now? We've always stopped before."

He stroked her cheek. "Because it wasn't right before and it is now."

Bella smiled. She loved the sound of Jeremiah's husky voice. "Why is now different?"

Jeremiah pressed a tender kiss to her lips and rested his forehead against hers. "Because we love each other. I've always loved you."

"I love you too." Those four words sealed their fate.

They separated as his hands slipped under her shirt and lifted it up over her head. Then they tugged his shirt off. She could feel the heat of his skin, the rapid beat of his heart and the thickness of his hair. Jeremiah made all of her senses come alive.

As if seeing her for the first time his gaze trailed up and down her body before returning to her face. His hand reached forward and rested on her cheek. She leaned into his hand and kissed the inside of his palm before her gaze took hold of his.

She knew how he felt and now he knew she felt the same. What they had was beyond physical. This would be a perfect exchange of the souls. He had been the only person she ever imagined being with. He gently settled on top of her then returned his lips to hers. One bra strap slid down, then the other before he removed it entirely. Jeremiah's skin felt wonderful pressed to her own. Shivers crept up and down her spine as his fingers trailed along her arms, ribs, and stomach. They were going to make love and she couldn't have chosen better. Still something bothered her. She remembered leaving with him, didn't she?

Letting go of whatever wrong nagged her brain seemed natural. He lifted up and put some space between them as his fingers trickled slowly down her stomach and hovered at the top of her jeans. His lips pulled from hers and he looked down at her as if asking for permission. She paused because something about all of this seemed wrong. How could it be wrong when it felt so right? Shucking the unsupported feeling aside she nodded. He unbuttoned her jeans then slid the zipper down and sat up so he could pull them off. Smiling she bit her lower lip as she watched him take his time.

His hands traveled up her bare legs pausing at her hips as he came back up against her and in that same husky voice said, "Beautiful."

With a coy smile she asked, "What is?"

"You are."

He snaked a hand under her back and pressed his bare chest to hers as he placed another kiss on her lips. She knew those rough hands and had no doubt Jeremiah touched her. She helped him get his pants off. Some part of her deep down screamed this was wrong. She refused to listen because the sensation made no sense. This was exactly how her first time should have been. It should be with someone she chose and someone she loved and who loved her back. Their love mattered despite all the bad stuff that happened. Nothing could take away this perfect night between her and Jeremiah. Nothing.

Chapter Twenty-Four

Bella opened her eyes. Darkness flooded the room so she couldn't immediately see anything. She rolled to her left a little and noted the dark sky outside. *Probably why I can't see.* She used her other senses while she waited for her eyes to adjust. She could feel the sheets and comforter, but the color blended in with everything around her. The one thing she could tell, she had no clothes on. And a body laid in the bed beside her. She recalled a night of passion with Jeremiah.

Slowly things became visible: the desk in the far corner, the large flat screen T.V. hung on the wall, a couple of unrecognizable posters of athletic stars. *Oh God!* With a little bit of light from the outside world shining through the window, she realized the one lying next to her... *No!* Shooting a quick prayer to God she lifted the covers and looked only to swiftly return them to their starting position. *Oh God!* She hadn't slept with Jeremiah last night. No. She had sex with David. *How the hell did I end up here? Hadn't I planned to leave with Jeremiah?* She saw and spoke to him at the hospital, right? *Was I that drugged up? No... I... Oh God! I am ruined. Miah will never forgive me.*

She felt the bed move as David shifted and rolled toward her. Quickly and quietly she shot to her feet. Scuffling around the room she found her shirt and jeans. She didn't care about the ache in her arm as she pulled her clothes on. The one thing she knew for sure, she had to leave. No time to search for her bra and panties and no reason to bother. Without shoes she tip-toed across the carpet and gently slipped out of the room. Bella turned just in time to run right smack into David's sister.

"Going somewhere?" Heather asked.

"Yes, I'm leaving. I need to go home."

"Why don't you wait for David to wake up?"

Lie. "Because I need to change clothes. I don't have any here."

"I'd let you borrow mine, but I'm about four sizes smaller than you."

Something to be thankful for. She started to walk around Heather, but before she left she needed answers. "How did I get here?"

"A taxi dropped you off."

Shit. Meant she had no way home aside from catching a taxi. What the hell went through her head last night? Had she been that drugged up? No purse, no phone, not to mention the consensual sex. "Will you let me borrow your car?"

"Why don't you just wait for my brother?"

"Heather, please. I'm begging you."

She narrowed her gaze and crossed her arms. "Do I look stupid?"

"What are you talking about?"

"You don't think I can tell you're not wearing a bra or underwear. Let's not forget the little walk of shame here and you reek of sex."

Shaking her head Bella stepped around her. "Never mind. I'll walk." She'd rather do that than stand there and get lectured by the school slut. Practically running the rest of the hallway, she made it halfway down the stairs before Heather caught up with her and grabbed her arm.

"Here," she said and placed a set of keys in Bella's hand. Holding on tightly she glared hard. "Let's just get one thing straight. If you hurt my brother, I will ruin your life. You'll wish for the hell I put you through before. Because by the time I'm done, you'll pray for death."

She didn't want to hurt David or Jeremiah. And one of them probably wouldn't be if she had remained single, but she had to deal with that choice. Only one thing could comfort Heather or she hoped it would. "Don't worry. I'll make sure he's cared for." Whether she left her confused or dumbstruck, she didn't care. She had her getaway and she took it without hesitation. Seconds later she had opened and closed the front door behind her, climbed into Heather's car, started the engine and sped off.

****

She planned to leave Heather's car in the school parking lot with the keys in the gas cap, except Bella remembered her car had been taken into police custody. If a taxi wouldn't cost so much, she would've stuck with her original plan. Needless to say none of that worked out. New plan. She'd run her two errands, then stick the car in the back lot at school where no one ever parked. Less of a chance anyone would see her and she could catch a taxi from there with ease.

Whether Heather realized it or not when she eloquently presented her threat, Bella had already made a long overdue decision. Now she just had to take care of business. After showering she pulled out the jeans and sea green blouse David had seen her try on a month ago in the mall. To date she hadn't worn the clothes. Instead she waited for a special occasion. Nothing could be more special than this. She opened the door for Rescate County's Assistant District Attorney. Inside to the left a woman occupied a desk. Bella had interacted with her a couple of times.

The secretary looked up at her arrival. "Miss Naughton. We weren't expecting you for a few more hours."

"I know, but I need to talk with him now. Is he available?"

"Of course. I'll let Mr. Perez know you're here."

"Thank you." Desiring space she walked over to the portrait hanging on the opposite wall. She didn't recognize the artist and the subject mattered little. It simply served as a temporary distraction from everything that played and replayed in her mind. She couldn't help but think over her past actions, including those she made last night. After the one failed attempt at sex with David, she knew she could never take that step with him. It only succeeded because she believed she made love to Jeremiah. She would never forgive herself for the harm caused to the people she loved.

"Miss Naughton," Mr. Perez stated.

Turning her attention to the prosecutor she headed his way and stepped inside his inner sanctum. Looking at the chairs, she considered sitting, but decided against it. She heard more than saw as Mr. Perez came around and leaned against his desk.

"I take it you're ready to go over your testimony."

"No. I won't be testifying," she stated quite calmly.

"Miss Naughton, I thought we talked about this."

"In length. Which was why it was important I see you right away. I'm withdrawing my complaint."

"I'm sorry?" He questioned as if her statement had been unclear in any manner.

"I take it back. He didn't rape me." Her first time using the word and she said it hadn't happened.

"If he's threatened you in any way, we can protect you."

"I'm telling you the truth. I lied before. I was embarrassed. Please, drop the rape charge."

"Miss Naughton —"

"Mr. Perez, the only thing you need to charge him with is attempted murder. He shot Jeremiah. My boyfriend deserves justice." *Even if I don't.*

He sighed. "I'll do my best."

"Thank you," she replied still as collected as when she came in. Finished with her first task she left the prosecutor's office.

****

When she showed up at her psychiatrist office to cancel all of her remaining appointments, bells went off because she had been pulled back to the doctor's office.

"Why are you canceling your appointments?"

"Your services are no longer required."

"Have you dealt with everything?"

"So to speak."

"Can you clarify that?" Dr. Filmore asked.

Yes, but the answer won't be satisfactory. It would provide enough reason for the doctor to believe she needed to commit Bella and that wouldn't accomplish anything. "I'm solving the problem."

"How?"

Again, she couldn't answer. Bella sighed because dealing with the doctor wouldn't be as easy as the prosecutor had been. She supposed that made sense. The attorney could only fight her battle as long as she willingly went along with the plan. The doctor on the other hand didn't have to plan, she had to pull strings. And Bella had held onto them tightly. Well, she lied before, so she could do it again. "I've accepted the rape."

"Is that what happened?"

"Yes. That's why my parents wanted me to see you. And now I don't need you."

"What made you accept it now? Has the culprit been punished?"

"No. His trial starts tomorrow. I have simply accepted that with every action there is an equal and opposite reaction." Bella told her. As with the attorney's office she hadn't bothered to sit. Neither had the doctor. Made it easier to move around the doctor and open the door to leave.

"Bella —"

"I have nothing more to say. I'm done, Dr. Filmore." Bella stepped out, headed down the stairs she had departed many times before. There had been no point to continue counting after the tenth visit. She came three times a week and none of it helped. Maybe things would have ended differently if she bothered to talk about any of what she felt, but she couldn't bring herself to do it. And now she really had ruined the one thing that should've been perfect for her.

Bella glanced up toward the window she believed to represent her psychiatrist office. She didn't know if the woman planned to call her mother. It didn't matter if she did. Nothing mattered. Now she could accept everything leading up to the shooting yesterday had been her fault. Whether she intended to or not she let it all happen. She'd like to believe things could have been different, but nothing could convince her of that. Every decision she had made had been her own. And if she had chosen another path, well... she had no clue what would've happened. She did know she wouldn't hurt anyone else ever again. First, she would make amends for the hurt she had caused.

Both of her tasks accomplished, she got back into Heather's car. She would drive to the school and leave the keys as originally planned. Then she would call and have a message delivered for the car to be found later. On her way to the school she called for a taxi and gave instructions for the taxi to wait in the back parking lot. She needed to be invisible for the drop off and that was the best place for that to occur. After she would return home. Bella didn't expect her mother to be there. It may not be the home she remembered, but she wanted it to be the last place she saw. She wanted to go with the memories that had once brought her peace.

Chapter Twenty-Five

"Heather!" Jeremiah called out and zigzagged through the throng of students.

She looked to him. "What?"

"Have you seen Bella?"

"Not since this morning. Why?"

As much as he wanted to get specifics on the *morning* portion of her answer, other information held a higher importance. "My dad called me and said she told the prosecutor to drop the rape charge."

Her gaze traveled from the book she had half way out of her locker to him. "Did she say why?"

"She said it wasn't true."

Heather looked back at her book, but hadn't bothered to pull it out any further.

"Whatever you know, I need you to tell me now." He didn't have time for patience or thinking.

Sighing she answered. "Bella was acting strange when she left the house this morning."

"Be more specific."

"She couldn't remember anything about how she got to our house last night. Nothing about me threatening her seemed to bother her. She just kind of blew it off." Heather said, but hesitated on anything further.

"There's more, isn't there?"

Slowly she shifted her eyes to his and nodded.

"Then tell me."

"I haven't even told my brother."

"Listen to me, this is important. I need to find her. She isn't in school. She hasn't been to any of her classes and I've gotten one strange phone call after another. To top it off she isn't answering her phone."

"What do you mean she hasn't been to school? I got a note like an hour ago saying she dropped my car off here."

"Now I really need you to tell me what David doesn't know."

She sighed. "I found her with a pill bottle a few weeks ago."

"And?"

"She might have freaked out when they spilled everywhere."

"And you didn't tell anyone?"

Heather shook her head. "She said she still took them for pain."

With this new bit of information, everything he feared when his sister first told him about all of those supposed panic attacks made perfect sense. He didn't even bother saying he had to go, he simply ran for the door. Good thing he drove and Bella lived about fifteen minutes from there. If what he suspected had come true, he prayed he got there in time.

****

Jeremiah put the car in park and threw the driver side door open. He didn't care about leaving the car running or the keys in the ignition. His feet pounded against the cement walkway as he ran to the front door. He'd seen Bella do this a million times and when he needed to remember it the most he couldn't recall where to look for the spare key. With every ounce of his soul consumed in fear he tried to calm down enough to pull the memory out of the storage compartment he absolutely needed to access. Frantically searching, he finally recalled the key had been put in the mouth of the frog by the door. Finding the key he pulled it out and unlocked the door. He threw the front door open and started down the hallway as he called, "Bella!"

The kitchen and den took less than two seconds to inspect. Fearful of what he would find when he got to her bedroom door he hesitated to open it. But courage didn't take long to push through the fear and force him to open the door. What he saw on the other side would haunt him for days to come. His heart raced as he ran across Bella's bedroom. Everything he saw overwhelmed all of his senses and made it difficult for him to think. Bella laid so still on the bed. One hand had fallen open. Centimeters away from those pale fingers sat an empty pill bottle.

His mind fought through all the mess that seeped into his brain and he pulled his cell phone from his back pocket. While he dialed 9-1-1 he checked for a pulse. The operator answering pulled him back from what he couldn't find no matter how many ways he checked. "I need an ambulance. My girlfriend isn't breathing. I think she overdosed."

"What's your location sir?"

"1113 Pecado Avenue in Nautica Valley."

"I've got someone on the way. Do you know how to administer CPR?"

"Yes."

"Then I'm going to ask you to do that until the paramedics arrive. I'll stay on the phone with you."

"Okay." He switched the phone to speaker and set it on the bed. He scooped her up and carried her to the floor where he laid her down. Once he had her settled he tilted her chin to open her airway and proceeded with chest compressions. He counted to thirty and then plugged her nose while he breathed into her mouth twice. Again he returned to the chest compressions then the two breaths when he heard the sirens approaching the house. He had started the third round as someone stepped through the front door and called out. Jeremiah replied, "Back here."

Two paramedics came in and he got up and stepped back to give them room to work. God he prayed he hadn't been too late. *Please, please let her live.*

He didn't breathe until one of the paramedics said, "I've got a pulse. Let's move."

"I'll be right behind you," Jeremiah told the men. He watched as they got Bella on a stretcher and rolled her out of the house.

****

"What the hell did you see?" Jeremiah asked Heather again. On the way to the hospital he called Vick and told him to get Heather, David, Sarresh, and Amanda out of class. They all needed to be there because he needed some answers. He gave the bottle to the officers who had waited under his father's instruction so they could test for residue. They needed to know what she took. Bella had immediately been taken back so her stomach could be pumped and her blood drawn. They all had one thing they wanted to accomplish, save her life. There they all stood as he hounded everyone for answers.

"I don't know what they were."

"Then describe them."

Heather sighed. "I don't know. I think they were round and white."

"Those sound like the ones her doctor prescribed," David inserted.

Jeremiah narrowed his gaze at the man claiming to be Bella's boyfriend. "These weren't prescribed asshole. The bottle wasn't labeled."

"Back off! I only know she told the doctor she was prescribed Oxycodone and Morphine."

"Prescriptions given by doctors are filled at pharmacies and have labels."

"Then she must've started taking something else. The only bottle I ever saw was the one her mother found when she went through her purse the day she disappeared, but it wasn't labeled. I figured her mother confronted her about it."

Jeremiah groaned because he really wanted to hit the guy again. If it felt good once, it would feel good again. "Did no one think unlabeled pill bottles were important? Did you even ask her about it?"

Heather sighed. "I'm sorry. I should've said something, but I tried to give her the benefit of the doubt."

"Why didn't you say something to me?" David asked his sister.

"I figured if something was wrong you would know. You were spending all that fucking time with her." Heather responded.

"Not all the time. She spent time with her friends." David looked at Amanda and Sarresh. "Didn't she spend time with you?"

Sarresh shook her head. "She stopped spending time with me after the miscarriage."

"And me before that." Amanda added in.

David turned his attention to Vick. "What about you? She was stuck with you in the cellar Saturday. You've known her the longest. Wouldn't you have noticed if she was off?"

Vick quirked a brow and looked at Jeremiah.

"Enough." Jeremiah held up his hand. This wasn't the time or place for the events of Saturday to come out. "You don't get it. We've all made excuses. She is in there because of us. I knew things weren't good, but I wanted to believe she was dealing. And she didn't. It doesn't matter what pushed her over the edge, but we all helped her get there. If we noticed or not, we didn't stop it." The doctor approached them and got Jeremiah's immediate attention. "How is she?"

"Her mother has given me permission to speak to you alone." The doctor took Jeremiah off to the side. "She's stable, but comatose."

"Will she come out of it?" Jeremiah asked.

"I don't know, but the next twenty-four hours are critical. Her condition will be monitored."

"Will any of us be able to see her?"

"I'll allow her friends a few moments. Her mother has instructed we allow you full access to her."

Jeremiah nodded. "Thank you." He glanced over to the group huddled together waiting on information. He rubbed the top of his head and headed for them.

****

Jeremiah rested his head with his arm outstretched as he held on to Bella's hand. He refused to leave her side and consistently prayed for her to wake up. His head popped up the moment the door opened.

"Did I wake you?" his father asked.

Jeremiah rubbed his eyes. "No. I wasn't fully asleep."

"Have you slept at all in the past few days?"

"A little. I keep hoping she'll wake up."

"Did the doctor say anything more about her coma?"

"No. Just there's no way to determine how long she'll be out." None of the news the doctor shared had been good. The longer she remained comatose, the more unlikely she'd wake up. Since they didn't know how long she'd gone without oxygen they had no way to determine if she suffered any permanent brain damage. Except the test all confirmed she had brain activity, which gave him hope she'd be okay and eventually wake up.

"Has anyone come by to see her?"

"Yeah. Her mother this morning, Amanda and Sarresh will be here later, and Vick left about twenty minutes ago." Amahl continued to fight for his life, so Jeremiah stayed with Bella while Behira stayed with her husband. Mrs. Naughton granted everyone permission to visit with Bella, except David and his sister. Not that he suspected Heather would ever show up. David was outraged when the decision had initially been made, but he stuck to it.

"That's good." Chief Detrone said and leaned against the wall crossing his arms as his gaze shifted to the ground.

"Dad? Is something wrong?"

He sighed. "The prosecutor called me a little bit ago. Quincy Harlem made bail."

"What? How did that happen?"

"When Bella recanted, the prosecutor had to drop the rape charge against him. The judge lowered his bail with only the attempted murder charge."

Jeremiah shook his head. "That's crap. Can't they do anything?"

"Unfortunately no. None of the threats tracked back to him. I've had the visitor log checked out and found nothing of significance on any of his visitors. We have nothing that puts him as the one ordering any of the threats she got. And the prints on that first note she got were useless."

He rubbed his forehead and pinched the bridge of his nose. Jeremiah sighed. "What do we do now?"

"I'm posting an officer outside her room and Amahl's room to make sure they're kept safe while they recover." The Chief pushed up off the wall and walked across the room to his son. He placed a hand on his shoulder. "I'm doing everything I can. We will get this guy."

"I hope so."

He squeezed Jeremiah's shoulder once and then headed over to the door. When he got to the door he paused with his hand on the knob. "Someone's out here to see you."

"Who?"

"David Warren."

"I don't want to talk to him."

"I know, but you should," his father said. "You aren't the only one who cares about her. How would you feel if you were on the other side of that door and he was in here?"

His eyes flipped up as he looked over to his father. If he planned a guilt trip, it worked. As much as he hated to admit it, he knew David cared about Bella. "All right. I'll talk to him."

"Good."

Jeremiah sighed and watched as his father left the hospital room. He looked back over to Bella, squeezed her hand and rose to his feet. Placing a kiss on her forehead he said, "I'll only be gone a few minutes." Even if she couldn't respond, he hoped if he talked to her enough it would give her reason to fight. Against his better judgment he stepped out of the room and made sure the door shut behind him.

"How is she?" David asked.

"The same."

"What about her dad?"

"As far as I know no changes."

David nodded. "Thanks for telling me. I know how her mother feels and I'm just glad to have some information."

Yeah, he could care less. "Is that all you're here for?"

"No," David replied. "I got a letter from Bella."

That caught his attention. Him, his sister, Vick, and Sarresh also received one. To his knowledge they had read theirs, but he hadn't read his. Whatever she had to tell him, she could do it when she woke up. "Okay."

"Did you get one?"

He nodded. "We all did."

"Have you read it?"

"No."

"Are you planning to?" David asked.

"No. She can tell me when she wakes up."

"And what if she doesn't?"

"I don't want to think like that."

"Have you destroyed it?"

"No."

David nodded. "Good." He hesitated on his departure. "Can I ask you something?"

"Yeah."

"Did you know how she felt about me?"

That was not a question Jeremiah had been prepared to answer. He didn't know what Bella told David in the letter she wrote to him. He had no clue how much she revealed, but he imagined it was a lot. "I asked her once, but she never told me."

"Do you know how she felt about you?"

Jeremiah nodded. Although he should have anticipated David's response, he didn't. So the blow to his face came as a surprise. He stumbled back a couple steps when David's fist hit his jaw. Last time Jeremiah punched back, but not this time. One, they were in a hospital. Two, Bella got pissed off last time. Even if she was in a coma, he didn't plan to upset her in any way. Instead, he just stood there.

David turned and started for the elevators. He paused and looked back to Jeremiah. "If she wakes up you can tell her it's over and not to contact me."

Jeremiah had no idea what happened. The only way he might understand would be if he read his letter or asked Bella when she woke up. He watched as David walked away. Then Jeremiah turned around and went back into Bella's hospital room.

****

Jeremiah pressed a kiss to Bella's forehead holding a small wrapped box in his hand. His mother had been released with the twins three days ago, but with Bella still in a coma he refused to leave. "Merry Christmas, Bell. I was hoping you would be able to unwrap this, but you still haven't woken up. This wasn't how I expected to spend our first Christmas." He took her hand in his. "I need you to do something for me. I need you to wake up. Then we can celebrate the right way. There are a lot of things you need to know, but I'm not going to tell you like this." He dropped his forehead against her hand. Jeremiah tried to remain hopeful she would recover, but the constant lack of response started to get to him. "Bell, please, I need you to wake up." No matter how many times he pleaded and begged, nothing happened. Only one good sign existed, her heart still beat. In all the concern she wouldn't come back to him, that one thing gave him faith.

The hospital door opened. "Hey son."

"Hey Dad. What are you doing here?"

"Your mother wanted me to check on the two of you. She's hoping you'll be home for Christmas dinner. Your grandmother came and helped Mandy cook. We want to see you and have you meet your new brother and sister."

Jeremiah shook his head. "I can't. I won't leave her alone."

"Has her mother been by since..."

"No. I saw her a couple days ago filling out paperwork, but she wouldn't come in."

Chief Jamar Detrone sighed. "I wish I could say I'm surprised."

"I — " Jeremiah started, but didn't finish. Bella's heart monitor sent off a flat-line signal. He popped up out of his seat and dropped the box in his hand. His dad hollered something, but he didn't hear what. Outside nurses and doctors gathered quickly and moved in his direction. "Come on Bell! Don't you give up!"

Bodies grabbed and pulled at him trying to get him out of the way. Jeremiah hadn't paid much attention until a doctor got in his face and said, "Come on son. I need you to move so we can get to her."

He barely acknowledged the doctor's statement, but he stopped putting up so much of a fight. As two people escorted him out of the room he cried out, "Don't you give up Bell! Don't you give up!"

In all the commotion the sound of the Christmas ornament breaking got lost. He stared through the window as doctors and nurses worked to bring her back. Somehow he mustered the strength to mumble, "Please don't leave me." Jeremiah watched and he prayed, but she didn't seem to come back. He'd do anything for another chance with her. Anything for his beautiful angel. Unable to watch he dropped to his knees. He was losing her again. *God, please don't take her away.* She had to come back. She had to. But that eerie sound of her heart giving out continued. *God, please don't take her away. I'll do anything, but please, please don't take Bella from me.*

Jeremiah looked up and pressed a hand to the window. Tears streaked his cheeks. He whispered, "Bella, I love you. Please don't leave me."

She came back once, but in his heart he felt like she wasn't coming back this time.

The doctor called for the nurses to stop.

Afraid of what the doctor was about to say, Jeremiah dropped his gaze from the window as he couldn't look when it happened. In a matter of moments he believed Bella would be pronounced dead. No matter how hard he prayed, he hadn't saved her. Just when he thought she really was gone, he heard his name whispered.

Miah.

He swallowed his fear and looked up. The doctor and nurses still surrounded Bella, but they no longer tried to revive her. Jeremiah didn't understand when he heard his name again.

Miah.

At that moment he realized Bella's heart monitor beeped normally. Jeremiah blinked tears free from his eyes. *Thank you, God. Thank you for bringing her back.*

The End

Acknowledgements

First I'd like to thank God. Every idea and word wouldn't be possible without Him in my life. I'd also like to thank my friend Alex. She has been a great support and soundboard for me. My editor has also been great. She guided me in education that school didn't teach me and helped me make the book what it has become. I am extremely proud of this book and grateful to all of my family and friends for encouraging me. I'm looking forward to the next part of this series.

About the Author

I was born and raised in Florida. Since high school I have had a passion for writing. I still remember the first short story I wrote. I'll never forget how I came up with the story or how my professor's response encouraged me. I hope my works can provide the same encouragement to not only my readers, but my support network. I have one brother and sister, both younger than me. I love them as much as I love my pets. I have a Jindo Mix dog with ten times more energy than I have. He's named after my favorite show, *Bones.* I also have a large cat named Bishop. They often help me write.

Check out my website www.krysfenner.co and follow me on Face Book, LinkedIn, Twitter, or Good Reads.

Made in the USA
San Bernardino, CA
04 March 2014